A hundred volting jet o... down on the first party of spectators, who died screaming. She threw boulders of fiery pitch into the largest buildings, demolishing them and setting the ruins on fire. Then the giantess took two quick steps and dived at the town. Her entire body soared through the air until gravity took hold and dragged her down onto her target. With arms spread wide and a gleeful war cry on her lips, she smashed into a row of storefronts and flophouses. The explosion lit the night sky and leveled blocks in all directions.

Tears streamed down Kei's face as he squinted into the carnage.

Engulfed in flames and screams, a third of the town was covered in tar. Fire, smoke, blood, and ooze all swirled together, and the giantess reformed, her feet planted among the wreckage. She held her arms high in triumph, and her hideous howl echoed off the waves.

EXPERIENCE THE MAGIC

ARTIFACTS CYCLE

The Brothers' War
Jeff Grubb

Planeswalker
Lynn Abbey

Time Streams
J. Robert King

Bloodlines
Loren Coleman

MASQUERADE CYCLE

Mercadian Masques
Frances Lebaron

Nemesis
Paul B. Thompson

Prophecy
Vance Moore

ANTHOLOGIES

Rath and Storm
Edited by Peter Archer

The Colors of Magic
Edited by Jess Lebow

The Myths of Magic
Edited by Jess Lebow

The Secrets of Magic
Edited by Jess Lebow

ICE AGE CYCLE

The Gathering Dark
Jeff Grubb

The Eternal Ice
Jeff Grubb

The Shattered Alliance
Jeff Grubb

INVASION CYCLE

Invasion
J. Robert King

Planeshift
J. Robert King

Apocalypse
J. Robert King

ASSASSIN'S BLADE

MAGIC LEGENDS CYCLE TWO • BOOK 1

SCOTT MCGOUGH

ASSASSIN'S BLADE

©2002 Wizards of the Coast, Inc.

All characters in this book are fictitious. Any resemblance to actual persons, living or dead, is purely coincidental.

This book is protected under the copyright laws of the United States of America. Any reproduction or unauthorized use of the material or artwork contained herein is prohibited without the express written permission of Wizards of the Coast, Inc.

Distributed in the United States by Holtzbrinck Publishing. Distributed in Canada by Fenn Ltd.

Distributed to the hobby, toy, and comic trade in the United States and Canada by regional distributors.

Distributed worldwide by Wizards of the Coast, Inc. and regional distributors.

MAGIC: THE GATHERING, WIZARDS OF THE COAST and their respective logos are trademarks of Wizards of the Coast, Inc., in the U.S.A. and in other countries.

All Wizards of the Coast characters, character names, and the distinctive likenesses thereof are trademarks of Wizards of the Coast, Inc.

Printed in the U.S.A.

The sale of this book without its cover has not been authorized by the publisher. If you purchased this book without a cover, you should be aware that neither the author nor the publisher has received payment for this "stripped book."

First Printing: December 2002
Library of Congress Catalog Card Number: 2001097185

9 8 7 6 5 4 3 2

US ISBN: 0-7869-2830-1
UK ISBN: 0-7869-2831-X
620-88627-001-EN

U.S., CANADA,	EUROPEAN HEADQUARTERS
ASIA, PACIFIC, & LATIN AMERICA	Wizards of the Coast, Belgium
Wizards of the Coast, Inc.	T Hofveld 6d
P.O. Box 707	1702 Groot-Bijgaarden
Renton, WA 98057-0707	Belgium
+1-800-324-6496	+322 467 3360

Visit our web site at www.wizards.com

Dedication:
For giving me a lifetime of good ideas,
this book is dedicated to my parents,
Bob McGough and Elaine St. Anne.

Acknowledgments:
This book could not have been completed without
the following individuals:

Jess Lebow, who helped map out the characters, plot,
and setting of the entire trilogy in a high-octane, two-hour,
two-pitcher brainstorming session
Rob King, an excellent editor who hit the ground running
and really helped strengthen the parts to make
the whole greater (and who really knows how
to smack danglers back into place)
The designers, developers, and artists who created
the Legends card set for all their excellent work
(certain card names notwithstanding)
Jezebel Schiro McGough, for inspiring and embodying
one of the most challenging and rewarding characters
I've ever written
Elena Kalikopuakea-o-Kualoa McGough, for her constant
support and enthusiasm, as well as making sure
I gave Jezebel fair dues
Carl and the Aqua Teen Hunger Force
(Master Shake, Frylock, and Meatwad) for giving me
a reason to stay up late

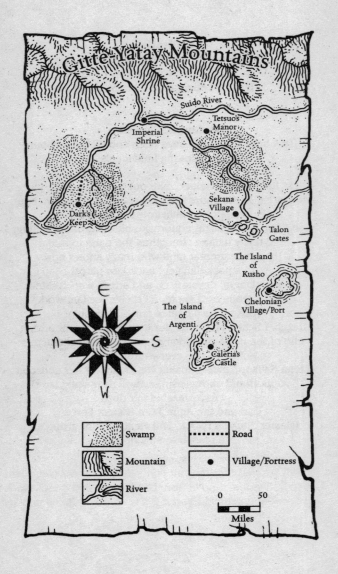

PROLOGUE

The burly man knelt at the foot of the altar, chanting words of supplication under his breath. Smoke rose from incense sticks and thick pillar candles at each corner of the altar. He had held the supplicant's position for over an hour, and the heat inside his ceremonial armor was becoming unbearable. Sweat pooled inside his helm and fell drop by maddening drop to the floor. Though his legs cramped and his bulging arms ached, he remained solid and untrembling, patient in his agony.

The shrine to Madara's emperor was a simple structure built into the side of a rocky hill on the edge of a river valley. Only the entrance was visible from without, and even it was plain and unremarkable. Only four stone columns and the yellow imperial banner testified to the site's importance.

As he knelt and chanted, Ramses Overdark heard his whispers echo and reecho off the polished gray marble. The interior of the shrine was as bare and utilitarian as the entranceway, and was devoid of sentries or staff. Except for the altar, Lord Dark himself, and the two servants who attended him, everything in the shrine could fit inside a single soldier's pack.

"My lord," whispered the male servant.

Dark ignored him but through slitted eyes saw what had alarmed the man. Smoke from the incense had grown black and now drifted straight to the floor, where it pooled and lay stagnant. The candle flames flared, briefly filling the room with a violent flash of light, and Dark felt the rapidly chilling air weigh heavy in his lungs. He continued to speak and eased his arm back to beckon the servants.

"Torches," Dark hissed without breaking the rhythm of his chant.

Both the male and the female bearers stepped up, and torchlight danced across Lord Dark's standard on their shoulders. The ink-black insignia showed a huge owl in flight with talons extended and two snakes in its beak. The snakes had knotted together and bared their fangs at each other over the bird's head. The standard was also etched into the dome of Lord Dark's helmet, and his signet ring likewise featured snakes coiling around his finger and facing off over his knuckle.

The pool of smoke on the floor started to swirl, creating a vortex around the altar and Lord Dark. He smoothly straightened into a standing position, his grace belying the pain in his muscles. With arms spread wide, he beckoned the servants closer to stand on either side of him.

"My venerable lord, my supreme master," Dark's voice boomed out from under his jagged, horned helmet. He had a deep, commanding voice, and the echo inside the shrine made it all the more impressive.

"My emperor," he continued, "ruler of all Madara and the surrounding seas—your servant stands in your holy shrine. I seek your blessing. I crave your wisdom. Will you hear me?

"As a token, the barest reflection of your divine brilliance, I offer light." He flicked his wrist, and the female servant stepped forward and illuminated the altar with her torch.

Dark's armored hand flashed out and froze into a claw before the woman's face. Her mouth opened as if gasping, but no air entered or escaped her lungs. Instead, a stream of thick, incandescent air flowed from her open mouth into Dark's palm. The torch-bearer choked and heaved, and her face went blue, but she stayed rooted in place as the softly glowing ball in Dark's hand grew larger.

"I also offer breath." Dark had not looked away from the altar. "For just as breath sustains the body, your grace sustains the empire." The servant's eyes rolled back in her head, and she dropped her torch. As she fell heavily to the floor, Lord Dark gently guided the floating ball of vapor up and over the altar.

Dark flicked his other wrist, and the remaining servant made a slight whimpering sound. The man came hesitantly forward even as terror-sweat rolled down his face.

Before the servant could raise his torch, Dark drove four stiff fingers into the man's temple. The blow left no mark, but the torch-bearer's left eye immediately flooded with blood. His head jerked violently to the left, and his entire body spasmed. Then he fell, and his torch thudded to the floor.

"Finally, I offer life, as you are the vital spark that created the empire and gave us all new purpose. We exist to serve you. I exist to serve you. Will you hear me now?"

The candles flared again, along with the abandoned torches, and then the room went black. Lord Dark pulled off his helmet and listened carefully. He had excellent night vision, and he could see his breath fogging in front of him, clinging around his head and forming tiny crystals of ice in his fine white beard.

Before him, the emperor's face appeared, a ghostly image with huge glowing eyes and an amused, predatory expression.

"Well met, my assassin. What is your desire?" The soft, hissing voice did not boom as Dark's had, but it was somehow louder and more powerful than Dark's stentorian bellow.

"Your Imperial Majesty," Dark said. The emperor's mere presence was overwhelming, his power palpable even in such a minor manifestation. Dark's mind spun as it always did, as he had counted on its doing. He dropped to the floor on one knee and both fists, paused, then bounced back upright. Once the offerings had been made and the audience granted, the emperor demanded brevity and concision. "The situation in the Edemi Islands grows dangerous. The secessionists—"

"I am aware of the situation in the Edemis. I will tell you when it becomes dangerous."

"Forgive me, Majesty. I misspoke. The situation in Edemi is . . . unacceptable."

"Agreed. What do you propose?"

Dark produced a small hand-carved effigy from a pouch at his side. "There is but one island that matters. Control it, and the rest of the chain falls into line. If it please Your Eminence, I suggest a simple removal of that island's ruler." With a short, sharp chop, Dark snapped the head off the figure. "Along with any who stand beside her. By your leave, my operatives will ensure that your enemies do not live to see fall become winter."

Dark remained outwardly calm in the silence that followed. He had rigorously trained for his entire life to control both mind and body through the force of his will. In the face of the emperor's staggering power and hellishly keen perception, Dark fought not to reveal more than was necessary to secure the god-king's approval.

"You can do this . . . efficiently?"

The stressed inflection of the final word unsettled Dark. Scores of imperial servants had been sent to the torture chamber for the sin of inefficiency.

"I can, Majesty."

The image of the emperor's face split into a wide grin as it faded. "Then carry on, my assassin. Do as you see fit."

The emperor vanished. Incense smoke surged upward, released from the terrible gravity of the imperial presence.

Lord Dark hooked his helmet onto his belt. Two spent torches lay on the marble floor, but the bodies of the servants had vanished.

Dark was pleased, but he did not revel in this minor victory. Here was but the first hurdle, the first step in a long and complicated path. His mind had already begun to map out the forks he would take on that path and the tracks he would obscure so that none might follow.

"For the glory of the empire," he said to the empty room. With a smile every bit as confident and predatory as the emperor's, Lord Dark turned and strode from the building.

PART ⬥ ONE:

IMPERIAL
SANCTION

CHAPTER 1

Tor Wauki ran easily across the rocky cliff top, his sandaled feet slapping the path in time to the pounding surf below. Though the path was uneven and he was but a single misstep from a hundred-yard fall, he ran as swift and sure-footed as a horse in a spring meadow. He felt the sea on his skin as the wind carried ocean spray and the scent of salt even to this great height.

The sun was high overhead, and as it burned off the morning mist, Tor could see two great pillars of rock jutting up from the waves on the horizon. The Talon Gates, as they were called, marked the only safe passage ships could take to or from this corner of the Madara empire. Hidden reefs, dangerous tides, and powerful spells awaited anyone who tried to steer around them.

Tor dragged his gaze away from the magnificent seascape and focused on his progress. His longbow was slung across his back, cinched snug between his shoulder blades as he ran. Less than a mile ahead, the path came to an end at another pair of stone pillars. These were far smaller than the Talon Gates, each a mere fifteen feet high, but they had been carved to resemble their larger counterparts in the distant sea.

Tor's vision was extremely keen, and he could see that beside the right-hand pillar was a small fruit tree. In the shade beneath the tree sat a white-haired figure dressed in a simple peasant's robe. She waited, cross-legged and patient, and watched Tor approach.

"Are you the champion?" The woman's voice was thin and almost inaudible against the wind and waves.

Tor did not reply. He was still too far away to answer without returning the yell and was determined to save his breath for running.

The old woman did not speak again until Tor was a stone's throw away and had slowed to a trot. She gracefully rose to her feet, cupped her hands, and shouted, "Hello, traveler. Are you the imperial champion?"

Tor continued to trot forward in silence until he was standing at arm's length from the old woman. He pressed his palms together in front of his chest and offered a shallow bow.

"Greetings, venerable," he said. "I am looking for—"

"Are you the champion? We sent for the champion."

"I am Tor Wauki," he said, "and I am second to the imperial champion. Who are you?"

"We sent for the champion," the old woman replied. "Is he coming?"

"He may, or he may not. First I must evaluate your petition. You are an elder from Sekana village?"

"I am the elder of Sekana. Singular."

"I see. You speak for the village council?"

"I speak to the village council. I offer advice, and sometimes they take it. I advised them to send for the champion."

"What is your—"

"Since it was my idea, they made me wait for him." The old woman rambled right over Tor's reply and kept rambling. "You'd think having the idea would have spared me the burden of seeing it through. I've spent all morning in the mist and the cold waiting for him."

"You have my sympathies. What is your name, venerable?"

"Bejahn." She waved her hand at the fuzzy green fruit on the boughs of the tree. "Would you like a temoya, Second? The village is famous for them." She sucked on her molars, turned, and spit a seed onto the ground. "They're not quite ripe, but I prefer them that way."

"No, thank you, Elder Bejahn. Please tell me why you have called for the champion. The message said there was a dangerous threat and the village needed help."

Bejahn pulled another green temoya from the tree. "There is, and we do, but there's no point in rushing until he gets here." The village elder sank her teeth into the tough skin of the fruit and tore off a mouthful, exposing the sweet yellow flesh inside. She offered it to Tor. "You sure you don't want one?"

"Elder," Tor's voice grew sharp. "You asked for help. Do you want it or not?"

"I want the champion's help."

"I am the champion's second," Tor said, "and I am here on his behalf."

Bejahn smiled through a mouthful of temoya. "I don't think you're up to it."

Tor unslung his bow from across his back. "Well, then, I will have to change your mind." He took an arrow from his quiver and nocked it onto the bowstring.

Bejahn held her hands up in playful surrender. "You're not going to shoot an old woman for eating fruit, are you?"

Tor let the arrowhead drift down to point at the ground. "Of course not. This is just a demonstration. Proof of my ability to represent the champion." He nodded toward the tree. "Which of those temoya looks best?"

"They get bigger as they get riper," Bejahn said. "Bigger,

sweeter, and softer. But as I said, I like them on the sour side."

Tor sighed. "Which looks best to you?"

Bejahn polished off the last of her temoya, tossed the skin aside, and licked the juice from her lips. She looked up at the tree, then pointed at a small green lump halfway up, about twenty feet from the ground. "That one."

Tor's first arrow tore through the temoya's thick stem, and the fist-sized fruit dropped from the bough. His second arrow split the falling morsel into two equal pieces in a spray of juice and seeds. His third arrow cut one of the halves into rough quarters, and his fourth pinned one of the quarters to the trunk of the tree.

Tor sprang forward and looped the bow over his head and shoulder. He caught the remaining two pieces of fruit before they hit the ground, one in each hand. He somersaulted over the hard ground and came up standing beside the arrow embedded in the tree. The archer smiled at Bejahn and popped the quarter piece of temoya into his mouth.

"Tangy," he said, "but you're right. They'd be too soft if they were any riper." He yanked the arrow out of the tree trunk and offered the skewered fruit to the elder. "For you, venerable."

The old woman stared at the archer and the fruit. Shrugging, she pulled the temoya chunk free and used her teeth to scrape the flesh from the skin.

"Follow me, boy," she said. She turned and went between the stone pillars, casting the skin carelessly aside. "I'd retrieve those arrows if I were you. You're going to need them."

Tor collected his weapons and jogged to catch up. He stayed respectfully behind Bejahn in observance of her age and the fact that she knew the way. They descended a narrow set of stairs that were carved into the side of the cliff itself.

"Our trouble started about two weeks ago," Bejahn said. "This . . . thing just showed up after the last harvest. She came with the first fog of autumn, when the temperature dropped and the seas got rougher."

Tor's muscles were eager to resume running, but he forced himself to stay in step behind Bejahn. "What kind of creature is it?"

Bejahn shrugged. "I've never seen anything like her before in any of my seventy-seven years. We thought she was a sphinx at first, but she doesn't have the right features. Now we're pretty sure she's some kind of dragon." They descended a few more steps in silence. "She's big."

Tor paused to offer Bejahn a steady hand as she navigated a sharp corner in the stairs. They were quickly approaching the rocky beach, and Tor could see the village in the distance.

"How big?" he asked. "The more you can tell me, the better. How many heads does it have? Does it fly? Or breathe fire?"

"Oh, she flies all right. She dropped out of the sky right there on the beach, between here and the village gate. Then she strolled into town, pretty as you please, and set up shop."

They reached the bottom of the staircase, and Bejahn led Tor across the sand and rocks toward the driftwood walls of the village.

"Wait," Tor said as they walked, "you mean it's inside the village?"

"No, that's the strange thing. She showed up and cuffed some of the younger men around when they tried to drive her off. They used poles and cudgels; she used tooth and claw. Then she curled up in the village square and demanded tribute. Some of the villagers tried to explain that we're a fishing village, that the only things we have in the way of riches are sea bass and temoya fruit. She cuffed them around, too. Finally someone brought her the day's catch, and after she had eaten three or four full nets, she flew off again."

Tor stopped Bejahn with a gentle hand. "It talks?"

"Not a lot," Bejahn said. "A few words here and there, but she makes herself understood, boy, believe me."

"What happened after she left?"

"She came back. Behaved much the same way, swatting people when they didn't get out of her way fast enough, plopping down in the middle of everything, and demanding a meal. That's how things have been for the past two weeks. She comes in, bullies us, eats our fish, then disappears for a day or so."

They were now at the entrance to the village, a narrow cobblestone street that opened up into a wide courtyard. Tor saw people milling around on the street and on the docks beyond, nervously folding nets and patching holes in their boats. A small party of four men and women came out of the gates to meet Tor and Bejahn.

"Is this the champion?" a man in the front of the group asked. He had a long, drooping mustache that fell down below his chin.

"No," Bejahn said, "this is the champion's assistant."

"Second," Tor said.

"Second. He's good with a bow."

"He'd better be. Look, Second—"

"My name is Tor."

"Sekana has always been loyal to the emperor, Tor. We bring in our share of fish, we pay our taxes, we even keep an eye on the Talon Gates. Our fruit graces every Madaran noble's table in summertime. We're entitled to the emperor's protection."

Tor nodded. "That's why I'm here. Though this sounds more like something for the kentsu than for the champion."

"We don't want soldiers here," Bejahn said. "They passed through our village five or six years ago, en route to some conquest or another. They took half our young women and all our young men. We can't afford their kind of help."

"Besides," the mustached man said, "this is a matter of imperial honor. This thing treats us like her subjects. She demands tribute and forces us to wait on her hand and foot. She makes us address her as 'queen.' If someone doesn't do something about this quickly, she's going to turn Sekana into her own private playground."

Tor's hand clenched reflexively on his bow. "That will never happen—and I wouldn't go calling her 'queen' out loud too often if I were you. The emperor hears all."

The man who spoke stepped forward and opened his shirt to expose four parallel lines carved into the skin of his chest. "I'll call her whatever she likes, boy. We're not warriors. Even if we were, the emperor has forbidden us from carrying weapons. This is your problem, yours and your master's, and we want to know what you're going to do about it."

Tor stepped up to the mustached man as the villager closed his shirt. They were the same height, but Tor was lean and hard where the man was soft and rounded. "I have come to address your problem, villager. That's all you get for now. After I'm done, we'll discuss the Sekanans's shocking lack of respect for the office I represent." Tor leveled his fierce brown eyes at the villager until the man dropped his gaze.

"Has anyone tried to follow this thing when it leaves? Do you know where it goes?"

"Of course," Bejahn said. She pointed down the beach, where a large rock formation loomed over the entrance to a deep natural cave. "She tends to patrol the coastline for miles in both directions. When she's done, she goes there to roost."

Tor unslung his bow. "Now we're getting somewhere. Do any of you care to come along?"

Bejahn tightened her robes against the stiff sea breeze. "I'll go. Might as well see this thing through to the end." She leaned forward and stage-whispered to Tor, "Not that any of these cowards were going to volunteer anyway."

Tor smiled. "You're not afraid?"

"Not at all. She usually attacks only those who bother her or try to sneak past without giving her fish. I think you're the one who's in danger." Bejahn followed Tor as he marched to the sea cave, leaving the villagers at the gate to grumble among themselves.

"Tell me again how big this thing is," Tor said.

Bejahn pointed to the docks, where a twenty-foot sampan was moored. "Put two of those end to end. Add a tail behind and big wing on either side. Four limbs, one head. She kind of looks like a cat, but I still say she's a dragon."

Tor nodded. "Thank you." They were now twenty yards from the mouth of the caves. Tor took a few steps closer, but Bejahn held back.

"This is as far as I go," she said. "I didn't get this old by taking stupid chances."

"That suits me, venerable. For your sake as well as the village's, you should stay where it's safe."

"Then we all agree." Bejahn smiled. "You're a good boy, Second. Be careful. Her teeth are sharp, and she's very, very fast."

Tor nocked an arrow and stood outside the mouth of the cave. The interior was dark. Anything could be hiding within, watching Tor's approach.

"You, in the cave," Tor called. "I am Tor Wauki, and I serve the imperial champion. In his name, and in the emperor's, I command you to show yourself. You are not welcome here, and you will not stay."

Tor's excellent hearing discerned a long intake of breath and the creak of massive joints flexing. A low growl of annoyance issued forth, and two glowing yellow eyes opened deep within the darkness of the cave. Tor tensed but did not draw back the string. The yellow eyes were ten feet above the ground, each as big as a person's head. The creature hissed a malevolent, feline warning.

"You may not address me." The creature's voice was low and sinister, midway between a growl and a purr. Then she hissed again, and the eyes closed, returning the cave to complete darkness.

Tor pinched all five fingers together over his arrowhead and whispered a quick incantation. His fingers flew apart, and the arrowhead burst into a light so brilliant it hurt his eyes.

"If you won't come out," Tor said, "I will come in and drag you out. Don't make me do that." Though he kept the arrow pointed at the ground, Tor calculated the distance to a spot on the cave ceiling halfway between himself and the creature. The illuminating arrowhead would give him enough light to pick a target on the thing's body and, if he were fortunate, would also dazzle the beast after her long nap in the darkened cave.

"This is your last chance." Tor looked back to make sure Bejahn was well out of harm's way. The old woman nodded at him encouragingly, but her face was pale and drawn with tension.

Tor turned back to the dark and silent cave. "So be it," he said, and raised the bow to take aim.

The creature's eyes snapped open, and something solid shrieked past his face. Tor caught a glimpse of a huge flat paw wreathed in luxurious, multicolored fur, but then he was blinded by wind-driven sand. He blinked his eyes clear and stared in shock at the ground in front of him.

His bow and arrow lay in pieces, shorn cleanly into segments as if by an expert swordsman. He still held part of the bow in his hand, and the glowing arrowhead sputtered and faded as it lay in the sand. His red leather breastplate bore four long slashes, similar to the ones on the villager's stomach. Tor felt a rush of vertigo as the shredded leather fluttered like flags in the wind. There was a burning sensation on the exposed portions of his chest, and to his disbelief tiny dots of blood appeared along the almost-invisible cuts in his flesh. The dots grew larger and larger, joining each other and forming four thin lines of blood. When Tor inhaled, the flesh separated farther. Blood began to stream from the wounds, sliding down his rib cage like water down a rock.

Inside the cave, the creature's eyes appeared. She hissed again, a warning tinged with scorn. Then the eyes closed.

Tor tried to press his breastplate over his wounds, but the movement opened them wider. He staggered back a step and felt a pair of delicate hands on his shoulder steadying him.

"Easy, Second," Bejahn said. "I told you she was fast."

Tor regained his balance and his composure and stood free of Bejahn's support. "Thank you, venerable," he said. "Officially, I hereby find you are correct. This situation requires the attention of the champion himself."

C H A P T E R   2

2 Lord Dark's diligence thundered along the only decent road through the marshlands. The road led from the banks of the river to the iron gates of Dark's castle keep and had been constructed to his precise specifications.

A team of four eight-legged imperial horses pulled Dark's carriage behind them. As usual, Dark was the only passenger, and there was no driver, for the horses were well-trained veterans. They knew the route and were familiar with the dangerous temper of their master. Also, there were no places to stop between the river and the keep and no alternate path for them to stray onto even if they tried.

Dark's castle was nearly invisible from the road, its turrets and vast grounds contained by a thick stone wall and further concealed by mist and moss-covered trees. The main gate was a huge, black iron slab fitted into a gap in the wall. Though it appeared to be unconnected to the wall itself, the gate had resisted both hostile forces and the ooze of the swamp for decades without toppling.

Dark inscribed a square in the air before him as the carriage approached the closed gate. He then placed his upturned palm beneath the figure he had just made and slowly raised his hand. Outside, the gate responded to Dark's motion, and it also rose, five tons of enchanted metal floating upward in the mist like a spider ascending its web. The diligence rumbled beneath the raised slab and onto the grounds. Lord Dark brought his hand down as soon as the rear of the carriage cleared the gateway, and the ingot of iron settled back onto the sodden ground.

Unlike the marsh road, the path from the main gate to the keep's front door curved and meandered, providing an excellent view of the castle's face. A groom stood ready to take the horses at the front entrance, and beside him a footman waited with a satin-upholstered stool. Dark was pleased to see his servants anticipating his arrival and obeying the proper decorum. He was less pleased to see the slight, oily-haired man dressed in cobalt and crimson robes standing beside them.

Everything about Boris Devilboon irritated Lord Dark, from his fawning, obsequious manner to the thin spiky mustache he continually waxed and fussed over. Though he intended it to be elegant and rakish, the little man's facial hair only added what appeared to be rat's whiskers to his already verminlike features.

The horses came to a halt, and the groom took their reins. The footman placed his stool and opened the carriage door just in time for Dark to step out. The lord of the manor ignored his servants and strode directly over to Devilboon.

"Welcome home, my lord." The blue-robed man bowed deeply, folding his staff behind his back so as not to trip his master.

"Irritant. What are you doing here?"

Devilboon smiled weakly. "My lord, you told me to report to you directly once I had completed my assignment in the Hakkan Delta."

Dark glared down, and Devilboon dropped his eyes. "You have completed your assignment?"

"Yes, my lord. The village elder you sent me to meet . . .

met in turn with a slight accident. There was a late night fire in his home. Neither he nor any of his sons survived."

"A pity." Dark went past Devilboon into the castle. He handed his helmet and his metal gauntlets to a waiting servant.

"Yes. My little friends are most efficient, but they are not known for their restraint." Devilboon produced a bag of coins and shook it for the sound. "The village then decided to pay the imperial tribute it was withholding." When he saw that Dark was not waiting or listening, he slipped the bag back under his robe and rushed up alongside his master.

"We . . . I stand ready for my next assignment, Lord Dark."

Dark removed his cloak and handed it to another servant. "I have nothing for you. Return to your hovel and await my summons. I have real work to do."

"Yes, my lord." The little man's face fell as he turned to go.

"Hold a moment, Devilboon."

"Yes, my lord?"

"Is Xira in the castle?"

"No, my lord."

"Of course not. Boy!" Dark's shout echoed down the granite hallway. A moment later, a terrified youth stepped out of the shadows.

"Send a runner to find Lady Xira and fetch her here. Set her up in her usual room, and tell her to meet me in my study at sunset tomorrow." He leaned down, his face mere inches from the boy's. "Be sure to tell her I specifically said 'at sunset.' Not when she feels like it or after she's changed her outfit three times. I have work for her. Go."

The boy nodded and dashed away.

"Are you still here?" Dark pushed past Devilboon.

"No, my lord."

"I thought not."

As Devilboon slunk back down the hall, Lord Dark loosened his breastplate and waited for the faint, nervous footsteps to exit the building and fade into the courtyard. Then he touched a nondescript stone in the wall, and a doorway opened. Dark disappeared into the secret passage and slid the entrance shut behind him, pleased to have scraped Devilboon off so quickly. The little rodent had his uses, but as company he was absolutely insufferable.

* * * * *

Lord Dark's hidden meditation chamber was the only place in the castle that allowed him to set aside the burdens of his office. Its location was obscured by architecture, spellcraft, and a genuine terror of Lord Dark himself. It was common knowledge among the castle staff that his lordship had myriad secrets to keep, and he kept them zealously. There was even talk among them about the chambermaid who accidentally happened across this particular hallway. The wilder rumors speculated that Dark had her skinned and made into a doormat. The truth was in fact far worse.

Dark now sat in the tiny stone room, cross-legged on the floor in the center of a circle of black candles. He rested his hands palm-up on his knees, his eyes clenched tight in concentration. A small pot of boiling hot tar steamed beside him, and he had used it to draw a complicated sigil on the floor. He was whispering.

When the smoking symbol on the floor began to hiss and bubble, Dark stood and opened his eyes. He held one open hand out toward the sigil and slowly inscribed a great circle in the air before him. As his hand completed the figure, he raised his other and traced out the same figure in the exact same space; but in the opposite direction. With both hands moving in smooth, tight arcs, he called out in his deepest, richest voice.

"My path has led me to your door," he intoned. His hands left cold, silver trails of light in their wake. "You are in your place of power, but you are still mine to command. Attend your master. I am coming through."

The circle of light was now steady and complete. It remained even as Dark brought his hands in and stepped up to it. The portal was at chest level, and Dark strode through it without hesitation and without resistance. He felt a buzz in his skull and spine and heard a crackle. When he opened his eyes, he was elsewhere.

Dark now stood on a small podium of rough granite that jutted up from a vast lake of burning, bubbling tar. Smoke and choking fumes rolled off the lake and swirled around him but did not enter his lungs. Though he could not see the walls or the ceiling, he knew by the echoes and by the long reddish stalactites that he was in a vast underground cave.

Carved into the rock below his feet was the same symbol he had drawn on the floor of his chambers. It was an ancient symbol, used by Madara's brutal warlords in the wild days, long before the emperor. This summoning sigil invoked one of the most vicious siege weapons ever conjured. As a younger man, Dark had spent nearly a full year tracking down this weapon and claiming it for himself.

"Lady Orca," he said, "come forth."

In reply, a massive bubble of tar formed and burst at the center of the lake.

Dark waited a mere moment longer, then savagely slashed his hand through the air. A wave of force flew out from his hand, creating a trench in the hot muck that ran all the way down to the lake bed and splattered tar high onto the cavern walls. Dark stared fixedly at the trench, and the smoking lake remained halved. He raised his hand again to cut the lake into quarters, but a tremor shook the entire cavern before he could complete his second gesture.

The lake began to bubble and boil more violently, and the flames on its surface licked higher, tickling the ends of the stalactites.

Dark nodded once, and the two separate halves of the lake were released, slamming into each other with a violent shudder and a sickening sound. The tar churned and swirled and finally formed a whirlpool around its center like a draining basin. Dark watched calmly as a column of semisolid tar rose from the vortex to the ceiling, snapping off the stalactites in its path. It thickened as it continued to draw burning tar from the lake below. While the lower portion of the column remained a solid cylinder, the upper part split into separate branches. A small blob pinched itself off near the top, and two thick tendrils flowed downward on either side of the larger mass. These deformities became a recognizably humanoid head and pair of arms, but they were featureless and without detail.

Suddenly, the entire figure froze. A small spark ignited on the crown of its head, and a thin veil of blue flame crawled over its entire surface from top to bottom. When the flames reached the surface of the lake there was an explosion of light and scalding, fetid air. In place of the tar figure now stood a gigantic bald woman with steel-blue skin and red-hot coals in her eyes. She seemed to be standing waist-deep in the lake, though Dark knew that here there was no distinction between Lady Orca and her home. Indeed, her body and her shimmering metallic robes merged with the burning surface of the tar, and there was a constant exchange of material between Orca's body and the lake.

"What do you want?" Orca's speaking voice was raspy and rough, as she rarely had occasion to utter anything but her terrifying war cry. Dark stared coldly at her until she dipped her head and added, "Master."

"I have sanction from the emperor," Dark said. "The secessionist leader of the Edemis is to be removed. I have planned the best way to achieve this, and you will be my instrument."

Orca's eyes flashed angrily. "Just the leader? Feh."

Dark raised his hand and clenched it into a fist.

Orca's head suddenly caved in and compressed, as if caught in Dark's grasp. She screamed and thrashed, sending waves of burning tar over Dark's phantom form without any visible effect on the assassin.

"If you would only remember to whom you speak, Lady, these meetings would be so much less painful. You will employ your talents as I say, when I say. Do we understand each other?"

"Yes! Yes, Master, I understand!"

Dark unclenched his fist, and Orca's head returned to its original shape. "To your point," he continued smoothly, "when have I ever asked you for precision? No, Lady Orca, you will act on the scale you are both accustomed to and suited for. Your theater will be the battlefield and your performance one of wholesale carnage and destruction."

Orca's eyes gleamed, and she smiled a black-toothed smile. "My master is feeling poetic today."

"Your master strives for brevity and elegance in all things. Now, prepare yourself. You must be ready at a moment's notice. I will send for you when the time comes."

"I hear and obey."

"Who do you serve?"

"I serve you, Lord Dark."

"And the empire. Together, we shall wipe her enemies from the very memory of the world."

Orca nodded, and the veil of blue flames crawled up her body from the surface of the lake to the top of her head. The humanoid tower of resin and pitch then collapsed in on itself, and the fiery lake churned and bubbled and roiled as before.

Dark took one last look around the charnel pit of Orca's domain, then circled ghostly hands to create his passageway home.

CHAPTER 3

As the champion's full entourage approached Sekana, an agitated and bandaged Tor watched from the shade of the temoya tree. The entire incoming party wore the champion's phoenix crest on their shoulders, and a bearer carried a phoenix standard at the head of the procession. Behind the crimson and black pennant came the champion's armorer Ayesha Tanaka, astride a small gray horse. On foot beside her was her student Kei Takahashi, a tall and gangly youth who wore the white-painted face of a healer in training.

Two more bearers followed Ayesha, pulling her heavy cart behind them. The armorer kept a complete set of tools and a functioning forge in her barrow, as well as a large supply of magical stones, gems, and metal that she could fashion into whatever the champion or his second might need. The cart was enchanted so that the interior was far larger than the exterior, and Tor had been forced to pull it himself on several occasions. He didn't envy the bearers' task. A final bearer came loaded with food, tents, and other essentials.

At the end of the procession rode the imperial champion himself, Tetsuo Umezawa.

Tor had been in Tetsuo's service for eight years as both apprentice and second, but he still flushed with pride at the sight of his master. Tetsuo rode high on a huge, muscular chestnut horse that had been given to him by the emperor himself. Like all imperial steeds, it had eight legs and could run for a week on a single meal.

Tetsuo wore a short sword on his right hip and a magically enhanced long sword on his left. Like Tor, he carried his bow slung across his back. Even laden with weapons and atop a spirited horse, Tetsuo was a study in grace and tranquility. His eyes maintained the same degree of deep, intense concentration at all times. Whether he was instructing his second on the finer points of combat magic, hurdling a four-rail fence on his monstrous horse, or fighting a duel to the death for the emperor's honor, Tetsuo's dignified bearing rarely changed.

Tor rose slowly, pressing down on bandages to keep his chest wounds from separating and bleeding anew. The standard-bearer halted a short distance from Tor's tree and the pillar gates and drove the phoenix emblem into the hard dirt. Ayesha and her student stopped opposite the standard, and the other bearers quietly fell in behind her and set their burdens down.

Tetsuo cantered his horse up beside the phoenix standard and dismounted. As he approached, the champion pulled the archer's message scroll from his belt and held it out with the broken seal visible to all.

"I received your report, Second. You did the right thing bringing me here."

"Master," Tor dropped to his knees, ignoring the pain in his chest. "I have failed you. I have failed the emperor. Forgive me."

Tetsuo's face did not change. "Stand up, Tor." He reached down and took Tor's shoulder, lifting the younger man to his feet. "Explain how you have failed me. You came to Sekana to see if my skills were needed and determined they were. Where is the failure?

"Unless," Tetsuo's green eyes narrowed slightly, "you sought to engage the enemy before you knew its strength." He poked his finger lightly into Tor's bandages, earning a wince from the archer. "Again."

"Worse than that." Tor reached into his hip pouch and produced the remains of his bow. "My weapon was destroyed before I could even draw the string." Tor's face fell.

Tetsuo frowned slightly at the pieces of Tor's bow. "That won't do. An archer needs his tools."

"I can make a new bow for him by sundown," Ayesha said. She stood with her arms crossed while she waited for Tor and Tetsuo to finish.

"No need," Tetsuo said. He unslung his own bow and held it out to Tor. "Until the armorer replaces your weapon, you shall use mine."

"But . . ." Tor's protest died as he turned the bow over and examined it from every angle. "What will you use?"

"A warrior should not become too attached to any one weapon," Tetsuo said. "I will face this thing with my swords and my wits. They have never failed me before.

"Now," he said, "show me this creature that attacks my friends and demands tribute from the emperor's subjects. I should like to see the creature that disarmed Tor."

So would I, Tor thought. He bowed and started for the sea steps. "Follow me," he said.

*　*　*　*　*　*

Tetsuo stood in the same spot his second had occupied two days ago, with Tor and Ayesha hanging back. The armorer had given Tor a special arrowhead from her barrow, one that exploded on impact. He had it nocked and ready in his borrowed bow as he waited for his master's signal.

"In the name of the emperor," Tetsuo said, "come out. You have invaded imperial territory and have terrorized imperial subjects. I am the Tetsuo Umezawa, the imperial champion, and I will have satisfaction."

The yellow eyes snapped open in the depths of the cave. The creature hissed in feline ire.

"You may not address me."

"You flatter yourself, creature. I serve the god-king of the Madara empire, and I am the keeper of his honor. There is none higher than me in all the world, save the emperor himself."

The creature let out a decidedly dismissive snort, and her eyes closed once more.

"Tor," Tetsuo called. "Smoke her out." He stood as patient as a statue, with swords sheathed and arms loose and ready by his sides.

Tor nodded and quickly detached the red crystal arrowhead from its shaft. Ayesha was ready and smoothly exchanged the exploding head for a smoking one. Once the modular piece was locked into place, Tor cupped all four fingers around the gray granite arrowhead and whispered an incantation. He then took aim and fired, sending the bolt parallel to the cave ceiling, high above the creature's eyes.

The arrow disappeared into the depths of the cave. Not even Tor heard it impact against the stone, but soon a stream of thick black smoke drifted out of the cave. Everyone heard the creature cough, however, and the angry growl that followed.

The smoke grew thicker until the creature once again exploded out of the cave. Removed from the action and with the benefit of experience, Tor was better able to follow the blur as the creature lashed out at Tetsuo. It was the same blow she had used on the archer, a punitive slap for an annoying child, but it was almost faster than the eye could follow and strong enough to shatter bone.

Tetsuo was faster still. As the colorful limb flashed out at him, he drew his long sword and caught the raking claws on the flat of his blade. The force of the strike drove him back a half-step, but the claws did not cut into his flesh.

For an interminable second the two combatants held this position, testing each other's strength, then the creature tried to yank her paw back with Tetsuo's sword still hooked in her claws. The champion merely twisted the blade free. The long limb disappeared back into the cave, which was now overflowing with smoke. Tor prepared another arrow.

A hideous, grating shriek split the air as the creature sprang from the choking smoke. She attempted to land on Tetsuo with her forepaws, but the champion leaped nimbly aside and slashed at the nearest limb.

Just as the blade was about to cut into silken fur, the creature snatched her leg back, and Tetsuo's blade sparked against the rocky beach. Champion and beast both back-pedaled, circling each other while they regained their balance and planned their next moves.

The creature was even larger than Bejahn's estimate. Except for her broad leathery wings she was entirely covered in rich, colorful fur like that of a mink or sable. The coat was a kaleidoscopic mixture of brown and black bands layered on a bed of rich orange-gold, with gleaming white accents throughout. Her tail was thick and rounded like a cat's, and her jaw was hinged so that when she bared her saberlike fangs, her mouth opened wide enough to swallow a person whole. Powerful muscles rippled under the silky fur, and each of her broad, flat paws was wide enough to pin two adult humans. From these paws extended retractable claws, razor-sharp and as long as daggers. She was fluid in motion, powerful and graceful like a cat but deliberate and calculating like a reptile. She stared keenly at Tetsuo, hissing and growling in purest outrage.

"What is that thing?" Ayesha said, but Tor simply shook his head. He clicked an exploding arrowhead onto a shaft and took aim.

"Stay back," Tetsuo called, his eyes never leaving the creature's. "Hold your fire."

The fuzzy dragon sat back on her haunches and threw a roundhouse blow at Tetsuo. The champion blocked with his sword, and once again metal barked against claw. The creature paused, measuring Tetsuo with her eyes, and threw another roundhouse from the opposite side, which was likewise blocked.

She unleashed a flurry of blows from both sides that even Tetsuo could not completely stop. Tor saw a seemingly liquid torrent of fur and claws rain down on his master and heard the distinctive ring of claws on steel seven times before one of the blows got through. The creature's paw slammed into Tetsuo's rib cage, slapping him through the air and into the exterior cave wall. The champion slid painfully down the rocks onto one knee, but he kept his sword up and ready to defend.

The creature stopped, losing interest just as she had obtained the advantage. She sniffed at the pad on one of her forepaws and ran her rough tongue between the digits. Keen-eyed Tor saw a few drops of bright crimson fall from the beast's paw before she spread her great wings and kicked up a minor sandstorm.

Tetsuo had regained his feet and stood ready to charge. The edge of his sword was glowing, and Tor watched as his master struck a series of three quick poses, the physical forms he used to channel mana through his blade. Before

Tetsuo could unleash his magical attack, the feline dragon launched herself and spiraled up into the rising mist.

Tetsuo completed the final form and violently slashed the air in front of him. A bolt of pure blue force erupted from the blade in midarc and soared up like a rising cannonball. The arcane energy slammed into the retreating dragon's underbelly, and she spun, momentarily out of control.

"Tor!" Tetsuo barked, and the archer let his red crystal arrow fly. He had targeted the thing's head, but she twisted her body and rolled under the arrow before it could strike home. She roared like a lion, spread her wings out wide, and dived back at Tetsuo. The champion sheathed his sword, centered his stance, and drew it out again. Another bolt of force flew up from the blade, this one purple and crystalline.

The creature dropped under Tetsuo's attack and landed short of the champion. As she spun to leap back into the air, she planted a solid, disdainful kick squarely on Tetsuo's chest.

Tor cried out as Tetsuo flew backward, but the champion had anticipated the blow. He twisted to minimize the impact, and as he soared he turned a somersault and landed firmly on the balls of his feet. He slashed down with his sword, unleashing a black bolt of energy that arced up over the creature's position and burst, forming a thick, dark cloud high over the dragon's head.

Tor loaded one of his own arrows, pinched five fingers above it, and splayed them wide to start it glowing. He fired the dazzling missile across the creature's field of vision, but she easily pulled her face back so that her eyes were protected.

"Enough, Tor. Fall back." Tetsuo launched another blue bolt at the creature. She instinctively lurched upward to avoid the attack and quickly found herself mired in the thick gummy cloud Tetsuo had made, unable to rise or fall.

While the creature was struggling to get free of the clinging, viscous smoke, Tetsuo spun his sword around his body. Chanting as he moved, he cast four separate fireballs from his sword, each in a different direction. The fireballs shot out, changed course, and converged on the dragon.

The creature screeched in fury as they bore down on her, with a look in her eyes that went beyond wrath. She dug into the cloud with all four limbs and tore a hole through the center of the clinging barrier. She shoved herself completely through the rift and twisted free.

Tetsuo's fiery attack slammed into the dense mass from below. There was a loud hiss and a foul odor as the cloud barrier exploded, but its density now shielded the dragon from the flames. Unharmed, she shook a few clinging tendrils of smoke and ash from her fur.

"Fire, Tor. Fire!" Tetsuo spun himself again, casting more minor blue bolts at the escaping creature. Tor nocked and fired arrow after arrow, but the creature swooped and rolled, avoiding every attack. She executed a short loop, her yellow eyes fixed on Tetsuo, then she rose up into the clouds and out of sight.

Tor relaxed the tension in his bowstring and looked to Tetsuo. The champion was staring at the spot in the sky where the creature had disappeared. His face was calm, but Tor had been with him long enough to know that his master's mind was racing.

"Ayesha. Tor," he said, "explore the creature's cave. If there are no other living things in it, I want the entrance mined. She must not be allowed to use this as her base while she preys on Sekana. When you are through, we shall go to the village to wait."

Ayesha stopped rummaging through her tool belt. "Wait for what?"

"For her to return. A creature as proud and as dangerous as this will try to punish her 'subjects' for summoning us. Also, with her nest compromised, she has nowhere else to go.

"When she arrives, she will find us waiting for her, and we will settle this once and for all."

Tor shivered at Tetsuo's tone. Once more he rejoiced in the life path that allowed him to learn from such a master . . . and also obliged him to serve Tetsuo's sword rather than face it.

Ayesha handed Tor several unprimed arrowheads, and he fired them, one by one, into the rocks around the mouth of the cave. When he was through, Ayesha strung conductive wire between them, humming softly to herself.

All the while, Tetsuo stood gazing out at the Talon Gates, unblinking in the stinging sea breeze.

CHAPTER 4

4 Lord Dark's servant boy ran all the way up the tower steps, pausing only to wipe the stinging sweat from his eyes. At the top of the stairs was a simple wooden door. A draft flowed under the door onto his feet, and a deep, steady buzzing sounded on the other side. He swallowed heavily, took a deep breath, and knocked.

The buzzing stopped. "Enter." The voice was musical and tinged with after-echoes, as though its owner were speaking through a long, hollow tube. The servant turned the knob and pushed the door open, but he did not enter.

Lavish decorations festooned the room. Bolts of red and green silk hung from the ceiling over an ornate four-poster bed with lace canopy that dominated the far wall. A huge, silver mirror stretched from floor to ceiling opposite the bed.

The most beautiful and opulent thing in the room, however, was its only occupant. Xira Arien stood gazing out the large window with one eye, while the other remained fixed on the boy in the doorway.

Xira stood a full six feet tall, but like many of Dominaria's insect races, her shoulders and hips were extremely narrow. She was an eumidian, a humanoid wasp with a brilliant gold exoskeleton and four huge, transparent wings.

Xira's face was oval and nearly featureless except for her large, green, compound eyes. Her chin came to a point and hung down over her throat, and her scissorlike mouth snapped open and closed as if she were biting breaths from the air around her. She wore a sumptuous brocade dress of blood red and dusty blue, with a huge triangular hat that stretched out far past her shoulders.

"What is it?" Xira did not turn to face the servant. Her voice was crystalline and beautiful, like a score of glass gongs sounding slightly out of sync. "Enter the room when you speak to a lady." The reverberation of her voice was accented by the perpetual low buzzing from her wings.

"My lady," the boy took exactly one step across the threshold, "Lord Dark requested your presence in his private study at sunset . . . roughly one hour from now. He has asked me to stress again how urgent this matter is."

Xira snapped her mouth shut twice. "Lord Dark thinks everything is urgent." She took up two handfuls of her billowing skirt. "I ask you, boy: Am I suitably dressed for an audience with his lordship? Of course not. I should switch to the yellow and black silk, shouldn't I?"

The boy remained silent, hoping Xira would answer her own question.

"Shouldn't I?" She snapped her mouth shut, and her wings stopped as she turned sharply to face the servant.

"No, milady." The boy kept his face turned to the floor. "I cannot imagine any dress that could improve upon your natural beauty."

The buzzing of her wings resumed. "Flatterer. Come here." The boy came slowly across the room, and Xira stepped around him, tracing a sharp finger across the line of his jaw and around the back of his neck. "You will help me change into the yellow and black silk. While I am between outfits . . . well, if Lord Dark is to wait, it will be because you needed extra time to dress me properly. I am a delicate creature, after all, and I require a gentle touch. His lordship will surely understand."

The boy gulped.

The buzzing grew louder. "What's wrong, my boy? You seem uncomfortable. Am I not beautiful?"

"Truly beautiful, milady."

"Isn't an hour or so with me worth a day or so of his lordship's ire?" The snapping mouth was very close to the boy's ear. "Duty must be balanced with pleasure, after all, or we are no better than soldiers."

"Milady, I cannot—"

"You can," Xira chided, "if you're bold enough."

The eumidian had disappeared from the room, but the servant could hear both her voice and the sound of her wings.

"Milady?" The boy scanned the room closely, from the last spot he had seen Xira to the farthest corner of the ceiling. "Milady, where have you—"

He was interrupted by a sharp stabbing pain in the back of his skull.

"Let this be a lesson to you." Xira was suddenly right beside him, purring in his ear. "It's quite rude to refuse a lady's request."

The boy's vision blurred, and his stomach rolled. His knees gave out, but the hard stone of the floor felt soft and diffuse, as if he had not fallen at all. Through a haze, he saw something sharp slide back up into Lady Xira's palm.

"I will go to Lord Dark," she said, "and I will see him in this outfit. Until then, you will entertain me. Then—" she gestured to the open window— "Lord Dark's moat monsters will have your remains to tide them over till feeding time."

Xira's wings buzzed, and she rose several feet off the floor. Through the haze of poison and pain, the boy watched her circling over him, floating gracefully like a feather on the wind. She came to rest with her feet on his rib cage.

Above him, Xira's scissor-mouth hungrily snapped open and shut. Though he screamed as loudly as his constricted lungs permitted, his cries barely echoed off the turrets on the castle walls.

* * * * *

Lord Dark quit his private meditation chamber and waited to receive Xira in his study. The master of the keep sat cross-legged on a woven mat in the center of the room, seemingly relaxed and dozing. Closer examination revealed a recurring restless twinge in the muscles of his face and eyes that danced behind closed lids. Annoyed, he slowed his breathing and tried to control his racing thoughts. All of the physical, mental, and magical disciplines he had mastered began with the same simple procedure: Clear the mind, relax the body, and focus on the self. If one mastered one's perceptions of the world, one could master that world and everything in it.

Dark imagined the forces that moved the empire, ones he had created and those he merely manipulated. They massed behind him to carry him forward or swelled before him to drive him back. He occupied a crucial position in the ebb and flow of power, one that put him at the very fulcrum of all vectors political, social, martial, and monetary. While these forces churned all around him, he was obliged to move cautiously or be swept away. His path was already forking before him, and he would need all of his guile and initiative to stay the course he had chosen.

As he breathed, Dark saw himself. He was on foot, walking along the banks of a lonely, meandering creek. The landscape on either side of the creek was dusky and obscured: Dark's mental image initially included only himself and the stream as they both progressed forward.

The image clarified as he took comfort from it. This was better than waiting. He mentally added an owl circling overhead and smiled inwardly. He had chosen this particular bird of prey as his standard because he honestly admired it. Its speed, its power, its predatory sharpness . . . but most importantly, its stealth. Unlike most plumage, owl feathers allowed for silent flight. Also, an owl's range of vision was almost a complete circle.

In his own life, Lord Dark also endeavored to see everything around him and strike so swiftly and silently that his prey had no chance to escape.

Dark's pleasant walk by the stream was interrupted by a furious hooting from the owl overhead. A flame flickered in the distant sky, and another bird of prey shrieked an attack cry. As this new flaming avian closed on the owl, Dark's stomach went cold, and his jaw clenched in anger.

The phoenix was much larger than the owl, but both birds attacked with equal ferocity. Dark watched feathers and flesh rain down from the sky as a cacophony of screeches, hoots, and wails echoed off the clouds. With some effort, he was able to look away and peer farther on up the stream's course.

A small wooden bridge spanned the stream a short distance ahead, with a footpath on either side that disappeared into the mist. A tall man armed with swords and a bow stood watching from the bridge as Dark approached.

Lord Dark instantly recognized the man and understood the true purpose of this vision. The only task Lord Dark had left undone was now facing him across the meditation plane.

"We meet again," the vision of Tetsuo Umezawa said, "assassin."

"Champion," Dark replied, "our paths cross because we are connected by our service to the emperor. But your presence, as always, is unwelcome."

Overhead, the two fighting birds vanished into the smoky mist, leaving their masters to take up the struggle.

"You are up to something. In the Edemis." The vision-Tetsuo was exactly the same as the real thing: suspicious, self-righteous, and full of loathing.

Dark sneered. "I am fulfilling the duties of my office. I am serving the empire."

"My office also has duties. Upholding the emperor's honor rarely aligns with murdering his rivals."

"I have imperial sanction. My office—"

"Your office is a disgrace. When I am done here in Sekana, I will examine your 'sanction.' I will then act accordingly. Have formal declarations been made? Have the generals in the kentsu been informed? There is not a shred of integrity among any who wear your crest, assassin. Power without honor is tyranny, and the empire should be above such things."

"Honor is your battleground, Champion. Leave power to those who know how to wield it." Dark fought back the wave of rage Tetsuo always inspired. "Come now. There is no reason for us to quarrel . . . not about this. The emperor has given me permission to act, and act I shall. In a sense, I am also doing you a service."

"Me? How do your actions serve me?"

"Your office, then. Leave me to my work and only the right people will die. The empire will be preserved and strengthened, and a potentially long and costly war will be averted."

Tetsuo's eyes remained cold. "How altruistic you are."

"Spare me your childish morality. Our roles are not so different, yours and mine. We both seek the one brick whose removal brings down an entire wall. Why butcher an army when you can slash a single throat for the same result?"

"We could not be more distinct," Tetsuo said. "You use the empire's majesty to inspire terror. I embody it to inspire respect."

"Yes, yes. Your tune never changes, does it? Happily, I don't have to indulge you on this occasion." Dark saw a new opportunity forming as they quarreled, and he quickly seized it, choosing his next words with extreme care. "Gosta and the others will fall. There is nothing you can do to stop me without risking the emperor's ire."

"You will do as you think you must. As will I." Tetsuo put his hand on his sword. "There is nothing I would not risk to preserve the emperor's dignity. Not even his ire."

Dark crossed his arms angrily. "So be it. Do your worst."

"I shall do my best," Tetsuo said. "The worst, I leave to you." The dream-Tetsuo began to drift away, and Lord Dark caught the briefest glimpse of a tall boy in white face paint standing in the haze behind the fading champion.

Dark raised his voice. "You've been warned, Champion. Stay out of my business." He angrily snapped out of his trance, furious that Tetsuo had tried to get in the last word.

Lord Dark rose from the woven mat and opened a large wooden trunk by the door. So, he thought, as he rummaged. As usual, the champion seeks to interfere.

Dark removed a slate tablet, a small writing brush, and another pot of tar.

Let him try, he thought. He hung the pot over a loaded brazier and set the fire burning. He had quarreled with Tetsuo often enough in the past to take the man seriously.

Tetsuo was a formidable warrior and battle mage, virtually invincible in direct combat, but he was a naïve and deluded child in the arena of global intrigue, when the scale of events themselves dwarfed his foolish concepts of integrity and fair play.

Yes, the way to defeat Tetsuo was to begin the battle before he realized one was underway. Force him to react rather than act; keep him constantly off-balance. Then a single swift and silent stroke from an unassailable position of strength would cut him down like any other obstacle.

"I," Dark smiled as he stirred the tar, "began this battle months ago."

*　*　*　*　*

Lord Dark sat in light meditation until he heard a faint buzz from the hallway and the sound of delicate feet coming to rest on stone. A moment later there was a gentle knock and Xira's musical voice.

"You sent for me, your lordship? I am here, eager to serve."

"A moment, Lady Xira." Dark did not open his eyes. He reached out, scooped up a blob of hot tar on the end of his finger, and smeared it through the sigil he had drawn on the slate tablet. The marred character let out a small pop and a hiss, and the tar stopped steaming.

Lord Dark opened his eyes, stood, and went to his desk at the rear of the room. He wiped his fingers clean with a mono-grammed cloth and leaned on the corner of his desk.

"Enter," he called.

Xira walked through the door, paused to adjust to the dim candlelight, and then closed the door behind her. "My lord."

"Milady. How fares the servant boy?"

Xira demurely turned her head aside. "Are there no se-crets from you, my lord?"

"Not in my own home, no."

43

Xira shrugged girlishly. "Dying, soon to be dead." She looked up into Dark's face. "He needed a lesson in manners."

"You need a lesson in self-denial. You indulge yourself far too often and too often at my expense."

"Forgive me, my lord. I was thoughtless and selfish."

"According to your nature." Dark smiled. "I have just the thing for you to repay me. I have seen the emperor, and he has given his assent. We have a warrant for Caleria, and if I deem it necessary, Magnus and Gosta as well."

Xira buzzed. "Is it necessary, my lord?"

Dark nodded. "All are to be sanctioned."

"His majesty was in a generous mood."

"His majesty saw the wisdom of my counsel," Dark said sternly. "Whatever his mood, mine is in no way generous."

"No, my lord."

"No, indeed. Now, then. You are to bypass Gosta on Kusho Island entirely. Travel to Argenti alone and unattended." He held up a hand to silence the protest he heard forming in Xira's throat. "As I said, you need a lesson in self-denial. Go via the Talon Gates."

"As you wish, my lord, but I don't see why I should slog through the mist alone like a carrier pigeon. At least send a boat with servants along."

"The next alteration you suggest to my carefully laid plans will anger me, Xira. Do as you are told."

"Yes, my lord."

"I will, of course, renew your enhancements. According to our arrangement."

Xira clicked nervously. "Yes, my lord. Now?"

Dark nodded. "Now." He leveled his gaze, and stared hard at Xira. They held their stare for a moment, Dark's cold eyes boring into Xira's until an eerie glow issued from his pupils. The energy meandered like smoke between the two, circling

Xira's head. Then, with a snap, the energy leaped into Xira's huge compound eyes. She and Dark cried out together, though only Xira fell back.

With a graceful wave, Dark bade Xira rise into the air. Xira's wings buzzed, and her whole body became engulfed in the smoky energy Dark had bestowed on her. She chittered madly as she floated, remaining aloft even after her wings stopped beating.

"Marvelous, my lord!" She flitted over to the huge window, up to the ceiling, and over Dark's desk.

"That should augment your natural abilities enough to get you to Argenti and back on my timetable. Now . . ." Dark covered both his eyes with his palms, then threw his hands out wide. Xira had time for a strangled half-screech as black lightning exploded out of Dark's hands and eyes. The bolts came together at Xira's head, slamming into her face and snatching her out of the air like a falcon-struck pheasant. Xira rebounded painfully off the wall of Dark's study, and fell facedown on his floor.

Xira lay still for a moment with air hissing in and out of her lungs. Then she sprang to her feet and snapped her jaws angrily.

"Was that entirely necessary, my lord?"

It was. Lord Dark's lips did not move, and he was smiling. *If you intend to complete the mission I have given you, it was absolutely necessary.*

Xira calmed, her wings slowing. *So,* she replied in her mind. *I'm to be monitored like an amateur?*

This is an important game we're playing, my dear. The situation will change rapidly once you're underway, and you will be my eyes and voice. You are the blade, but I am its wielder.

Xira clicked petulantly. "Yes, my lord," she said aloud.

Dark held her gaze for a moment, then casually inspected his manicure. "There is one final detail. Before you go through the Talon Gates, you will stop in the coastal village there. It is called Sekana." He waited for Xira to complain, but the eumidian kept silent. "There you will find the imperial champion on some foolish errand or another. When you do, report back to me."

"I have heard of the place. A miserable little collection of peasant huts that reek of fish. You are quite sure the champion is there?"

"I am. Tetsuo and I have a great deal in common, despite what he says. We are connected by our disciplines as well as our service to the emperor. It is difficult for us to keep our actions or our locations hidden from each other for long."

Xira's eyes glittered. "Do we have a warrant for him, as well?"

Dark's face was cold and blank. "Perish the thought. As I just explained to one of your peers, Tetsuo's death would be a severe tragedy for all of Madara. Something like that shouldn't even be discussed." Dark stared hard at Xira until she nodded.

"So as far as you're concerned, there is no warrant for Umezawa. Unless I explicitly tell you otherwise, you are only to engage him verbally. Verbally, and nothing else. Do you understand?"

"I do, my lord."

"Excellent. Leave at once. I will await your report once you reach Sekana and have made contact with the champion."

Xira nodded. "A question, my lord?"

"Ask."

"Am I alone on this mission? Am I free to operate according to my methods, or are you going to partner me with that tiresome Devilboon?"

"I have other plans for little Boris. But you will have a partner, Xira. One who enjoys working alone as much as you do. I have taken pains to keep you two out of each other's way."

"Dare I ask who my associate will be?"

Dark smiled. He stood, and indicated the cooling pot of tar on the floor beside Xira. "I have already dispatched Lady Orca to Kusho," he said. "Before you engage Caleria and Magnus, she will engage Gosta."

Xira's mouth snapped, and her wings buzzed. She could barely contain her glee. "Will she continue on to Argenti?"

"She will. If you want there to be anything left when you arrive, I'd advise you to depart immediately."

CHAPTER 5

Tor emerged from the fisherman's hut that served as Tetsuo's makeshift headquarters. He checked the position of the just-risen sun and approached Ayesha's barrow. The armorer already had her miniature forge working and was tapping something into shape with a metalsmith's hammer.

"Anything happening?"

"Nothing I'm aware of," Ayesha replied. "We should be able to see more once this fog burns off. "

Tor scanned the sky and turned back to the forge. "And you, armorer? What are you tinkering with so early?"

Ayesha did not look up from her work. "I am making grapeshot arrowheads for you. I thought they might be more effective against this creature than the single-impact kind. If we can hole her wings, the fight will be half-won."

"Another excellent idea." Tor paused. "Have you had time to think about a new bow for me?"

"No." Ayesha stopped pumping the bellows. "The grapeshot requires a heavy weapon to launch it high enough. I don't carry the materials to make you such a bow, and the local trees are better suited for growing fruit and fueling fires. I was hoping you could continue using Tetsuo's."

"That," said the champion as he came over the rocky dunes, "will not be a problem."

"You're sure you don't need it?" Tor had the champion's bow in his hand, but he wasn't eager to give it up.

Tetsuo nodded. "Keep it for now. I need you armed and ready to protect the villagers when this thing comes back." He looked down the rocky beach at the village in the distance and back down along the coastline. "Where is Kei?"

"Inspecting the local fauna for medicinal herbs. It's part of his training. Why? Do you need him here?"

"I would like to speak to him, yes."

Ayesha stood up, placed her index and middle fingers in the corners of her mouth, and blew two short whistles and one long one. "He's on his way." She dropped back to her knees and resumed hammering.

"There are other matters that will shortly concern us all," Tetsuo said. "It would be best if we could end things here quickly."

"Perhaps we could bait the creature," Tor said immediately. "Draw her out and lure her to a place of our choosing."

"A sensible plan. What would we use as bait?"

"She likes fish," Tor said. Ayesha stopped hammering and looked at him in amusement, Tor shrugged, and added, "I had time to speak to the villagers after I was injured. They said she's given to sneaking into houses, plopping herself down in the middle of things, and demanding fish. Virtually every home on the water has been invaded at one time or another."

Tetsuo turned on Tor, his voice sharp. "You mean this thing has entered the village by stealth in the past?"

"Yes. Many times."

"You told me that she came in through the main gates, and terrorized the town square."

"At first. Once she had the villagers running scared, she came and went as she pleased." Tor's voice rose in concern.

"What's the matter, Master? Have I done wrong?"

Tetsuo glared at Tor for an extra second before he said, "Has anyone been to the village this morning?"

Tor shook his head, and Ayesha set her hammer down. "I've been at the forge since I woke up." She handed Tor three round metal balls with sockets for arrow shafts. "You think she's inside the walls?"

The village alarm bell sounded in the distance, its plaintive peal almost lost among the sound of breaking waves.

"If she wasn't before," Tetsuo said, "she is now. Come. It seems the creature is now baiting us."

*　*　*　*　*

The feline dragon sat in all her colorful splendor, regally cleaning her massive paws with her tongue. She faced the village square. Behind her stood the central storehouse, a large single-room edifice with one wide entrance, which she now blocked.

Tetsuo entered the square, followed by Tor, Ayesha, and a still-panting Kei.

The dragon paused to sniff the air. She then resumed grooming herself.

Tetsuo marched resolutely down the path to the storehouse. The street was deserted, and when Tetsuo was thirty yards away the dragon began to purr loudly.

"Who is queen?" The creature's tone was all smugness and tease.

"Madara has no queen." Tetsuo stopped walking and crossed his arms over his chest. He raised his voice only slightly.

"Perhaps not," the dragon said sweetly, "but this village does."

Tetsuo drew his long sword. "You go too far. Sekana called me, desperate for my help. Do you really think holding their provisions hostage will stop me from killing you here and now?"

The dragon tilted her head in playful confusion. "Provisions?"

Just then, Bejahn's face appeared in the doorway behind the dragon. There were two more terrified faces on either side of the elder's.

"By the emperor's eye, Champion," Bejahn called, "help us."

Without looking, the dragon lashed out with one of her back paws and shattered the door frame above Bejahn's head. The villagers cried out and ducked to avoid the storm of debris and splinters.

"Earlier—" the dragon paused to bite an errant shard of wood from between her claws—"you roused me from a sound sleep and drove me off. I am fully awake now, two-legs. Can you dance with your sword faster than I can destroy the building? The whole village?" She lashed out again, scoring on the broad front wall and shaking the storehouse to its foundations. "One solid blow in the right place, and this entire barn comes tumbling down."

She yawned. "Perhaps you'd like to launch more fireballs at me? You probably won't miss this time, but if you do, it would save me the trouble of wrecking the building myself." She settled down on her haunches, yawned, and closed her eyes. "Leave me now."

"I'm not going anywhere. The empire demands satisfaction."

The dragon cracked open one eye. "And I demand silence. Begone, little monkey, or there will be blood on the streets of Sekana."

"Master," Tor called. Tetsuo turned and saw his second with an exploding arrow trained on the creature's head. "I can take her."

"Lower your weapon," Tetsuo said. He glared at the dragon. "She thinks we can do nothing to her without endangering the villagers we came to protect."

The dragon's eyes twinkled. "I do think that."

"But she doesn't know the empire. Or the emperor. She doesn't know that if I fail, the kentsu will return to confront her. I may die in disgrace, but she will die in agony. The soldiers are not so concerned with the fate of Sekana and its inhabitants. The orchards will be burned and plowed under. The entire coastline will be swallowed by the sea, and every living thing for miles in all directions will be put to the sword."

The dragon's eyes narrowed, and a low angry growl rumbled from deep in her chest. Tetsuo stared hard at her.

"You cannot stay here," he said. "The emperor will not allow it, and the most powerful forces imaginable are sworn to his service."

"Let them come," the dragon snarled. "I have killed armies before."

For the first time, Tor heard uncertainty in her vainglorious voice, and a thrill ran through him. Could Tetsuo actually talk the monster into leaving? He knew the champion was not bluffing or exaggerating the imperial response. The soldiers of the kentsu were notoriously savage and had conquered whole nations for the emperor's glory. No sane creature could hope to stand against them. Tor regarded the posturing dragon and wondered just how sane she was.

"You cannot stay," Tetsuo repeated, "and I cannot leave. We are going to fight, dragon, and no matter who wins our contest, you will be dead within a week. Either I kill you now, or the kentsu kills you later."

The dragon sniffed, unimpressed. "We shall see. Perhaps I shall kill you, and your followers, and this entire village before I find a new place to build my home."

"Or," Tetsuo said, "I have an alternative."

The dragon closed her eyes again. "I'm bored. I declare you to be the champion of blather and nothing else."

Tetsuo ignored the taunt and removed a carved jade talisman from around his neck. It was in the shape of a phoenix rising, and he tossed it to the ground between himself and the dragon.

"I am Tetsuo Umezawa, the imperial champion," he said, "and if you will tell me your name, I will challenge you to prove my claim to that title. Your weapons and skill versus mine. Face to face, with no outside interference and no retreat until one of us either surrenders or dies."

The dragon opened her eyes. "After I spent all morning herding these two-legged sheep into one place? You're a noble fool, Champion. Why would I give up my advantage to participate in your childish showdown?"

"Because if you defeat me in a formal duel, you will become the imperial champion. My associates, the villagers, and just about everyone else in the empire will be at your service. You can roost here in Sekana for the rest of your life, if you like."

"Unless your emperor sends his army or someone better than you to destroy me."

Tetsuo's face was like stone, his voice even and sure. "I earned the right to my office through combat. By definition," he said, "there is no one better than me."

The dragon lifted her head and stared up at the clouds. She licked her chops and then tilted her head at Tetsuo. "You would bargain with a dragon?"

"I would serve the empire."

"Well, then. If it's a bargain you seek, let's make it a proper one. We will fight. If you win, I will be dead, which is what you want. But if I win, you will be dead, and I don't care about you one way or the other. You must offer something other than your life and your station."

"Name your stakes."

"Six months in Sekana. I wish to be left alone and unmolested by you grubby little apes. The villagers and your servants remain here at my service and in silence. Not one word of my presence or your death is reported to anyone until I am gone."

Tetsuo looked back at Tor, Kei, and Ayesha. "They are not my servants," he said, "but I can ask for their compliance."

Tor started to disagree, but the armorer's voice stifled his protest.

"Suits me," she said.

Kei nodded, adding, "I follow my master."

"Ayesha," Tor whispered, "we can't agree to—"

"Surely you're not suggesting your master will lose?"

Tor's face colored. "Of course not." He raised his voice, "We agree, Master. We will remain silent."

Tetsuo turned back to the dragon. "It is done."

"Not quite. I require assurances. You must swear to our bargain with whatever oaths are sacred to little monkeys."

"I give you my word of honor." Tetsuo's eyes flashed. "There is nothing more sacred. And you, dragon? What oaths are inviolable for your kind?"

The dragon smiled. "None. But I give you my word anyway." She rose and stretched, a shudder of muscular power rippling from her head all the way back to the tip of her tail. "Shall we begin?"

"Away from the village," Tetsuo said. "Else who will be left to serve you once I am dead? There is a final formality. I have given my name and issued a challenge. You must give yours and accept."

The dragon sneered. "That sounds rather binding, Champion. You're not trying to hex me before the fight begins, are you?"

"It is ritual combat we fight. A formal duel, and we are bound by its conventions."

"Once I declare my name and intent, the duel begins?"

"It does."

The dragon stretched out her wings and fluttered them in a spectacular display. "Then we shall remove ourselves to the dueling place. Prepare yourself for the next world, Champion. My name will be the last thing you hear in this one."

Tetsuo turned and headed down the road leading out of the village. The dragon padded softly after him.

Ayesha waited until they were both well clear of the storehouse door, then nodded to Kei. "There may be wounded in there. To your work, healer." The white-faced youth opening his medicine pouch as he went up to the storehouse.

Tor locked eyes with Ayesha for a moment then slung the champion's bow over his shoulder. "And to mine. A duel such as this requires a formal witness."

"We will get the villagers to safety," Ayesha said, "then follow along." Led by Bejahn, the villagers were streaming out of the storehouse and heading for the docks. Several were bruised and bleeding, and Kei pulled these aside and questioned them softly.

"You'd better hurry," Tor added. "I don't think the fight will last that long." He started down the road after the combatants, sparing one last look at the confusion in the square.

Ayesha directed the former hostages out of the building, away from Tetsuo and the dragon. Kei was trying to talk to and treat four people at once, and they were on the verge of trampling him.

Tor also spotted a woman standing far in the distance on the roof of a villager's hut. She was tall and thin, with the rising sun behind her so Tor could not clearly see her features or mode of dress. The harsh light outlined her figure in dazzling brightness, however, and in the glare Tor thought for a moment that he saw large translucent wings jutting out behind the woman's shoulders.

The archer paused briefly, but then ran to catch up to his master.

* * * * * *

Tetsuo led the dragon to the seaside. The tide was receding, and the beach was like stone, having been pounded flat by the waves and dried by the harsh morning sun. They were two hundred yards from the village, near the beach where the fisherman tethered their largest boats.

Tor jogged into view, and Tetsuo stopped him well clear of the spot he had chosen. He motioned the archer over near the sea. Tor nodded, unslung his bow, and circled around the two combatants. Halfway between his master and the ocean, Tor rested the bow's bottom tip on the toes of his left foot.

Tetsuo was keeping him clear of the duel but also using him to stand between the dragon and the fishing boats. Even now, villagers tentatively approached the shore, no longer safe in their own homes. Tor held the bow lightly with both hands, but his right twitched as he fought the urge to rip an arrow from his quiver and let it fly at the dragon.

"Tetsuo Umezawa, imperial champion of all Madara." The champion drew his long blade and held it tip-first at his opponent. "In the name of his majesty, the emperor, I challenge you to a duel. The victor will claim my title and all accompanying responsibilities."

The dragon's eyes were open wide, her pupils dilated for combat. She was actually salivating, her hinged jaw hanging wide and her all-black eyes twinkling.

"My name is Wasitora, queen of the nekoru. We are rarely found in these parts. That will soon change, for I accept your challenge." The dragon seemed to explode at Tetsuo, and the champion let out a war-cry as he also sprang forward.

The line of villagers bound for their boats stopped as the two combatants rushed each other. Without taking his eyes off the duel, Tor barked, "Keep moving! If you're going to go, go!"

Queen Wasitora drove straight at Tetsuo, counting on her superior speed to prevent the champion from casting any spells with his blade. Tetsuo anticipated this approach and instead of casting a spell simply slashed at the dragon's paw.

Wasitora abandoned her strike just as her extremity touched the edge of Tetsuo's sword. She leaped up and over the champion as he struck. The two fighters' momentum carried them past each other, and they both landed unharmed.

The champion raised his sword to his face and blew several strands of luxurious nekoru fur from its blade.

"My *coat*," Wasitora hissed. She glanced at the cut the sword had made in her fur then opened her mouth wide and roared.

Tetsuo waved his sword out in a wide arc to his right. Before he could finish the maneuver, Wasitora kicked up a wad of wet sand and rocks. She beat her leathery wings, and flying debris peppered Tetsuo's face and shoulders, momentarily blinding him. In that moment, the dragon queen struck again.

Even without sight, Tetsuo was ready. Wasitora had not committed herself as heavily as she had the first time, merely lunging forward and slapping at Tetsuo's head. The champion slid the flat of his blade between his face and the dragon's claws, but the blow still landed.

Her paw glanced off his jawline, and Tetsuo staggered back on one foot. As he teetered, he viciously slashed his sword through where Wasitora would have been if she'd pressed her advantage. The dragon merely sprang alongside Tetsuo, however, correctly anticipating his counterstrike.

Tetsuo's eyes had cleared, and he saw the dragon, poised mere yards away for her killing blow. The duelists' eyes met, and they both struck as one. Tetsuo threw his long sword at Wasitora's head, spinning hard and fast enough to split the dragon's skull.

The nekoru queen was already striking low at Tetsuo's legs, and the sword whirled high and wide, missing her entirely. As she sailed forward, she spread her wings slightly to keep her bulk from crashing into the sand and stretched her forelimbs far out ahead of her. Tor tried to cry out a warning, but in the time it took him to inhale, Tetsuo struck again.

The champion drew his short sword, holding it tip-down and blade-forward as the dragon's claws came at him. He hopped forward and tucked his knees. This minor effort carried him a few feet off the ground and a few yards forward.

Wasitora's paw soared under him, and as the rest of her body followed, Tetsuo jammed the tip of his short blade into her shoulder. The dragon shrieked as the blade tore along her right side, leaving a deep incision from the shoulder joint all the way past her wing.

She landed heavily in a storm of rocks and sand and ocean spray. Tetsuo came down lightly on the balls of his feet then calmly walked to retrieve his long blade.

Tor stifled a cheer, but only because his master had been furious the last time he'd broken decorum during a duel. The dragon lay in an undignified heap, panting and scratching at the ground as she tried to get her injured wing and forepaw to respond.

Tetsuo sheathed his short blade and took hold of the long sword, turning to face the dragon where she sat. She glared back with a look of pure hatred, injured but unbeaten, and she hissed.

Tetsuo sheathed the long sword and stared at the dragon. He pressed his palms together in front of him and bowed to his opponent.

"Wasitora, queen of the nekoru," he said. "Good-bye."

Tor felt an galvanic thrill run through him. The champion's wide array of finishing maneuvers never failed to impress him.

Tetsuo drew his sword and slashed it up high at arm's length, the motion accompanied by a whisper of steel echoing off the rocky ground. Wasitora struggled, but Tor could not determine if she was trying to approach Tetsuo for one last attack or simply to get out of his way.

The champion brought his blade down to his right hip, and pointed behind him, with his left hand palm-first to the dragon. The air in the blade's wake started to hum as Tetsuo focused his power. He slowly raised the sword so that it was straight out to his right at shoulder level. Thin streams of vapor energy trailed behind it.

Before he could complete the last form in his attack, Tetsuo was interrupted by an ear-splitting roar. A chorus of screams and the sound of splintering wood quickly followed. Tor, Tetsuo, and the dragon all turned as a monstrous wave rose up on the shoreline, carrying two fishing boats laden with villagers high above the beach. Another boat had capsized farther out to sea, and the three remaining craft were tossed and buffeted by sudden and violent swells.

The two wave-tossed boats came crashing down on the beach. Cries of pain and panic from the villagers were all but drowned out by the sound of the wave's fury. The others still at sea screamed for help as yet another huge wave rose.

Some of the villagers closest to this new wave abandoned their boat and started swimming . . . not for shore but farther out into the ocean. Tor's eyes darted from the wreck to the wave to the interrupted duel. Wasitora had risen on her three good legs, but she did not attack. Tetsuo had abandoned his maneuver and stared hard at the towering wall of water.

The big wave crested like a mountain rising from the deep and began to drain away. There was something huge at its center. Amid the sea foam and the salt spray, it was impossible to determine its shape, but everyone could appreciate its size.

The great beast rose up at the water's edge, its pale white scales dripping with brine and seaweed. Its head was as big as the fishing boats, and its eyebrow ridges rose high over its forehead to form a bony carapace. It dredged massive fore-limbs out of the wet sand, flicked a long, forked tongue, and roared loudly enough to make even Tetsuo wince.

"Madarans," the giant land wurm bellowed, furious at the forced swim from the Talon Gates to the shore. "No longer shall you raid and murder your peaceful neighbors. Caleria cries, 'enough.' She demands payment for the innocent dead.

On behalf of the independent Edemi Islands, she declares war on your empire." The beast glanced down at the villagers on the beach before it. "Prepare to die."

As the villagers scrabbled to their feet, the wurm pulled the rest of its vast bulk onto the shore.

CHAPTER 6

Xira Arien watched from the roof as Tetsuo and the cat dragon postured. She couldn't hear what they were saying, but it was easy enough to piece together: The beast was preying on the villagers, and the champion had come to stop her. Tetsuo threw his talisman at the dragon's feet, and they marched off to settle their differences like obedient little children. Tetsuo's boy had spotted Xira, but that didn't truly matter. She had come to be seen.

She sank her clawed feet deeper into the main roof beam. Xira usually went shoeless only if she was wearing an outfit that covered her all the way to the floor, and she cursed Lord Dark for sending her out so miserably underdressed. She was currently wearing a skintight blue bodysuit with a basic silk hoop skirt that ended just below her knee. She felt naked without her accessories, her shoes, and her fancy hat. With no servants or even a change of clothing, she would soon be just another peasant who wore the same outfit every day. Xira crouched slightly so that the skirt hung down to the roof thatch, partially covering the gripping claws on her feet.

The champion's armorer directed aimless villagers across the square and out of the village. A tall boy, painted like a healer, meanwhile isolated the wounded and performed basic first aid.

Xira stood to her full height, buzzed her wings, and rose into the air. If Lord Dark insisted on forcing her to be drab and awful, she saw no reason to drag the assignment out. Besides, she thought maliciously, the best way to cure misery is to spread it around.

She landed in the village square, evincing cries of surprise and pointed fingers. The painted healer looked at her blankly, as if he had seen a hundred eumidians and simply didn't recognize this one. The armorer, however, went all tense and dour. As Xira swatted some of the dust from her skirt, Ayesha whistled sharply and motioned to the healer.

"Kei to me."

Interesting, Xira thought. The boy's name is Kei, and he's apprenticed to the champion's glowering bulldog.

"Lady Ayesha," Xira called sweetly. She curtsied. "Well met."

"I disagree, insect," Ayesha said, "and you must call me 'armorer' or simply 'Madam Tanaka.' I dislike false titles." The white-faced boy stood close behind her, tall enough to see clearly over her shoulder.

"You misunderstand, dear," Xira chimed. "I address you as an equal for the sake of expediency. Otherwise, I would never speak to you at all. Now will you introduce me," she stepped around Ayesha and offered her hand to Kei, "to this luscious servant of yours?"

Ayesha's hand fluttered near the short sword she wore on her hip. "Xira Arien, this is Kei Takahashi, my apprentice and a healer-in-training. Kei, this is Xira Arien, a stuck-up killer from Lord Dark's stables. She fancies herself a lady, so don't spit on her just yet."

Xira snapped her jaws at Ayesha, then smiled and stepped forward, her hand extended to Kei. "Charmed."

The boy started to reach out, but Ayesha glared so fiercely he quietly dropped his hand and stepped back.

"Lady," he said.

"So what brings the champion's entourage to this quaint little collection of hovels and fishing boats? Don't tell me you're having trouble with that nekoru."

Ayesha fixed her eyes on Xira. "You know what that thing is?"

"I have traveled far and wide in the service of the emperor," Xira said airily. "I saw one once before, in Jamuraa. They're supposed to be extremely dangerous—" she shrugged—"but the one I saw was much bigger than this one. It should be no trouble for your noble master."

"Why are you here, Lady? Is your master so bored he sends spies to watch the champion's day-to-day activities?"

"I am on imperial business." Xira bared her shoulder, presenting the assassin's crest to Kei. She winked, then turned the owl and snake brand toward Ayesha.

The armorer's hand stayed on her sword. "Is your business with us? Or are you simply going to throw yourself at my apprentice until he gags and runs screaming from the square?"

Xira's jaws clicked angrily, but she quickly smiled again. Her tone was soft and casual. "Careful, armorer." She extended her right arm straight down at her side, flexing her long, thin fingers. "You go to far."

"I am always careful around you, Lady."

Xira felt her stinger, retracted and ready inside her forearm. She could easily skewer and envenom Ayesha before the armorer could defend herself. Eumidians were much faster than humans.

But Lord Dark had been quite clear . . . she was not to attack without a direct order, and that order had not yet been given. Then again, he had specified Tetsuo as the one to be left alone. Xira could always claim that she thought the armorer and her boy were fair game.

Just as Xira decided to try her luck against Ayesha and work out her explanation to Lord Dark later, something strange happened. The white-faced boy flinched, gaped at Xira, and pulled his master back a step. Ayesha started at his touch but allowed herself to be pulled back another step then put her hand on top of Kei's.

"Kei," she said. The tall youth blinked and looked with some surprise at his hand on Ayesha's shoulder.

"Forgive me, Master," he mumbled. "I thought I saw something."

"Perhaps you did." Ayesha was staring hard at Xira. "If you'll excuse us, Lady. We have constructive work to do."

Xira's mind whirled. The boy had sensed the danger to Ayesha at the precise moment Xira had chosen to attack. There was more to the gangly youth than met the eye. She filed this information away for future use . . . and her report to Lord Dark, of course.

"Forgive me, armorer," Xira said at last. "I didn't realize you had that kind of master-pupil relationship." She smiled cruelly, opening up her arms and inviting Ayesha to attack. "I would never poach on your private reserve."

The boy flushed behind his face paint, and Ayesha's glare was sharp enough to cut glass. Xira congratulated herself. If the armorer struck at her, Xira would not even have to lie to her master. She could kill two of the champion's entourage and justifiably claim self-defense.

A chorus of screams echoed over the west seawall, and a terrific crash sounded. Half the villagers ran to investigate the sounds; the other half ran in the opposite direction. Without taking her eyes off Xira, Ayesha backed away, Kei's hand in hers.

"Get to the beach," she said. "If any villagers are wounded, treat them as best you can. Otherwise, wait for me." Kei nodded and ran for the main gate.

"We'll have to continue this some other time, assassin." Ayesha drew her short sword and pointed it at Xira. "You will answer for those insults and for your presence here."

Xira smiled with sharp mouthparts. "You won't have to look far to find me, dear."

From the other side of the seawall, a huge beast roared, freezing the villagers in their tracks. Ayesha spent one last second glaring at Xira, swore, and ran after her student.

Xira glanced around at the chaos in the square: villagers running to and fro, an unseen beast rising on the other side of the seawall, the terrified and wounded crying out. She flexed her wings, vibrated them until they caught the air, and rose elegantly into the sky.

That is no nekoru roar, she thought. She crossed her arms over her chest, and a smug expression filled her face. She rotated as she rose, scanning the area in all directions until she spotted Tetsuo and a small crowd of others on the shoreline.

A huge wurm crawled over a boatload of villagers, en route to the champion. Behind Tetsuo lay the female nekoru, bleeding from a shoulder wound but still active and hissing malice.

Xira closed her eyes and felt Lord Dark's enhancement take hold, keeping her aloft while she focused her thoughts inward. The sounds below faded, and she floated in a vast, misty void.

My lord, she thought. *I have arrived in Sekana. I have seen the champion but am currently unable to engage him. At this moment he is standing between two fifty-foot dragons who seem bent on tearing him to pieces. It appears we may not need to sanction him after all. How shall I proceed?*

Xira waited. Just as she was about to go forward without further instructions, Lord Dark's voice boomed through her brain.

Well done, Xira. Keep a close watch on the situation, and take nothing for granted where Tetsuo is concerned. Contact me again when the battle is over.

Xira opened her eyes and resumed hovering under her own power. In accordance with Lord Dark's wishes and her own, she gleefully streaked across the beach to get the best possible view of the champion's demise.

* * * * *

Tor fired a red crystal arrowhead, which exploded noisily but harmlessly against the wurm's throat. The wurm stretched and roared at Tor, allowing the villagers on the beach more time to stumble, roll, and otherwise get out of its way. As Tor loaded another arrow, a giddy, random thought crossed his mind: What about the duel?

Even Tetsuo seemed caught off-guard. His sword was still out, but its tip and the champion's eyes darted back and forth between Wasitora and the new interloper.

Tor let the second arrow fly and loaded a third. The wurm rose high on its hind legs and came thundering down on the beach. The resulting tremor jarred villagers off their feet and the arrow from the Tor's string before the archer could let it fly.

Tor caught the arrow in midair and froze as a painful roar of fury ripped through the cold sea air. A great blur bounded past him and onto the land wurm's neck.

Wasitora pounced, the claws on her uninjured limbs extended before her. She screeched and hissed in purest hatred, her wounded forelimb and wing trailing her.

The land wurm fell back, and it bucked and bellowed as it tried to toss her off. Wasitora had her teeth sunk deep into the wurm's shoulder, and the claws on her good legs were hooked into the seams between the wurm's scales. She hung from the great beast as it tossed its huge head from side to side. Her sharp back claws tore long strips of flesh off the wurm's torso.

As the two dragons fell and rolled in the surf, Tor saw the remains of half a dozen villagers in the craters created by the land wurm's stomping feet.

With sword drawn, Tetsuo charged past. "Get these people back inside the village." Tetsuo raced to the grappling beasts and thrust his sword deep into the land wurm's belly.

Enraged, the wurm finally threw off Wasitora. The nekoru queen took a huge mouthful of flesh with her, and the land wurm roared again, this time in pain. Wasitora spit the bleeding chunk into the wurm's face and hissed angrily.

Tetsuo twisted his blade inside the monster's gut and leaped back to avoid a sweeping blow from the land wurm's tail.

Wasitora ears were pinned close to her skull, and her great jaws were open wide. Her wounded leg and shoulder still hung limply at her side, but she bounded forward again and took a position between the wurm and the fleeing villagers.

"Mine," she growled.

"White wurm," Tetsuo called nearby.

It turned away from the villagers to face him and Wasitora both.

Tetsuo's voice rose, and sparks of greenish-yellow light flew from his eyes. "You claim vengeance on behalf of murdered innocents. You declare war in response to unprovoked attacks. What are these villagers, if not innocent? What is your attack, if not unprovoked?" Tetsuo raised his sword and pointed it at the land wurm. "Stand down, or Caleria herself will suffer for your bloodlust."

"Madarans," the wurm said loudly, repeating its declaration, "no longer shall you raid and murder your peaceful neighbors. Caleria cries, 'enough.' She demands—"

Wasitora lunged at the wurm, and her huge paw passed like a shadow across the dragon's face. Flesh ripped, and blood splashed across the dragon's brow. It screamed in pain and thrashed in the sand.

Wasitora calmly sat back on her haunches. Her wounded shoulder would support no weight, and she curled her other paw around something. When the wurm's thrashing slowed, Wasitora held out the eyeball she had just excised so that it was in plain view of the wurm's remaining eye.

"Leave now," the cat dragon said calmly, "before I play with you some more." She inverted her upturned paw, and the grisly trophy fell to the sand.

The sight of its ruined sight seemed to drive the land wurm insane. It whirled to snap at Tetsuo with its jaws and cracked its tail like a whip across Wasitora's body. She was unable to dodge effectively, so the nekoru queen leaned forward and took the blow solidly across her back. She flew like a stone from a sling and landed in a great splash of sea foam and blood.

Tor, who had dived away from the wurm's flailing tail, snorted sand from his nose and tried to recover his feet.

The wurm reared up in triumph and came down heavily once more, creating another tremor. It turned and lumbered toward the village.

"White wurm," Tetsuo called. "Turn and face me."

Something about the champion's voice made the dragon pause. Weeping blood tears from its hollow socket, the land wurm growled menacingly at the champion.

"You have declared war on Madara?" Tetsuo said. "So be it. I *am* Madara, and your war ends here." The wurm snarled, and Tetsuo smoothly drew his sword. Repeating the careful, elegant motions he had performed against Wasitora, he raised the blade high above his head then down behind his hip, with his left arm extended. He held the form for a single moment as the dragon slithered closer then brought the sword up and around his body in a wide, looping swing. The blade left an arc of blue-black energy in its wake, and the arc expanded, growing brighter and brighter as it flew toward the wurm.

The monster howled as the edge of the energy wave sliced through its body, separating a length of tail, its forefoot, and part of its snout. The crippled beast's cries were muffled but even more pained.

Tetsuo repeated the motion, releasing another scything arc of energy, and the top half of the mutilated creature dropped heavily onto the sand.

"Madarans," it coughed through its ruined face, "no longer shall you raid and murder . . ." The great beast's voice trailed off, and it shuddered.

Tetsuo stood over the dying wurm. He sheathed his sword, exhaled, and drew it again with a loud, piercing cry. The sword seemed to leap out of the scabbard into Tetsuo's outstretched hand, and a white-hot bolt of heat flew from its tip and slammed into the pieces of the wurm's devastated body.

Tor dropped and covered his head.

With blinding light and deafening noise, a gigantic explosion blotted out the world. The last thing the archer saw was Tetsuo standing tall as the killing force of the explosion blew sand, water, and viscera past him like a swarm of furious bees.

Tor coughed sand from his lungs and looked up.

Tetsuo stood with his sword pointed forward. The ground below his feet, and indeed for a hundred feet in all directions, was fused into a great circular platform of cracked and smoking glass.

It was eerily quiet in the battle's aftermath. One boatload of villagers still clung to their vessel in the choppy waves. Most of the others had fled inside the village walls. Tor saw Kei approaching in the distance, with Ayesha close behind. Tetsuo himself finally moved, sheathing his sword and walking purposefully into the waves.

"How long have you been there?" Tor called.

"Since the dragons started fighting each other," Ayesha called back. She and Kei were quickly closing the distance between them. "It seemed best for us to let things play out."

"Another wise decision." Tor slipped his bow over his shoulder and started after his master. Tetsuo was knee-deep in the surf, scanning the waves. When he spotted something, he called out to Tor.

"Over here," he said. "I need more hands." Tetsuo waded deeper into the ocean and bent at the waist, plunging his entire body under the water.

When he stood, he had his arms wrapped tightly around Wasitora's head. The nekoru was far too large for him to move on his own, but he was able to raise her face out of the water. The cat dragon's eyes were closed, and her spiky tongue lolled clumsily out of her mouth.

"Tor," Tetsuo prompted, and the archer took hold of the champion's burden. One of Wasitora's eyes opened a slit, and she sneezed salt water from her nose.

"Don't touch me," she hissed, but her voice was weak, and she made no effort to pull free. Her eye slid shut once more, and she drew her tongue in behind tightly clamped jaws.

"Ayesha, Kei," Tetsuo called, "help us." He turned to the handful of villagers who were inching their way back to view the scene. "And anyone else who wishes to repay a favor. Help us get her clear of the waves."

* * * * *

My lord. Xira hovered high above the waves. *The champion survives.*

That is a habit he has been cultivating for years, Dark's voice replied. *It's past time we cured him of it.*

I am ready, my lord.

Has he seen you?

I cannot be certain. Others in his party definitely have.

Excellent. Now, listen carefully. I want you to provoke him. Do whatever you like to whomever you like, so long as you do not engage him directly, but make sure he comes after you.

Understood. Where shall I lead him, my lord?

Straight for Kusho Island. Xira could hear the malicious grin forming on her master's face. *While he wastes his time there, you will make for Argenti. There you will receive your final instructions. Do you understand?*

Your orders are clear, my lord.

You will obey. Say it, Xira.

I will obey you, Lord Dark.

A faint buzzing rose in Xira's head then died down. She could feel the connection to Lord Dark, but her master was no longer in direct communication with her. She scanned the beach below

A squad of villagers, the champion, and his second bore the nekoru toward the village. Just outside the procession stood the healer, tending to the poor unfortunates wounded by the wurm.

Xira darted inland and descended onto one of the larger dunes of sand and rock. Her huge green eyes were fixed on the white-faced boy.

"Provoke him," she whispered. She stood, staring from Kei to Tetsuo to Ayesha and back again, sharp mouthparts snapping open and shut in anticipation.

CHAPTER 7

Despite the angry mutters of the Sekana villagers, they placed Wasitora's unconscious body in the storehouse. In addition to the deep slash on her shoulder, one of her wings and several of her ribs were broken. She would bully no villagers in the near future. She could barely breathe, much less stand. Tetsuo ordered her wounds bound and called for volunteers to watch over the dragon while she slept. Only Bejahn came forward, to the annoyance of her neighbors.

"I'm the only one old enough to understand," she said cheerfully. "The champion solved our problem, but not in the manner we expected. You learn to accept what the emperor gives you."

A handful of men and women lingered behind to stare at the sleeping nekoru, but most of the villagers filed out as quickly as they could without looking back. Tetsuo had Tor usher out the last few stragglers, and they closed the storehouse door. Beyond it, Wasitora slept on·a pile of grain sacks, and Bejahn stood safely clear of her long reach.

"Master," Tor waited until they were alone on the street. "Is this a good idea?"

"She shamed me," Tetsuo said gravely. "Even wounded, she leaped to the defense of the villagers while I was still separating friend from foe."

"She was protecting her favorite toys, Master. If you had

struck the wurm first, she would have been on your back as soon as it was turned."

"Perhaps," Tetsuo said, "but the fact remains: She risked death and suffered injury for the benefit of Sekana. The empire owes her something not easily repaid."

Tor considered. "So what do we do with her?"

"Help her recover," Tetsuo spoke without hesitation. "When she is fully healed, we will discuss her future in Madara.

"I must find Ayesha and speak to the village council. Find Kei and bring him here. I want to be sure Wasitora hasn't suffered any internal injuries."

"Consider it done."

"When Kei is through examining her, both of you return to our quarters outside the village. The armorer and I will meet you there."

Before the two warriors could separate, Bejahn's head poked out of the storehouse door.

"She's awake," the village elder said. "She wants fish."

Tor looked at his master, and Tetsuo shook his head. "Tell her to wait until our healer has examined her."

Bejahn glanced over her shoulder nervously. "You tell her. I agreed to watch over her, but I'm doing it from across the room, thank you very much. I still don't feel safe."

"I will talk to Wasitora," Tetsuo said. To Tor, he repeated, "You find Kei."

* * * * *

Xira stood utterly still and silent as the champion reentered the storehouse. Generations ago, her people had perfected the art of ambush, and Xira's natural gift for standing motionless was augmented by a mystic camouflage she could employ at will. To all but the most sensitive eyes and ears, she was invisible until she struck. She also knew the reasons for Lord Dark's warning about Tetsuo, and so she lurked in the farthest darkened corner of the building, well clear of the champion's combat-honed senses.

Tetsuo spoke calmly to the nekoru and bade her wait for the arrival of the boy healer. The dragon hissed and grumbled, but she was too weak to do anything more. Xira smiled in cold satisfaction. She had chosen the right place to wait, and her prey would soon come to her.

Tetsuo departed, leaving an old woman behind to mind the dragon. Once he was gone, Xira was free to move, albeit slowly, without fear of detection. She silently lifted one clawed foot and set it down less than an inch from where it had started then did likewise with the other foot. She paused to make sure that neither the nekoru nor the old woman had heard then repeated the process. While she inched along, Xira amused herself by mentally plotting out the best way to attack and kill both the villager and the dragon before they could raise an alarm.

Her fortitude was rewarded a short while later when Kei entered. Xira was still tight against the wall of the storehouse, but she had traversed the length of the building and now stood a mere stone's throw from the dozing dragon. The nekoru stirred as the white-faced boy entered, and she opened one huge yellow eye to stare at him.

"Easy," he said. "I'm here to help."

"Fish," Wasitora said. She shut her eye again, but she also stretched out her neck to give Kei access to her wounded shoulder.

The boy ran practiced hands along the dragon's wing and shoulder blade, but he stopped as he approached Wasitora's rib cage. The nekoru issued a low, warning growl.

"That hurts, doesn't it?" Kei reached into his medicine bag and pulled out a small sprig of blue-green leaves. He wrapped the leaves in a swatch of gauze, sprinkled it with the contents of a yellow vial from his larger pack, and cupped the bundle between his hands. He whispered an incantation that created a soft pop and a waft of juniper then gently smeared the magical poultice across the dragon's wing, shoulder, and side.

The effect was immediate. Wasitora's muscles relaxed, and she exhaled in a long, slow whistle as the tension drained from her entire body. She settled in on the pile of sacks, and her breathing slowed and grew deeper.

Kei turned to Bejahn. "She will sleep deeply for the next several hours, venerable. When she wakes, I'm going to have to bind her ribs and wing so the broken bones set properly. We'll probably need the champion for that . . . and a half-dozen strong men with heavy ropes. Between now and then, she may stir and call for water. All you need to do is give her some. No more than a dipper at a time. Can you do that?"

"Easily," Bejahn said. "So long as she's not ordering me to bring her food or looking at me like I'm her next meal, I can handle just about anything. Well done, healer."

"Thank you, venerable." Kei nodded and turned for the door.

Xira stepped forward and clamped her hand on the underside of Bejahn's chin. "Yes, healer. Well done. And don't cry out. You might wake the patient." Bejahn struggled, but Xira's iron grip kept the elder both silent and still. "You might also startle me, and I don't know my own strength when I'm startled." She squeezed Bejahn's face. "I might pop this wrinkled fruit right off the bough."

Kei held his hands out, empty and open at his sides. "I'm

unarmed," he said. "Don't hurt anyone. What do you want?"

"You mean you don't know already? You fairly read my mind earlier." Kei shrugged helplessly, and Xira hissed with glee. "I want you to deliver a message to your champion." Xira snapped her jaws at the healer. "Actually, I want you to *be* a message to your champion."

Xira shoved the heel of her hand upward, slamming Bejahn's teeth shut with a clack. She then opened her grip to allow a long, tubelike stinger to spring out of her wrist. As soon as the pressure on her jaw vanished, the old woman pulled her head back with surprising speed and spared herself an almost instantaneous death. The stinger still scored, tearing the flesh along Bejahn's cheek and injecting powerful venom as it went.

Letting the old woman fall, Xira leaped into the air.

The boy froze, as all threatened healers did. His body wavered between fight and flight.

Xira invoked her camouflage and vanished against the storehouse roof. She couldn't keep her jaws from snapping in anticipation as the healer, now totally unnerved, took a half step closer to the old woman and fumbled with his medicine bag.

Xira pounced, and Kei's face snapped up at the sound of her ecstatic chittering. There was nothing wrong with the boy's reflexes, she thought. It's his battle strategy that needs work.

Her weight and momentum drove Kei down and onto his back. He managed to catch both her hands and keep her stinger away from his flesh. Xira laughed, her voice chiming and echoing across the storehouse.

Something strange happened then, something that hadn't happened since Xira was very young: Her prey slipped from her grasp. It was as if he had ceased to exist for a moment and her claws had passed right through his ghostly arms. She was confused, but she quickly recaptured Kei's hands before he could escape completely.

The assassin buzzed her wings and hauled backward with all her might. Kei flew up over her head, but she held onto his hands so that they both turned a full somersault in midair. As they came around, Xira released Kei and sprang off the healer's chest with both spined feet. Kei slammed hard into the storehouse wall then staggered back into the center of the room. Xira planted her feet as he stumbled and drove the full length of her stinger up between his ribs, deep into his chest cavity.

Kei gasped, and Xira relished his shock-widened eyes, mere inches from her own.

"Did you see that coming?" Xira's voice was high, grating, awash with excitement. "Did you anticipate it would feel like this?

"You will be my message," she whispered. "When he gets it, the champion will see the folly of interfering in Lord Dark's plans for Kusho and Gosta Dirk."

Kei grabbed Xira's shoulders and tried to push himself off her stinger, but her other hand clamped the back of his neck, and he could not withdraw more than a few inches. Xira could control the amount of venom she injected, and in other circumstances Kei would have been dead long before. She had been nursing the germ of a wickedly wonderful idea since her last conversation with Lord Dark, however, and she was hoping to make something splendid of the boy now that she had things her way.

Xira concentrated, calling up something from within that was far more primal than venom. She was steeped in Lord Dark's enchantments, but her kind had its own savage type of magic that was as organic as wings and stingers.

Light cascaded across each facet of Xira's eyes. Her stinger bulged as something squeezed from Xira's wrist into the hollow tube. The bolus passed through the stinger between Xira and Kei's bodies then stopped when it reached Kei's torso. Xira grabbed a fistful of Kei's hair and forced his head back, squeezing the muscles in her stinger arm as hard as she could.

There were three things eumidians did whenever they had the opportunity. The first was kill. The second was consume. The third Xira now performed on Kei's helpless, thrashing form.

With a violent cry, Xira forced the contents of her stinger tube into Kei's body. The healer's eyes rolled back in his head, and he gasped like a beached fish.

Xira's stinger slid back into her wrist, and she released the back of Kei's head so the boy could fall to the floor. Panting, she surveyed her work.

Bejahn lay motionless across the room. Kei twitched silently on the floor. The nekoru enjoyed the initial throes of the healer's tranquilizing poultice and actually purred, her eyes tightly shut.

Xira raised her arms above her head, opened her scissor-jaws, and screeched in triumph.

"Provoke him," Lord Dark had said. If the champion weren't inflamed by this, the man was colder than a graveyard stone.

Chiming musically to herself in her crystalline voice, Xira straightened her skirt, flexed her wings, and disappeared into the lengthening afternoon shadows.

CHAPTER 8

"I should have stayed with them."

The thought crossed Tor's mind a hundred times as he kept vigil by the storehouse, which was quickly becoming a field hospital. Tor was also acting as sentry, but there had been no further sign of the wasp-woman who attacked Kei and Bejahn. He had missed all the action and left his colleague unprotected.

The sun set over the water, and Wasitora shifted, awake and restless on her pile of sacks. Bejahn remained in a deep, deathlike sleep, but her breathing was regular. Both her temperature and her color had improved over the past hour, and she seemed to be slowly recovering. The only one who was still in danger was Kei.

In Sekana, the village healer was also the village blacksmith, and he uncomfortably admitted that he was far better with a hammer and tongs than he was with herbs and healing spells. He did what he could to stabilize the patients and keep them comfortable, but Tor suspected that the blacksmith was most interested in getting out of the storehouse before Wasitora regained her feet.

Ayesha's rage was like a cold, dense fog that permeated the air around her. After the initial frenzy of action when the victims were discovered, Tor watched the armorer withdraw around the rear of the storehouse and heard her string together endless filthy names and dire threats with Xira's name tossed in every few breaths. He had witnessed the armorer swearing at her tools and threatening her material while at the forge, but he had never heard anything like the skin-peeling hatred Ayesha expressed for the insect assassin.

By contrast, Tetsuo seemed to feel . . . nothing. A look of dire concern crossed the champion's face when they first entered the storehouse, but since then he had been as stoic as a stone. He sat down next to Kei's makeshift sickbed and simply stared at the stricken healer, watching the youth toss and moan and shake with fever.

Ayesha came out of the village council hut and marched up the road to Tor. "They want to talk to Tetsuo." The armorer's teeth clenched as she spoke. "They want to know what's going to happen next."

"He's meditating right now, arm—"

"I can see that, Tor. Stand aside and let me speak to him."

Tor's eyes dropped, and he stepped aside. "Of course."

Ayesha paused. "This wasn't your fault, you know. You couldn't have stopped her."

Tor bristled. "I could have sunk a shaft in her neck as she flew away."

"If you had been there, she would have taken you out first. You were armed."

"I should have stayed with them."

"No," Ayesha said. "I shouldn't have let him go." She turned and stormed up the path to the storehouse.

Tor watched her until she was on the threshold then turned back to scan the road. There was no one in sight, and not even dust moved across the square. Keeping his eye on the approach to the storehouse, Tor backed up the path until he stood in the circle of torchlight just outside the entrance.

Inside, he heard Ayesha's rage-choked voice speaking in a low, ominous tone. "The villagers are frightened," she said.

"They're afraid you're going to leave the wounded nekoru here for them to take care of. They're afraid you're going to abandon them to catch up with Xira."

Tor waited, but Tetsuo didn't answer.

"We are going after her, Champion," Ayesha said. "Aren't we?"

"We are." Tetsuo's voice came from a standing position, but Tor had not heard his master rise. "I'm more concerned with your healer right now. She may have done worse than kill him."

Tor started. Ayesha gave voice to his surprise. "What do you mean? What's wrong with him?"

Tor stole a glance into the room. By candlelight and torches, he saw Ayesha and Tor standing over Kei's bed. Tetsuo had his hand extended palm-down above Kei's forehead, and he wore the same expression of grave concern.

"He's a sensitive, isn't he? That's why you took him in."

Ayesha nodded. "Low-level precognition. He'd had a tough life by the time I met him. He only ever used it unconsciously, to avoid his foster father's blows. Why do you ask, Tetsuo? What did she do to him?"

With a feather-light touch, Tetsuo lowered his hand to Kei's forehead. "I don't know exactly what she did," he said, "but I know what it's doing to him."

The champion withdrew his hand and faced Ayesha. "He's dreaming. While his body is here, his mind runs rampant. 'Here' and 'now' are no longer barriers to his senses. He's seeing things he shouldn't see, learning things he shouldn't ever know.

"If the wound doesn't kill him," Tetsuo said, "I'm afraid the dreams might."

* * * * *

Kei was flying. Wind rushed past his ears, and his top-knotted hair whipped behind him as he soared. Moonlight reflected off white-capped waves thousands of feet below. Tiny ice crystals hung suspended in the nighttime clouds as he rushed through them.

It must be cold, he thought. So far out to sea, so high in the air, so close to winter. Why am I sweating?

Kei spotted a land mass ahead and immediately recognized it as the north coast of Kusho, first island in the Edemi chain. He came down and landed on the beach just off a large wooden pier. The white coral-sand beach was damp and silent, but in the distance humans and chelonian turtle-folk alike milled around the outskirts of town.

A hiss and a crackle to his left caught his attention, and Kei turned. A large stone stuck out of the sand just clear of the waterline. As Kei stared in fascination, a sigil inscribed itself on the weathered rock. It was an ugly, jagged symbol, all harsh lines and sharp angles, and it sizzled and smoked as if the ink on the author's brush were aflame. The character ate its way into the rock for a moment then Kei heard a painful crack, like the sound of splintering bone. Several drops of smoking black ooze formed in the etched sigil, running down the face of the rock and collecting in the sand below. The drops became a steady stream, the stream became a rush, and the rush became a fountain as steaming goo poured from the rock.

Soon the viscous pool beneath the rock was twenty feet wide, and the fountain kept on streaming. The thick mass did not flow down to the sea behind him, nor did it seep into the sand. Instead, it thickened further and became the beginnings of an oily heap.

A single great eye opened at the top of the rising mass, and Kei cried out. The eye was at least three feet across, and its pupil was a glowing red coal. A second eye formed beside the first, and both coals scanned right past Kei and locked onto the coastal town.

Kei took another step back. He willed himself to fly away, to rise into the safety of the sky, but went nowhere. Instead, he watched as the heap grew a head then a pair of shoulders. Kei felt rooted to the spot he occupied, unable to move.

The smoking black mound formed itself into a giant humanoid shape. There was a flash of blue flame, and when Kei opened his eyes, the thing was complete. She stood over seventy feet tall, her ebon skin swathed in steel robes of blue. She opened her cruel mouth and roared, drawing an empty hand back as if to hurl a stone at the town.

Chelonians, merfolk, and human sailors emerged from shops and taverns to see what was the matter.

The giantess cast her arm forward, and as her hand moved, a huge ball of flaming tar formed in it. The missile arced high over the pier and crashed down at the structure's midpoint, splintering the dock and setting the boards on fire. A second flaming mass shattered the far end of the pier, taking two moored ships with it. A third destroyed the shore end. The giantess roared again and took a huge stride. The sand sizzled under her feet, and the ground shook with each new step.

Kei screamed a warning to the witnesses at the edge of town, but his words were lost in the monster's fury. He wanted to reach the survivors of the ruined boats at the end of the pier, but as he took his first step, he was yanked roughly into the air and pulled high up over the lagoon. Though he kicked and struggled, he could not come down and could not fly off. From this vantage point, Kei could do nothing but watch the slaughter.

A hundred yards from the town, the giantess spewed a revolting jet of hot tar from her mouth. The deluge rained down on the first party of spectators, who died screaming. She threw more boulders of fiery pitch into the largest buildings, demolishing them and setting the ruins on fire. Kei thought his shock and horror were complete until the giantess took two quick steps and dived at the town. Her entire body soared through the air until gravity took hold and dragged her down onto her target. With arms spread wide and a gleeful war cry on her lips, Orca smashed into a row of storefronts and flophouses. The explosion lit the night sky and leveled blocks in all directions.

Tears streamed down Kei's face as he squinted into the carnage. Engulfed in flames and screams, a third of the town was covered in tar. Fire, smoke, blood, and ooze all swirled together, and the giantess reformed, her feet planted among the wreckage. She held her arms high in triumph, and her hideous howl echoed off the waves.

Chelonian soldiers began to surface in the lagoon. Each was young and lean, armed with a razor-tipped spear. The turtlefolk's shells were studded with large triangular teeth, and their extremities were encrusted with organic, coral-like armor. They wore thin metal helmets that had a single sharp fin on top for cutting through water and enemies alike. Kei counted twenty soldiers in the first wave, with more groups surfacing all the time.

When the first spear pierced the giantess' side, she turned. She noticed the platoon of heavily armored, fighting-mad chelonians swimming forward to protect their home, and she paused. Then, she clenched her huge hands into fists and roared with sadistic laughter. The grinning giantess cast both arms out straight ahead, her fingers splayed wide. A wide, thin sheet of gooey oil sprayed from the giantess's fingers. She waved her arms back and forth, covering much of the lagoon's surface in a layer of oily black gunk.

Most of the chelonians were still in the water, and they coughed and gagged as the horrid stuff clogged their throats and coated their faces. Those who submerged to wash off the foul oil found that it clung to them, resisting both seawater and turtle claws. Arriving squads stayed submerged, but the tar oil quickly spread to covered the entire lagoon and would not be dispersed by wind or tide.

The giantess spread her arms wide, exposing the crest on the front of her robes. Kei gaped at the standard, his brain refusing to accept what he saw. With her eyes open wide and her pupils rolled back in her head, the monster let out another mind-numbing cry and brought her hands together with a tremendous boom.

The oil and tar coating the lagoon instantly burst into flame. All the chelonians bobbing on the surface were caught in the inferno, and their otherworldly keening filled the air. Even those who had fled below the waves were not spared. The tar that still clung to their bodies ignited, magically burning underwater.

The half-dozen or so chelonians who had made it ashore paused only a moment for their doomed comrades. They formed into a pitifully small phalanx and extended their spears for a final charge. The giantess laughed again and lifted her foot as if to squash them like hard-backed beetles.

"Enjoying the show, boy?"

Kei craned his head to both sides, but there was no one in the sky but him and the moon.

The craters on the moon shimmered and ran together. A thin cloud passed before that shining circle. Kei suddenly found himself looking into a handsome, cruel, dark-skinned face with a white mustache and small beard.

"Lord Dark," Kei whispered. He had never seen the master assassin's unobstructed face before, but he recognized the man's patrician bearing and his cold, cold eyes.

"I understand you're something special, little healer," the moon-face said. "So you can deliver the following special message to your champion." Kei's vision blurred again as he blinked away phantom tears, and when he could see clearly again, the clouds below him had taken on the shape of Tetsuo's care-worn face. .

Dark spoke to Kei, but also to the cloud-image of Tetsuo. "The assassin's blade is aimed at Kusho. If Umezawa insists on meddling in imperial business, he will find that blade has also skewered him."

Kei stared into Lord Dark's features, memorizing every detail of his expression. The face in the moon noticed Kei's close inspection, and it smiled.

"I've always held—" the face tilted to take in the charred and blistered bodies on the sea below—"that the best thing about chelonians is they come in their own bowl. Once they're dead, you can just toss the whole corpse onto the fire. Then all you need is a fork and something to crack the shell, and you've got a fine meal." The face squinted, peering as if trying to get a clearer view. "In this case, I think we can dispense with the fire."

Kei's vision spun, and he felt himself being hauled away from the scene of the massacre. The giantess was still in the ecstatic throes of her destructive rampage, roaring and laughing as she flattened building after building and burned the survivors as they ran. The features on the moon faded into craters and passing clouds, but Lord Dark's mocking laughter remained, ringing in Kei's ears even as the black void swallowed him up.

CHAPTER 9

"If you're determined to see this through," Bejahn said, "I certainly can't stop you. In fact, I think it's quite an elegant solution, but I don't think the council will agree."

"Thank you, venerable," Tetsuo said. "Circumstances being as they are, none of us has much choice in this matter."

Bejahn was on her feet, speaking softly to Tetsuo and Ayesha. Tor remained on sentry duty, but he was well within earshot and had been contributing throughout the conversation. They had been talking for quite some time.

"I would speak to the council now, venerable. Are you able to gather them and bring them here?"

"Oh, I should think they're already together, waiting for you to tell them what's what. Even if they aren't, they'll fall over themselves to hear what you have to say. You won't be waiting long." Bejahn made her shaky way past Tor. "Stand ready with that bow, archer," she said. "You might need to help quell a riot." Smiling, Bejahn teetered off.

From inside the storehouse, Kei groaned and stirred. Tetsuo nodded at Ayesha, and the armorer hurried in to her student's bedside.

"Master," Tor said when Ayesha was inside. "Will Kei live?"

Tetsuo nodded. "The immediate danger has passed. The long-term danger, however, is just beginning."

"What did she do to him?"

"She injected him with something his body cannot tolerate. If I am correct, then she has cursed him with a slow, painful ordeal that will ruin him inside and out. Within a few weeks, Kei will be unrecognizable. He may ask us to kill him before it's done. Though it seems impossible now, we may find ourselves considering his request."

Tor shook his head in anger and frustration. "But why? What does she gain from torturing a healer-in-training?"

"Don't waste your energy trying to unravel Xira's motives," Tetsuo's voice was cold. "She rarely has any, beyond vanity and cruelty. Remember who our true enemy is. Xira is Dark's creature. She acts on his orders, according to his purpose. He sent her here to spy on us, perhaps to slow us down while his schemes play out. Her attack may even be a simple diversion to distract us from Dark's real objective."

Tor tightened his grip on his borrowed bow. "It won't work, will it? You can go on and confront Lord Dark. Ayesha and I will hunt Xira down and force Kei's cure out of her."

Tetsuo shook his head. "It won't come to that. Even if it did, splitting up would only serve Dark's agenda." Tetsuo peered over Tor's shoulder. "The village council is approaching. Please go inside and ask Wasitora to come out. She is awake and has been listening to us for some time now."

Tor nodded and went into the storehouse. The huge nekoru was curled up, her head nested among all four feet and her eyes tightly shut. Tor approached carefully.

"Wasitora," he called, but the great beast did not move. He remembered Tetsuo's words and went no closer.

"Wasitora," he repeated. "Come on, big kitty, we know you're awake." He took a small stone from the floor and tossed it gently at the base of the dragon's tail.

Without opening her eyes, the furry dragon struck out with her hind leg and caught Tor's stone. The rest of her body remained still as she held the stone above her own spine, pinned almost daintily between the tips of two needle-sharp claws.

"*Queen* Wasitora." The nekoru opened one eye. She spotted Tor and flicked his stone back at him, bouncing it off his head before he could dodge. Tor yelped, and Wasitora opened her other eye.

As regally as she could manage, Wasitora rose. She minimized her limp as she sauntered past Tor. The archer rubbed his forehead and swore softly to himself. Then Tor looked over at Ayesha and Kei. The healer's eyes were open but glazed, and he appeared to be in pain. He was whispering to his master.

When Tor stepped outside, Tetsuo gestured for the archer to stand by him. Wasitora sat to the champion's left, her back straight and all her weight distributed on three legs.

"Sekanans," Tetsuo said. He was speaking in his loudest, broadest voice, the one he used for formal declarations and crowd control. "You called me here to deal with the challenge presented by Queen Wasitora." He pointed to the nekoru, who snorted. The dragon managed to sound bored, disdainful, and put-upon all at the same time.

"I have met her challenge. I have fought against her then beside her. She is an honorable creature . . . ignorant of our ways, perhaps, and too proud of herself . . . but honorable nonetheless.

"She did not overly abuse her prisoners in the storehouse. She fought fairly in a formal champion's duel. Most importantly, she rushed to the defense of you and your village when the land wurm attacked, even though she herself was already injured."

Tetsuo turned his profile to the villagers and faced the reclining dragon. "Queen Wasitora, I hereby offer you a commission in the service of the empire. Be my deputy here in Sekana. Watch over the village and the Talon Gates in my stead, and the villagers will extend to you the courtesy due an officer of the empire."

Bejahn stepped aside so as not to stand between Tetsuo and the angrily muttering villagers. Wasitora herself narrowed one eye and licked her lips.

"And if I refuse?"

Tetsuo placed his hand on his sword. "If you refuse, we shall resume our duel. I have no more time to spend here in Sekana. It will be a quick and brutal affair. You will not survive."

"Wait one minute, Champion." The mustached council member's face was flushed. "We brought you here to get rid of her, not give her a job." The other council members voiced their agreement, but none stepped forward. The mustached man glanced at his peers and added, "How is this different from before you came? We still have to serve and feed her, and she still treats us like her toys. The only difference is that now it's official."

Tetsuo stared at the mustached man for a moment. Then, in his formal tone, he said, "Your oath to the emperor binds you, as it binds us all. Tend to Wasitora's wounds, provide food and shelter, do all the things an imperial guest deserves.

"In turn—" he faced the nekoru again—"she will protect you as I would. You have two obligations here, Wasitora. The first is to make sure that no one under your care suffers violence . . . from anyone or anything." Wasitora's eyes narrowed, and she growled, but she did not challenge Tetsuo's words. "When I return—and I *will* return—there will be an inspection. Anyone who has violated the terms of my agreement will answer to me."

Wasitora shifted uncomfortably under Tetsuo's penetrating glare. "You said 'two,' Champion. What is the other condition?"

Tetsuo drew his blade and extended the flat out to the dragon. "That you swear an oath to honor my terms. You may keep the title of queen so long as you accept the fact that you are in Madara and subject to Madaran law. The emperor has many vassal kings and queens throughout the world. If you would stay here, you must agree to behave as one. You are a working guest, performing a vital function on behalf of the emperor. You do so at his sufferance."

The mustached man broke in. "Sekana does not accept your terms, Champion." He pointed at Wasitora. "She will have us waiting on her hand and foot, bearing her from place to place on a litter. I will appeal to the emperor himself before I allow—"

"No one has offered you terms to reject," Tetsuo said. "As far as you are concerned, I am the emperor's voice in this matter. By rite of office, I speak for him. I speak for everyone here when I tell you to keep silent from now on." He dipped his sword closer to Wasitora. "What say you?"

Wasitora glanced at the sword, then at the mustached villager. She lowered her head and leaned forward so that it was under Tetsuo's blade.

"I accept your terms, Champion."

Tetsuo touched the sword lightly on the crown of the dragon's head, then sheathed it. Wasitora lifted her face, narrowed her eyes, and licked her lips again. She purred maliciously and tossed her head at the mustached man.

"I hadn't thought of a litter. The more I stay off my feet, the faster I'll heal. Why don't you—" she carelessly tossed her head in the mustached man's direction—"gather a crew and start building the chair?"

The outspoken villager sputtered in outrage, but Bejahn stepped forward before he could speak. "He'll get right on that, O Queen." To Tetsuo, she said, "Thank you, Champion. We shall sleep better knowing that a dragon protects our shores." She stared around the assembly, challenging anyone to disagree.

The villagers' muttering was no longer so loud or so angry.

Wasitora stood and turned her back on the villagers. Without looking back, she went back inside the storehouse.

The crowd of villagers broke up into smaller clusters of fours and fives, speaking to each other in hushed tones. Bejahn stood alone, gnawing on a piece of temoya fruit and smiling at Tor.

Ayesha came out of the storehouse. She spared the milling villagers a quick glance then strode up to Tetsuo.

"Kei has had a vision," she said. Tetsuo motioned for Tor to come closer.

"What did he see?" Tetsuo asked quietly.

Ayesha glanced at Tor, and then back at Tetsuo. "He saw a massacre on Kusho. He's still feverish, and he's not completely coherent, but he described some sort of giant that all but wiped out a chelonian village."

Tetsuo nodded grimly. "It has begun. Lord Dark is attempting to bring the Edemi chain back under the emperor's control."

Ayesha nodded. "It gets worse. Kei described the giant as wearing an imperial crest during the attack. The phoenix crest." She took hold of Tetsuo's robe and pulled a flap of it forward so Tetsuo could see the emblem there. "Your crest, Tetsuo."

Tor could not contain himself. "What? Who would dare impersonate—" He stopped himself as the answer to his own question became obvious. "One of Dark's monsters?"

Tetsuo nodded. "There is nothing Lord Dark would not do to advance his own position. But as always, he goes too far too fast. While he faces me on the meditation plane, his thugs injure my deputies and commit mayhem under my banner. He leaves taunts and threats for me everywhere I go. He is making sure that I involve myself in this matter."

Ayesha stared coldly at Tetsuo, her anger clearly rising again.

"What will we do?" Tor asked.

"We will do as we always do. Fulfil the office I hold. Represent the emperor and defend his honor." He looked to Tor and said, "Gather the armorer's tools and bearers. We are going to Kusho.

"And you," he said to Ayesha, "will help me procure and prepare a vessel for our journey."

* * * * *

Sekana was a fishing village, so there was no shortage of seagoing craft to choose from. Ayesha accompanied Tetsuo as he inspected the available boats and offered critical opinions of each one's seaworthiness. Tetsuo eventually selected a medium-sized sampan large enough to bear the weight of his entourage and Ayesha's barrow but small enough to make the journey under oar power alone if need be. While the bearers waited to load the boat with supplies and Tor watched from the dock, Tetsuo and Ayesha completed a powerful pre-voyage ritual.

The armorer fitted the front of the boat with a rough piece of driftwood, and Tetsuo walked from stem to stern with a stick of smoking incense. At the bow, Ayesha knelt and lowered a dipper into the water while Tetsuo did the same at the stern. They chanted as they scattered seawater around the perimeter of the main deck, finally meeting behind the mounted piece of driftwood. There, they clasped hands and emptied their dippers over the makeshift figurehead. Steam rose from the driftwood, and a cold gust of wind blew up from behind, whipping their hair and clothing forward. Tetsuo wedged the smoking incense into the driftwood then gestured for the others to join them onboard.

"Is the sea that rough between here and Kusho?" Tor asked. "It's only a day and a half away."

"Less than a day," Ayesha corrected. "If we all take our turns on the oars and the wind is favorable." She smiled humorlessly. "It will be, or it will answer to me."

"The approach to Kusho is treacherous," Tetsuo said. "It is protected by natural and mystical defenses, but it has been years since they were directed at imperial ships. We must be on our guard."

"Hence the voyager's charm." Ayesha took the dipper from Tetsuo and put it back inside her barrow.

Kei came onto the dock with Bejahn at his side, and Ayesha frowned. Neither her student nor the village elder seemed fully recovered from Xira's sting.

"Permission to come aboard," Kei said. He smiled weakly.

"Denied," Ayesha said. "You're staying here, far away from anymore danger."

"Come aboard, healer." Tetsuo extended his hand and helped Kei up onto the sampan.

Ayesha stared in anger and confusion.

Tetsuo said, "He has to come with us. I fear Xira's attack has not yet run its course and may yet prove lethal. We will do all we can to prevent that, but Kei must be with us if we are to help him."

Ayesha still stared at Tetsuo, unconvinced.

"Trust me for now, armorer. I will explain more when we are underway."

Ayesha tightened her jaw and nodded. Kei came aboard and took up his position behind and to the left of Ayesha.

"You and you." Ayesha pointed at the two burliest bearers. "You're taking the first shift on the oars." She fairly sneered at Tetsuo. "May I take my student with me below, or do you have something else in mind?"

"Actually," Tetsuo said, ignoring Ayesha's rancor, "I do, and it requires both of you."

* * * * *

Without further delay, they left Sekana. Bejahn waved from the docks and wished them well. Tetsuo stood quietly by Kei as Ayesha summoned a favorable wind, and they were off. Between the charmed wind and the bearers' efforts at the oars, they made it through the Talon Gates and were out in the open sea by midday.

Ayesha made sure that everything was stowed securely and that Tor had clear instructions to keep him out of trouble. Tetsuo wrung obedience from Tor through the commanding force of his presence, but he allowed the archer too much freedom otherwise. Ayesha didn't trust the archer to sit still and didn't trust her own patience if Tor started to play acrobat on the masts or practiced his marksmanship on passing birds.

Finally Ayesha reported to Tetsuo, who led her and Kei to the rear of the main deck and bade them sit on the boards. The champion untied his long sword and scabbard and sat facing Kei, his weapon across his folded legs. Tetsuo's eyes bored into Kei's.

Ayesha had been in Tetsuo's service longer than anyone

else, and she trusted him, but he had been far too cold since the insect's attack, sterner and more distracted. He clearly suspected something awful. Ayesha wanted to know what was weighing so heavily on him that it rattled his placid exterior. It couldn't be worse than what she herself was imagining.

Tetsuo closed his eyes and simply breathed for a few moments. After watching the champion draw and expel air several times, Kei glanced to Ayesha. She nodded, and Kei closed his eyes and prepared for deeper meditation. When they were both breathing deeply in unison, Ayesha closed her own eyes and fell into their rhythm.

"You know what has happened to you." The champion's voice was low but powerful. It was oddly reassuring to Ayesha, despite her anxiety.

Kei replied. "She put something in me," he said, "and it's still there. I can feel it."

"How much do you know about wasps?"

Ayesha continued to breathe, but her jaw clenched tight.

"I know how to treat their stings . . . well, those of the smaller variety. I haven't studied the insects themselves."

"Yet," Ayesha added.

Tetsuo voice was concerned but encouraging. "You and your master must walk with me now, Kei. There is something you both need to understand." The champion started chanting to himself, intoning the same long syllable until his breath ran out and then starting over again. Kei and Ayesha did the same. Between the gentle rocking of the ocean and the calming effect of the chant, Ayesha felt her mind drifting up and away from her body.

"You did not choose the path you're on," Tetsuo said.

"No," Kei answered. "My master chose it for me."

Ayesha felt a rush of pride at the confidence in Kei's

voice. He had resisted the healer's path at first, but now she heard how comfortable he had become with her decision.

"The healer's way is an excellent choice. Ayesha believes, as I do, that everyone should have a path. All paths are different, however. No two walk exactly the same course. The armorer's is different from Tor's, which is different from yours, which is different from mine."

Kei and Ayesha had recited the basics of this catechism together countless times, and they did so again now: "But all lead to the same destination."

"Your path has intersected mine. Overlapped it. Often, as we make our way through the world, we find both companions and enemies alongside us, but the paths always diverge eventually."

An overlap between Tetsuo and Kei was news to Ayesha. She blocked out her own selfish curiosity and pique, focusing on her breathing and the expected response.

"But all lead to the same destination."

"You saw part of my conversation with Lord Dark," Tetsuo said.

Ayesha paused, half-entranced, at this departure from the traditional form.

"Yes," Kei intoned.

"And I saw portions of your vision. The massacre on Kusho, as you described it to Ayesha. Show it to us now."

Suddenly and unbidden, ghostly images rose behind Ayesha's eyelids: a giantess burning chelonian troops. Kei moaned as he relived the awful sight.

"Yes, this is what I saw."

"The taunts from Lord Dark. The warning. The cruel joke he made of the chelonian's deaths."

Ayesha saw the master assassin's face superimposed on the moon. She felt Kei's fear and her own anger.

"Yes," her student said.

Tetsuo's voice grew tight. "He is a user. He uses his slaves to commit murder and to confound his enemies. One of them, in turn, is attempting to use you. Do you understand how?"

"Yes . . . no. I only understand that I was spared so that I might suffer and distract you from your purpose."

Tetsuo let out a long, slow breath. "How much do you know about wasps?"

The nightmare vision of fire and death on Kusho faded. Ayesha now saw a green spring meadow with tall grass waving in the wind. A single fallen tree lay in the distance. Kei was there, and she saw his face wrinkle in concentration. He raised his hand to Ayesha, and she mentally returned his greeting.

"Over here." They both turned toward Tetsuo's voice, but the champion was not in the meadow. His voice had come from the fallen tree, which shimmered closer into sharp detail.

A cloud of wasps buzzed around a melon-sized hive built into the end of the tree. Some of the insects crawled across the rotting bark and the waving grass, while others flew tight circles in the air.

"Look closer, Kei. Look closer, Ayesha."

Side by side, the healer and his master focused on the far end of the tree, where a palm-sized spider waited at the corner of its web. A large brown wasp had become entangled in the thin silver strands, and the arachnid was inching along the web to inspect its catch.

Fascinated, Ayesha and Kei peered closer.

The spider slowed as it recognized its mortal enemy and carefully circled the portion of the web that contained the wasp. With deliberate efficiency, the spider cut each strand linking the wasp to the larger web. When it had completed a half-circle, the tangled wasp dropped and waved in the gentle breeze, connected by one large strand and a handful of silky tatters.

Suddenly, the wasp broke free and launched itself at the spider. Though much larger, the spider tried to spring out of the way. The wasp was faster, however, and it flew directly onto the spider's back and quickly stung it behind the head.

The spider curled up and tried to roll the wasp back onto the web, but the insect held fast, stinging the spider several more times.

The venom took hold, and the spider's struggles slowly ceased. The wasp let it go, and the spider's paralyzed form dropped onto the log below. The insect rose into the air, hovered for a moment, and then casually buzzed down to its victim.

Even with the detailed view of her mind's eye, Ayesha could not determine what the wasp was doing to the spider's motionless body. When it was done, it flew a short distance down the log and landed, facing the spider.

Suddenly, the sun dropped from the sky, and the scene went dark. The moon blazed across the darkness overhead, and the sun shot up again on the opposite horizon. Three days passed in mere moments as the course of the sun and moon inscribed streaks of light and color across the sky.

On the third sunrise, the bright yellow orb slowed and seemingly stopped as time returned to normal. Disoriented, Ayesha looked back at the log. The wasp still waited by the spider's body. It began to twitch.

Ayesha heard a sickening sound as a sharp insect head burst out of the spider's abdomen. The newcomer bit and tore and clawed its way free of the spider's body, ripping the fleshy coffin to pieces as it struggled free. The infant wasp was much smaller than its parent and reddish-black in color. It had eight legs and a definite spiderlike quality to the shape of its body. The horrid thing flexed its translucent wings, bit off another shred of dead spider, and rose into the air. The parent wasp also took off, and the two insects buzzed back to the hive.

Kei gasped. Beside him, Ayesha opened her eyes. Kei was falling backward, and she lunged to catch him before he could crash onto the deck. She gently lowered the healer onto his back as the boy retched and shuddered and moaned.

"I'm to be killed," Kei whispered, horror flooding his eyes. "I am host to a parasite that will kill me and eat me even as it is born."

Ayesha winced in the face of Kei's panic. She squeezed his hand and gently brushed stray hairs from his face.

"That is my fear," Tetsuo said. He looked at Ayesha as he spoke to Kei. "I'm sorry to have shown you this, but you need to understand: This thing is already killing you. You must resist it will every ounce of will you possess. Any physical harm that comes to you now will only accelerate the process. You are in a fight for your life, and it is a fight you must win."

"Can I be cured?" Kei whispered. "Can this tumor be removed?"

"That is my intent," Tetsuo said. He took Kei's hand from Ayesha. "The only way I know to help you is to find Xira. She did this to you, and she will tell us how to undo it. I expect she is already on Kusho, taking advantage of the distraction provided by the massacre in your vision."

Tetsuo's voice trailed off, and he seemed to forget Ayesha and Kei were there. "Gosta Dirk had best beware until we arrive. The assassin's blade is poised over his head."

Tetsuo locked eyes with Ayesha once more. "Do not despair. Lord Dark and Xira are treating this like a game. They bluff and maneuver and waste their energy on tricks and distractions. Thus, we have an advantage. We understand the stakes of life and death far better than assassins ever could. To them, these things are mere coins to be traded and bartered."

Tetsuo turned back to the trembling boy on the deck. "Trust in me, Kei, and in your master. We will not allow you to leave this world as a pawn in some political display of dominance. I swear as the imperial champion of Madara, that you will not die so that another killer like Xira can be born."

Tears streamed down Kei's face, carving tiny paths in the white makeup he wore.

Ayesha stifled the rejoinder that reflexively rose in her throat. Now was not the time to drill Kei on his composure.

The healer collected himself enough to ask, "What should I do?"

"Rest now. We can do nothing at sea but wait. Be ready. We should arrive on Kusho by sunrise tomorrow. And then—" Tetsuo's green eyes flashed—"I will break the assassin's blade across my knee."

Ayesha nodded grimly. "And force the pieces down Xira Arien's throat."

PART TWO:

IMPERIAL ENEMIES

CHAPTER 10

Lord Dark's diligence stopped just outside the imperial shrine. He lowered the armored helm onto his head and stepped onto the crushed stone pathway. His servants waited alongside their coach fifty yards back, forbidden to approach the shrine without his direct instructions.

Lord Dark snapped his fingers impatiently, and the loud crack echoed across the silent road. Boris Devilboon stepped imperiously from the servant's coach onto the path. He swept past the servants toward Lord Dark, and a brown-haired woman with a covered urn fell in behind Devilboon.

"My lord." The little man bowed so deeply that the hood of his robe touched the path.

"Be silent," Dark snapped. He took the urn from the servant woman and dismissed her with a flick of his eyes. "Listen, little Boris. You are a nonentity as far as the emperor is concerned. You will stand well behind me when he manifests. You are not to be seen or heard. If I notice you during the next half hour, I will personally tear your ears off and feed them to you."

Devilboon nodded with eyes downcast but did not reply. Dark was pleased the little rat knew what was expected of him.

With the urn in his hands and Devilboon trailing five paces behind, Dark made his way into the shrine. The perpetually burning candles flickered and cast mad shadows on the walls as Dark placed the urn on the altar. He removed the lid, stepped back, and began the invocation.

"My venerable lord, my supreme master, my emperor—your servant stands in your holy shrine. Will you hear me?" Dark reached forward and nudged the urn. The vessel toppled, and glittering gems scattered across the altar and onto the stone floor.

"I offer the treasures of Madara, mined by loyal peasants and shaped by the most skilled of gem cutters." Dark fixed his glare on the stones, and they burst into tiny, brilliant, multihued glows. "There is no wealth, no triumph, no victory without your blessing. Will you hear me now?"

The candle flames flared and went out. The room cooled, and light from the glowing gems slowly faded. One by one, they all disappeared.

When the room was pitch black, Dark removed his helmet and peered into the air above the altar. No vision had appeared, but he sensed the emperor's presence.

"What do you want?" The emperor's soft voice was distorted by echoes that hung in the air long after the words were spoken.

Dark did not hesitate. Dealing with the emperor's disembodied voice was only slightly less dangerous than facing a physical manifestation.

"Guidance, Your Majesty. My agents are poised in the Edemis, ready to carry out your wishes, but there is an impediment." The emperor did not reply, and Dark continued. "The imperial champion has sworn to interfere. My function is a delicate one, one that depends on secrecy and stealth. His blundering will make success far more difficult to achieve. Even now he is en route to Kusho, and he intends to hinder our work."

Dark waited through another long silence then said, "The

champion and I are . . . equals in your eyes. I cannot command him to stay away. Only you can do that."

Silence. Dark risked a glance back at Devilboon crouching in the shadows.

"Will you order the champion to stand down, Your Majesty? At least allow me to remove him, as I would any other obstacle to your will."

While he waited, Dark carefully reached out with his mind to Devilboon's. All of his minions were subject to his will, and he exerted that will now on little Boris. Dark slipped into the man's mind, deep into the most primal part, and flipped a switch that he himself had planted there. Devilboon stiffened, but he made no sound.

"What shall I do, my emperor? I would not lightly deprive you of Umezawa's service, but I cannot carry out the Edemi sanctions with him confusing the situation. What is your will?"

There was a long pause, and the room grew colder.

"My will," the emperor hissed at last, "is unchanged. I gave you power and position to command the machinery of the empire in my stead. I also gave you the freedom to act as you see fit. Do so, and do not trouble me again."

"Your Majesty. You bestowed similar gifts on Tetsuo Umezawa. Now we stand opposed to one another, and our paths are unclear."

"This audience is over," the emperor said. "I did not set you above all Madara so you could come whining to me at the first sign of disharmony. Settle your conflict with the champion. Carry out the task I have given you. Return here only when you have succeeded or failed, that you may be appropriately rewarded.

"Do not petition me again with trivialities." There was a loud implosion of air, and the candles sprang back to life.

The room was exactly as it had been when Lord Dark had entered. Except that the urn and the jewels were gone, he noted sourly.

Dark spun and stormed out of the shrine. Devilboon stood wide-eyed and slack-jawed, his full weight leaning against the wall. Dark grabbed Devilboon's hood as he went past, dragging the stuporous little man behind him.

Outside the shrine, Dark snapped his fingers, and all of his servants stood rigid. "Begone!" The servants led the horses around, and the carriage started back up the road.

When they were well out of earshot, Dark dragged Devilboon over to the master assassin's diligence. The servants had already turned it away from the shrine. Dark roughly threw the smaller man through the door, onto a cushioned bench. Dark then climbed in, bolted the carriage door, and whistled for the horses. They quickly built up speed as each of their eight legs dug into the road.

Dark waited until they were clear of the shrine. He looked into Devilboon's vacant eyes, noting with disgust a slight trail of drool that dribbled down the little man's chin. Dark held his hand in front of Devilboon's face and reached once more into his mind. He found the switch he had triggered and gave it another mental push.

Devilboon's eyes glowed with azure energy. His hanging jaw began to work, bobbing up and down as he tried to form words but producing little more than random syllables. Steel-gray smoke rose from his eye sockets and wreathed his head like a crown.

"What did you see, Boris?" Dark's voice was low but insistent. "What do you know? Your master commands." He raised his voice above the humming energy from Devilboon's eyes. "Proclaim."

The little man's voice rose, and the arcane light from his

eyes crackled. He stood inside the cramped carriage and spread his arms to the sides. When he spoke, his voice was high and tinny, and though it grated on Dark's ears the master assassin strained to absorb every syllable as it flowed effortlessly from Devilboon's mouth.

> *Our god-king speaks a single word,*
> *But mood and tone his thoughts betray.*
> *More vital than the things you heard*
> *Are leges that he didn't say.*
>
> *No sanction for the champion's head,*
> *No succor for the servant true,*
> *But fangless in a serpent's bed*
> *He dies, and no blame comes to you.*
>
> *His majesty has other realms*
> *Distracting him from this regime.*
> *One pawn deceives, one overwhelms,*
> *And thus you stand alone, supreme.*

Devilboon stared vacantly at his master for a single moment after the last syllable left his lips, then he groaned, his head rolled, and his eyes slammed shut.

Dark let him fall back onto the cushioned bench. He pondered the meaning of the little rodent's proclamation. The first inkling of a brilliant, terrible idea formed in his mind.

Dark whistled for the horses and spoke the name of their next destination. In response, the horses whinnied and redoubled their speed.

Lord Dark carelessly shoved Devilboon's limp body onto the floor of the cabin. Little Boris did have his uses, but Dark

still preferred him unconscious. The ride to the kentsu headquarters in the east would be long and tedious enough without the sycophant's endless chatter.

As he rode onward, Dark called out to his castle keep with
his mind, issuing instructions and preparations for his pending return.

* * * * *

Tor stood with Kei at the fore of the sampan while yet another wave crashed over the bow. He struggled to keep his
footing as the boat pitched and rolled beneath him, and he
decided then that he would never be a great sailor.

Shortly after the champion's vessel had lost sight of the
Talon Gates, the waves grew angry, and the wind blew in all
directions. The ship became almost impossible to steer. Tor
wondered about the voyager's charm and how far they'd
have gotten without it. Even now the armorer worked simply
to maintain the protective spell while the champion wrestled
with the rudder.

Another huge gust shoved the ship sideways in the water,
and a cascade of brine and foam coated the main deck.
When Tor squinted and shielded his eyes he could see the
edge of the charm that blunted and deflected the wind-
driven rain. It was holding for now, but if the storm grew
worse . . .

Lightning split the sky above, and Tor reflexively dropped
into a crouch. The ship rose under him and sent him rolling
clumsily into Kei, knocking the slender youth flat onto his
back.

Tor clamped onto Kei's shin and held fast. He wasn't sure
he completely understood what was happening to the healer,
but the champion had pulled him aside and made it clear:

Kei was to be protected from all harm until the sampan made landfall. Tor kept Kei's legs pinned until the sea's fury abated. Then he rolled off and pulled the healer to his feet.

"You didn't have to shield me like that." Kei cupped his hands around his mouth to be heard over the roaring sea. "I'm not an invalid yet."

"I wasn't shielding," Tor shouted back. "I was clinging for my life. Your leg was handier than the railing." Tor grinned, and the healer fought off a smile.

"Tor! Kei! Inside!"

They turned to Ayesha's voice, which somehow cut through the noise of the storm. Tor glimpsed a momentary flash of fear from Kei, then he nudged the healer. "I bet you don't often get away with 'Sorry master, I didn't hear you.' "

Kei smiled but quickly regained the stoic expression under his running face paint. "Ayesha Tanaka refuses to repeat herself." He pressed his hands together and bowed to Tor. "She never has to. Her voice cuts through time itself."

Tor laughed then fixed his own face into a somber mask and followed Kei toward the stern.

* * * * *

Under the canvas, Ayesha waited with her arms crossed. Tetsuo was at the rudder behind her, the chords in his neck bulging as he maintained their heading. She and the champion had been reviewing their options since the sun had set and the storm had worsened. Someone or something was consciously directing the weather and sea against the sampan. The solution was clear, but it presented a problem of implementation.

Kei and Tor arrived.

Ayesha spared Kei an assessing glance then locked eyes with Tor. "We're not going to make it to Kusho," Ayesha said. "Tetsuo and I can keep us afloat and on course, but the boat simply wasn't made for this kind of storm." She nodded to Kei. "We're not turning back. Even if we wanted to, it wouldn't do us any good. The storm is keeping pace with us, stalking us."

Ayesha shifted uncomfortably, unfolding her arms. Tetsuo held the rudder with difficulty, but he nodded encouragingly to the armorer.

The ship pitched violently to the left, and Tor staggered clumsily down to one knee. As he rose, he eyed Ayesha's steady stance enviously.

"So what do we do?" Tor blurted. "We can't go on, we can't stay here, and we can't go back. Are we doomed?"

"Of course not," Ayesha said. "I think we can safely get where we're going. We just need to add more fuel to the voyager's charm."

Tor shrugged. "Sounds good. What can I do?"

Ayesha refolded her arms. She had not expected the archer to make this easy on her, but here he had volunteered. Perhaps Tetsuo's lenient approach with Tor was not entirely without merit. "Tetsuo and I need to gather up and focus the local blue mana," she said. "We need quite a lot, and channeling it into the charm will be delicate work."

Tor nodded. "So you want me to steer? Do I get to steer?" He stumbled again as the stern rose sharply. "Maybe Kei should steer. I could do something I'm more suited for, like falling down."

"Tor," Tetsuo called from the rudder. "Be still and listen."

The archer rode another sideways roll then stood firmly, his feet planted and his arms wide for balance. "Sorry.

We're about to sink, then." Tor stood a little straighter and took the bow off his shoulder. "Just tell me where to aim."

Tetsuo laughed, and even Ayesha smiled.

"Little archer," the armorer held her hands out, presenting the black clouds and lightning jags just outside the wind-whipped canvas. "Your target is the storm. Do you think you can hit that?"

* * * * *

As they led him up onto the heaving deck, Tor began chanting to himself. His original archery instructor had been fond of songs, and this was the first tune Tor had learned when he started training with the bow. It was a young boy's song, a student's song, with a confident and joyful look ahead to all the adventures an archer might have.

Tetsuo cut through the main mast with a single stroke of his long sword, and Tor stopped singing.

Ayesha had explained the plan very carefully to him. Since someone controlled the storm, breaking free was simply a matter of wresting that control away. To do that, Ayesha needed to cast a spell from the deck of the ship while someone else set off a series of gemstone devices high above the storm's eye. Tor was that someone.

The bearers lowered the section of mast onto the deck, and the other two fixed sturdy beams across the top and bottom. Under Ayesha's direction, they stretched the canvas sail tightly between the cross beams and nailed it in place. The entire contraption began to look like a crude children's kite, an impression that was completed when Tetsuo lashed the thick mooring rope to the ends of both cross beams. The champion looked up at Tor, smiled encouragingly, and motioned the archer over.

Mechanically, Tor planted his feet on either side of the mast just above the lower cross beam and lay down on the kite's wooden skeleton. Ayesha sprinkled some foul-smelling oil across Tor's stomach and whispered a few words. Tor felt the oil harden around him, binding him tightly to the mast. As he lay supine, rain pelting his face and thunder booming in his ears, Tor fought to recapture the melody of the archer's song.

"This," he muttered, "is the worst plan ever."

His tongue lay heavy in his mouth as the armorer handed him the bow and placed three arrows in his quiver, two with blue crystal arrowheads and one with white. Tor's arms were free, and he croaked a dry thanks to Ayesha as he looped the bow and the quiver over his head. He nodded at Tetsuo.

Tetsuo gave the signal, and the bearers stood the giant kite on its end so that Tor stood on the crossbeam, spellbound to the vertical mast. As two of the bearers held the kite up, the other two secured the ropes to the deck, connecting the contraption to the ship.

Tetsuo waited until all the knots had been tied and tested then inspected the entire array. Finally, he came around and clapped a hand on Tor's shoulder. The master locked eyes with his pupil and smiled then went back to the rudder.

Ayesha rummaged around in her pack and came out with a vial of blue-white dust. "This will work," she yelled, her face barely a foot from Tor's. "My makeshift glider is enough like a kite that it might even fly on its own in this wind, but with this powder, you'll have no trouble staying aloft."

"Armorer?"

"When you see a bright blue flash on the deck, shoot all three arrows down into the heart of the storm, one after the other. The sequence is blue, white, blue. Understand? Space them out as much as you can, but make sure they don't go farther than one hundred yards or so away from the sampan. Understand?"

"I understand! Armorer?"

Ayesha leaned her head in so that her ear was right next to Tor's mouth.

"Are you sure this will work?"

Ayesha pulled her head back and grinned. "I've been breaking things a lot longer than I've been making them. Someone's controlling this storm, and I'm telling you for certain: Yes, I can break that control."

The armorer took two steps back and uncorked the vial. She threw the glittering dust over Tor's head and cried out, "Fly!"

The bizarre contraption immediately lurched up. The canvas filled with wind and lifted Tor off the deck, but his stomach stayed at sea level.

Ayesha walked under the kite and held her clenched fist above her head. Her eyes flashed in the darkness like distant stars on a cold night.

The kite continued to rise. Tor took one last look before his head rose through the protective barrier around the sampan, and then he lost sight of everything. The cold north wind slapped his face like an iron hand, and he squinted against the driving rain. Once the entire kite was clear of the sampan's protection, it soared upward on a heavy gust until the ropes that lashed it to the boat snapped tight. His head slammed into the mast behind him.

The sampan was now hundreds of feet below him. Tor was both amazed and heartened by the dramatic change in the weather at this altitude. The wind was far less cold and violent, and the rain fell gently rather than pounding down like a volley of nails.

As Ayesha had hoped, Tor could now see the shape of the storm. It clung around the sampan like a tight-knit cap. The darkest clouds and the largest waves clustered around the boat in an ugly knot, with distinctly lighter and calmer weather radiating outward. At the center of the angry mass of wind and rain, there was a bubble of relative calm. The voyager's charm had created an artificial eye at the center of the artificial storm.

Tor's eyes adjusted to the dim light, and he scanned the sky around him. He checked to make sure that he was as high as the ropes would allow then strung one of the blue-tipped arrows onto his bow.

Wind gusted around him, and Tor waited to make his first shot. Inside the charmed bubble, Ayesha was waving some kind of baton and tossing white powder to her left and right.

Come on, you blue flash, Tor thought. He added "great pilot" to the list of things he would never become and mentally rehearsed making all three shots in quick succession.

A huge waterspout suddenly erupted from the sea beneath the kite, and Tor almost dropped his arrow. The column of saltwater and wind swirled up before the archer, and the top formed into a human face.

"WHO . . . ARE . . . YOU?" The face in the spout was definitely male, with a long, sharp nose and a huge shock of hair that covered it from crown to chin. Only his eyes, his forehead, and his long nose were visible under the thick mane. His features were twisted in exertion.

The watery apparition lunged toward Tor, and the kite twisted and rolled, its ropes straining against the deck far below. There, a dim blue light sparked from Ayesha's position. Abandoning his chosen pattern, Tor fired all three arrows at the looming face. As they flew, Tor slipped the bow over his head and brought his hands together.

Three distinct explosions bloomed behind the face, and the bearded apparition roared in anger. Each crystal released a burst of mystical static, which combined with the raw power of the elements to destroy any control over the storm. Energy cascaded toward Ayesha, who channeled it into the voyager's charm.

"IMPERIAL . . . DOG!" The waterspout lost cohesion, and the bearded face deflated. It glared at Tor as the waterspout collapsed beneath it.

The wind was still strong, but now it blew the dark clouds away from the sampan rather than herding them toward it. The seas grew calmer, and the wind died down.

Tor's kite dropped as slack formed on the tethers. The barrier around the sampan became slightly more visible and started to glow as the storm dissipated.

"Right on schedule," Tor yelled to anyone who could hear him. Their plan had worked. Apart from some pants-wetting fear, he'd never had a doubt.

Below, Ayesha and the bearers began the laborious task of hauling in the sail-kite. It approached the deck one arm-length at a time. Tor peered out to the clearing horizon and saw a faint gray rock.

"Kusho Island!" He pointed at the smudge of gray barely visible at this distance. "We're almost there."

CHAPTER 11

The kentsu made its eastern headquarters in the foothills of Madara's Gitte-Yatay Mountains. Dark's team of imperial steeds made the journey from the shrine to the kentsu camp in under a day. Devilboon had eventually awakened from his trance, but a few hours after that Dark had put him to sleep again. Now the little man sat silent and wide-eyed as the first daggers of daylight stabbed into the diligence.

The steeds approached the perimeter of the camp and were halted by armed sentries. A team of eight imperial soldiers stood with spears at the ready, and two of the elite imperial guards waved the horses to a stop. Lord Dark permitted this inconvenience because he respected General Elsdragon's dedication to the security of his camp.

The imperial guards approached the carriage, their blueblack armor shining purple in the gathering light. Each carried a long sword and bore the kentsu standard on their chests, a rampant falcon with lightning bolts clutched in both clawed feet.

"You, inside the carriage. Come out and identify yourself."

Dark looked at Devilboon, still gaping at the mountains all around them. The master assassin swatted his minion alongside the ear and hissed, "Get out and announce me, thickwit."

Devilboon gathered his staff and as much of his dignity as he could muster. He pushed open the door and called, "Lord

Dark, the emperor's assassin, has come to meet with your commanding officer." Boris planted his staff and stood tall. "Stand aside and let us pass."

The two guards shared a glance then turned back to Devilboon. The one who had hailed them spoke again. "Well met, assassin. If Lord Dark will but present himself, we shall not hinder him further."

With real fear in his eyes Devilboon looked back at his master. The carriage was silent and motionless for a long moment. Then, slowly, Dark slid his right hand out of the window and clenched his fist, his signet ring facing the guards.

"Here is my seal," Dark's voice boomed out of the shadowy interior of the coach, "which is more proof than you deserve. If the way is not cleared for me in the next ten seconds, I will present myself to you fully, and General Elsdragon will need to order ten fresh graves dug and post ten new fools at this gate."

The elite guards each took a step forward and inspected the ring. They shared another glance, shrugged, and waved the spearmen back.

Devilboon sneered at the assembled sentries and climbed back into the carriage. Dark drew his arm inside and whistled for his horses. In response, the huge steeds cantered easily through the open gateway and made their unhurried way into the camp. Dark nodded to himself when one of the elite guards sent four of the spearmen after the assassin's coach. Their presence as escorts was both a courtesy to a visiting dignitary and a warning against any hostility.

The carriage and its escort crossed the camp, passing semipermanent barracks that could house up to ten thousand of the emperor's finest troops. There was a similar camp to the northeast and an even larger one to the south.

The full might of the army had not been assembled in years, and Elsdragon had distributed his forces throughout Madara so that no corner of the empire was unprotected. He made his own camp here, close by the imperial shrine and nestled among the Gitte-Yatay. The eastern mountains were especially rich in red mana, the magical fuel that allowed a general to build an army and send it against the emperor's enemies.

The carriage came to a halt in front of the general's command tent. Armed escorts fanned out behind the coach, and Devilboon stepped down. At last, Dark swept out of the coach and stood, his arms folded.

Two men emerged from the general's headquarters to greet the new arrivals. Lord Dark did not recognize the smaller of the two, a broad-shouldered grunt with a big belly and a huge tangle of curly black hair. He had brown skin and a wide flat face, and it irritated Dark that he could not place the man's name or his tribe. The squat soldier wore a kentsu helmet and a simple peasant's costume. His two reddish-gold wristbands matched a braided rope of cloth tied across his chest. The kentsu falcon standard was tattooed on his naked shoulder, and other markings that Lord Dark could not decipher covered the exposed flesh on his arms, legs, and throat.

Beside the unfamiliar man walked Jorgan Hage, and Lord Dark knew him well. Hage was the general's second-in-command and by all accounts both a fierce warrior and an effective battlefield leader. He was of low birth, from the wild and bloodthirsty Ærathi tribe. Hage wore his long red hair berserker-style, flowing out loose around his shoulders. A thin metal diadem kept it clear of his eyes. Except for this Ærathi affectation, he wore the standard armor and uniform of an elite kentsu officer.

"Greetings, Lord Dark," Hage called. "If the general had known you were coming—"

"I will speak with Elsdragon now." Dark started past Hage and the tattooed man, but the Ærathi brute stepped in front of him.

"*General* Elsdragon," Hage growled, "is waiting for you inside. Sergeant Meha," Hage indicated the smaller, rounder man beside him, "will escort you."

Dark looked Sergeant Meha up and down. The tattooed man smiled pleasantly. Lord Dark did not.

"I need no escort." Dark turned to Devilboon, and said, "Nine hells, little Boris, look at the state of them. Not a civilized Madaran among them. Has the kentsu conquered so many savages only to be conquered itself from within?"

Hage snarled and reflexively grabbed the huge war hammer strapped across his back. Devilboon stepped out of harm's way, but Sergeant Meha put himself between Dark and Hage before the situation grew violent.

"This way, my lord." Meha's eyes twinkled as he bowed, more amused than offended. Dark nodded to the oddly dressed soldier and started down the path to the tent. Meha stopped to open the tent flap for him. "General," he called. "Lord Dark is here to see you."

Dark waited at the threshold until a clear, languid voice called out, "Thank you, Sergeant. You are dismissed. Please enter, Lord Dark. It is a pleasure to see you, as always."

The inside of the tent was lit by a glowing red gem fixed on the end of a spear and jammed into the ground. Dark approached the fire crystal and the man standing beyond it.

Marhault Elsdragon had been in command of the imperial army for twelve years, twice as long as anyone else had ever held the post. He was a large man, but slender, tall and sinewy where Dark was broad and burly. Elsdragon wore black and gold armor polished to a mirrorlike sheen, and rich brown hair swept straight back from his forehead to expose tall, pointed ears. He was rumored to have elf blood in him, a claim that not even Lord Dark had been able to prove or disprove. Regardless, Elsdragon was a powerful man in charge of the emperor's most devastating military forces, and Lord Dark did not care to antagonize the general as openly or as lightly as he had Marshal Hage.

"General." Dark pressed his palms together and bowed slightly.

"Assassin." Elsdragon returned the bow. "What brings you to my headquarters?"

"If you please, General. I am Lord Dark in public." Elsdragon nodded, and Dark continued. "I am currently acting on imperial orders concerning a matter in the Edemi Islands. Tetsuo Umezawa seeks to delay or deny the successful completion of my mission."

"You are in conflict with the champion." Elsdragon nodded. "Again. I have already heard, in a dispatch from the emperor himself."

Lord Dark smiled and cocked his head to one side. "Then you know I have proper sanction for what I do."

"That is so."

"You know the emperor has left it to me to resolve this latest conflict between his officials."

Elsdragon nodded thoughtfully. "I do. But tell me. What does your latest squabble with Umezawa mean to me?"

"Nothing," Dark said evenly, "but it might. If it did, I would hate for any miscommunication to create confusion between us."

"There is nothing to miscommunicate. The kentsu have not been ordered into the Edemis."

"Of course, but the situation there is escalating quickly.

Already Caleria sends her beasts to raid our shores. But to the point, General: If matters in the Edemis continue to cause friction between owl and phoenix, I would know which side the kentsu supports."

Elsdragon raised an eyebrow. "The emperor's, of course. We all serve the emperor—assassin, champion, and kentsu alike. You and Tetsuo would do well to remember that more often than you do."

"With respect, General, do not lecture me on my responsibilities. I serve the emperor as I always have, faithfully and ardently. It is the champion who works against all our interests."

"My lord," Elsdragon said, "at this time I have no imperial orders to move against you or the champion. I shall not move at all until the emperor issues orders to do so."

Dark smiled. "Then I can rely on no interference from the kentsu, should Tetsuo and I come into open conflict?"

"You can rely on my strict adherence to the emperor's wishes. Neither I nor any of my troops will move an inch until he expressly states those wishes."

Dark bowed again. "Thank you, General. It is always a pleasure to deal with true servants of the empire. So much unpleasantness can be avoided if men like us simply sit and talk."

Elsdragon smiled a cold, lifeless smile. "Indeed. Was there anything else, my lord? You and your servant are welcome to linger, but I imagine you have much more important things to do elsewhere."

"In fact, I do. If you will excuse me now, I will not take up any more of your time. May I add that I regret my pending success in the Edemis. In completing the task the emperor gave me, I deny myself the pleasure of seeing your troops in action once more."

Elsdragon's face was like stone, betraying nothing. "There is nothing to regret, my lord. If you and the champion both fail in the Edemis, then the kentsu will march. You are the emperor's first resort. We are his last. Thus his dominance is forever assured."

"Long live the emperor." Dark turned and exited the tent, without even a glance at Meha holding the flap for him.

Outside, Dark watched Devilboon's sweaty face in the coach window as Marshal Hage and the four spearmen lurked nearby. Either the Ærathi savage was afraid to trifle with the assassin's crest or he was too respectful of the imperial steeds to molest the coach. Dark swept up the path, and the soldiers cleared the way before him.

"Farewell, Marshal," Dark called jovially as Devilboon opened the door and stepped out. "Thank you for minding my servant and my horses. If you ever decide to leave the army, I can always use a talented groom. Provided, of course, that you can rise above your roots and resist your inclination to eat them."

"Good-bye, my lord." Hage flushed and nearly shook with rage. "Our paths will cross again soon."

Dark paused a moment, still beaming as he stared hard at the soldier. He could hear the naked threat in Hage's words, could feel the hate in his heart. He casually swung himself into the coach.

"Come, irritant," he called to Devilboon. To himself, he added, "It is time to prepare a serpent's bed for the champion's final rest."

* * * * *

With the storm gone, the currents and the traveling spell favored Tetsuo's sampan all the way to the shores of Kusho.

As they approached the wedge-shaped island's northern tip, the champion expertly maneuvered them through Kusho's notorious hidden reefs. Tor stood alone at the fore of the ship, carefully scanning the coastline for a place to land.

"There's a lagoon up ahead." Tor kept his eyes fixed to the fore.

"I can't see anything." Kei's voice made Tor jump.

"You're getting sneaky in your old age," Tor said. "You haven't been staring as long as I have." He pointed. "Look there. You can see rocks and sand when there's a break in the haze."

"*You* can."

"I can hear waves on a shore nearby, too. Trust me, this is one of the things I'm good at." He smiled, but Kei merely walked away.

Tor shrugged and resumed his vigil. The healer had gone silent when they first spotted the island, and he had grown ever more somber as they approached. Maybe whatever was inside Kei was starting to wear him down.

The wind gusted, and the haze covering the water thinned out. "Dead ahead!" Tor cried. "There's definitely a beach to land on." He whispered a silent prayer and whistled a few bars of the young archer's song. Soon he would be on the ground again, good old solid ground. He longed to walk a hundred yards in a single direction, or even five paces on a surface that wouldn't drop from under his feet.

Ayesha came to the middle of the ship. "Are there any people on the beach?"

Tor squinted. "Yes . . . no, wait. There's something there, but I don't think it's alive. Hold on." Tor inched out onto the driftwood figurehead and shaded his eyes with his hand.

"There are rows and rows of . . . shields, I think."

"Shields?"

"I think so. Round shields, stuck in the sand. One, two
. . . three rows of about thirty each." Tor looked back at
Ayesha. "I don't see anything moving. Just rows of shields,
like an entire platoon is camping here on the beach before
they move on." Tor slid down off the figurehead. There was
the distinct smell of smoke, and Tor could see the remains
of a ruined pier scattered across the beach. "We're getting
close now. You should be able to see it for yourself in a
minute."

Kei had come back up on the deck and spoke softly to
Ayesha. She answered sternly and pointed at the beach. He
nodded, and Tor thought again how tired the healer looked.

Ayesha shook her head and called out to Tor. "Kei says
those aren't shields, and that isn't a bivouac." She turned and
went back to the rudder, where Tetsuo still steered.

"What is it, then?" Tor called again, louder. "Ayesha? What
. . ." Tor's voice lost all its force as the sampan ran up on a
sandbar less than twenty feet from shore. All of the sampan's
passengers stumbled forward, and Tor clung tight to the rail
to keep from pitching over the bow.

Wind carried the smoke and vapor out to sea so that the
view was clear. Tor stared at the beach, eyes wide, as the
tide gently slapped the hull of the boat.

The white sand beach ahead was covered not with
shields, as Tor had guessed, but with shells. Row upon row
of giant, empty tortoise shells. They were partially buried
in the sand so that each stood on its end, as tall as a
person and covered in brilliant markings. The half-hidden
sun glistened off iridescent swirls and metallic colors or-
ganically grown through each hardened plate. Many of the
shells were marred, however, burned and blighted as if
they had been carelessly doused with lamp oil and set
aflame. Some were broken and missing pieces, and Tor's

keen eye saw that some had been shattered and reconstructed for display.

Tor whirled from the eerily silent scene and found Kei, Ayesha, and Tetsuo standing in the middle of the deck. Each stared past Tor to the array of empty chelonian husks. Kei looked as if he might collapse, and there were tears in his eyes.

"This is what they did," Ayesha spat furiously, "in your name, Tetsuo. Under your standard."

"They have much to answer for," Tetsuo said. The boat suddenly listed to one side, and an agonized groan rose up from the rudder. "We have more pressing problems."

Tetsuo turned around to see a heavy chelonian warrior hauling himself onto the deck. Seawater gushed off his shell as the turtle man rose and pointed his spear at the champion.

Tetsuo charged, swinging his sheathed sword at the amphibian's face. The turtle man's head retreated inside his shell, and Tetsuo altered his swing so that the sheath rammed end-first into the center of the chelonian's chest. Tetsuo planted his feet and lowered his shoulder, and he shoved the chelonian backward over the sampan's rail.

A strange lump of coral and stone landed on the deck. Tetsuo took one look at it and said, "Ayesha."

The armorer quickly stepped up to the ticking, vibrating chunk and held her hands over it. "It's a mine," she said. She shut her eyes, and Tor heard a rush of air. The ticking ground to a halt. Ayesha smiled at Tor and said, "I'm a breaker, remember?" With a flick of her foot, she flipped the deactivated explosive over the rail.

A grappling hook arced up and latched onto the deck railing at the rear of the ship, and a second landed near the center. A third hook bit into the railing a few feet from where

Tor stood, so he jerked it loose and dropped it back into the sea.

"We're being boarded," Tetsuo called. "Abandon ship." The bearers and the other servants promptly jumped off the sides of the ship and made for shore.

"My barrow—" Ayesha began.

Tetsuo grabbed her wrist in one hand and Kei's in the other. He dragged them across the deck to where Tor waited.

Webbed chelonian hands grasped the rail, tilting the ship as the heavy creatures tried to climb aboard.

"My tools!" Ayesha snatched her hand away from Tetsuo, but the champion dropped Kei's hand and caught Ayesha by both shoulders.

"Leave everything," he said calmly. "We can't fight them here. We probably don't need to fight them at all. We just need to defend ourselves until we can calm them down enough to listen." He released her, pried a nearby chelonian off the rail, and shoved her back into the sea.

Tetsuo turned to Tor. "We must not kill anymore turtle-folk. Agreed?"

"Of course." Tor had his bow ready, but he looped it back over his head. "First we get off the boat, though." He made as if to vault right over the figurehead. "Right?"

"Right," Tetsuo waved Tor on. "Go, Tor, get to the beach."

Tor stood up on the rail, but before he could jump into the surf Ayesha grabbed his foot.

"Wait," she said. She glanced at Kei for a split second. The healer stepped up and offered Tor his hand. The archer pulled Kei up onto the rail. "On three?" he said. Kei nodded.

"Stay close to Tor," Ayesha muttered.

"Yes, Master."

Tor grabbed him by the shoulder and yelled, "Three!" He leaped over the side of the sampan, dragging Kei with him.

Cold water stung him, and salt spray made it nearly impossible to see. Tor was grateful the narrow strip of ocean between the sandbar and the shore was too shallow for chelonians to lurk in. At least he didn't have to worry about tripping over one.

With Kei's robe clenched in his fist, Tor made his way toward the sand. A breaking wave caught the healer full in the face. Tor released Kei, who fell heavily onto his hands and knees, coughing up water and gasping for air.

"You." The voice was loud and clear, its tone a mixture of sadness and anger. "The one from the sampan."

Tor staggered back into the surf, wiped the last of the salt-water from his eyes, and looked up the beach at the voice's owner.

A huge man with a thick mane of white hair and an even thicker white beard stood at the edge of the beach near a scrub forest. His long nose jutted angrily out of the cloud of hair. Tor recognized the face he had seen in the waterspout, only now it was flesh and blood. The man carried a curved chopping sword and a round wooden shield.

More warriors emerged from the scrub forest, humans and chelonians as well as a few species Tor did not recognize. They all carried swords or spears or, in some cases, driftwood cudgels studded with shark's teeth. The huge man with the white mane leveled his blade at Tor and Kei.

"Imperial dogs," he said, "I am Gosta Dirk, and as long as I live, Kusho will be free." His voice grew louder until his words echoed down the length of the beach. "Come, brothers! Kill these murdering cowards where they stand! We'll send the pieces in a box to their precious emperor!" Gosta's warriors roared their bloodthirsty assent.

Tetsuo and Ayesha were knee-deep in the surf, and Kei gasped nearby on the sand. Tor always knew how many and what kind of arrows were in his quiver, and as he eyed the oncoming mob, he knew he didn't have enough.

"Nine hells," he whispered. "I should have stayed on the boat."

CHAPTER 12

Tor grabbed Kei by the collar and yanked him back into the ebbing tide. The healer fell on his side in the water, sputtering and flailing as another wave broke over his head.

"Sorry," Tor said. Even so, Kei was better off close to Ayesha, with Tor between him and Gosta's small army.

Most of Kusho's defenders howled for imperial blood, and a few had drawn their weapons and were already charging. Tor reckoned he had about thirty feet of space and ten seconds of time before they were upon him.

Tor drew, aimed, and fired at the first Kushan warrior. The human male fell, wailing with a bolt in the meaty part of his thigh. The second and third attacker jumped over the thrashing form, then each met Tor's arrows and fell. They blocked the flow of angry warriors.

Despite their turtlelike bulk, the chelonians were actually fast on dry land. A large female with a spear in either hand lumbered at Tor, and it took him a moment to aim properly due to her bizarre, wobbling gait. Tor let fly dead center at the warrior's chest plate, but the arrow simply bounced off.

The chelonian lowered her head and aimed her sharp helmet fin at the archer. Tor started to panic as the sheer number of incoming threats almost overwhelmed him, but he forced himself to let his training take over. If he relied on reflexes alone, he would not live through the next few minutes. Instead, he controlled his breathing, planted his feet wide, and cleared his mind.

The charging chelonian roared in triumph as Tor's bow fell useless at his side. She raised one spear over her head and thrust the other out in front of her, kicking sand up on either side of her as she waddled-ran within striking distance.

Simultaneously, the chelonian threw her raised spear over Tor's head and stabbed the other one out at chest level. If Tor leaped up or stayed put, he'd be skewered. If he ducked or rolled to the side, her broad body would crush him.

Tor dived over the thrusting spear but under the thrown one, twisting his body and legs around the two missiles and the oncoming turtle shell. He landed on his hands and tumbled like an acrobat, pressing his face and torso into the soft sand. He rolled onto his knees then his feet. Tor drew and sighted an arrow as his foe tried to stop her forward momentum and sank a shaft into the shell's shoulder seam.

The chelonian screamed in pain and rage. She whirled and, with her good arm, threw the remaining spear at Tor. Tor easily avoided the point then incapacitated two humans and a merman with an arrow through each sword-bearing wrist.

"Fire and flood!" Gosta cried. "We outnumber them twenty to one."

Attackers still menaced Tor with weapons and words but stayed clear of his bow and scattered when he turned to face them.

Gosta warbled out a few syllables in the low-pitched language of the chelonians, and a squad of four advanced in formation, with Gosta in the lead. Two of the turtlefolk marched with their backs to Tor, lurching and wobbling in unison. The other two stayed in step, a spear jutting forward in either hand. Gosta must have spent a great deal of time drilling with the turtlefolk, for he also mirrored each crazy tilted step in their advance.

In effect, the squat formation was a mobile fortress, safe from Tor's arrows as they advanced on his position. Once they got close enough, Tor expected all four to turn and immobilize him through sheer weight while their leader hacked him to pieces.

Tor scanned the field, breathing steadily. Before the idea had fully formed, he put it into action. He drew one of the grapeshot arrows and clamped it between his teeth then nocked a normal arrow and sighted it onto the oncoming turtle shells. Tor drew back, lowered his aim, and sank the shaft into the coral on a turtle warrior's right leg, puncturing the flipper beneath.

The wounded chelonian let out a screech and stumbled. Both defensive members of the squad fell over each other into the sand, one landing belly-up and the other facedown on top of the first.

Tor quickly aimed the grapeshot arrow and let it fly. The round gray arrowhead shattered against the two sprawled chelonians. A hundred jagged bits of shrapnel flashed out in all directions. The initial volley stung the standing chelonian's exposed faces, and the turtlefolk instinctively pulled back inside their shells. The rest of the vicious payload ricocheted off their sealed armor and deflected straight toward Tor's intended target: the unprotected Gosta Dirk.

For a big man, Gosta was fast. He managed to get his shield up in front of his face before the sharp pellets blinded him. His sword arm remained unprotected, however, and a half-dozen tiny wounds opened on his shoulder and biceps.

The two fallen chelonians croaked in seeming agony. Gosta's sword fell from a fist that could no longer clench, and for a moment all was silent and still on the beach.

Gosta slowly lowered his shield. He glanced at his wounded arm and at Tor. The archer measured Gosta's expression of pure ire and calmly loaded another arrow as the bearded man knelt and retrieved his sword with his left hand.

"Bastard," he spat. He pointed the sword at Tor and yelled, "Chelonian spears at the ready. If I don't take his head on the first pass, pin him to the beach." Gosta practiced a long, smooth swing with his left arm and advanced on Tor.

"Stop!" Tetsuo's voice rose over the moans and battle cries of Kusho's defenders. Tor felt the champion's powerful hand on his shoulder, and he exhaled. With his arrow still trained on Gosta, he took one step back as Tetsuo came forward.

"Listen, citizens of Kusho. You have a grievance against the empire. I am Tetsuo Umezawa, the imperial champion. I am here to learn the truth. I am here to listen to you. There is no reason for us to fight."

All around him, the members of Gosta's battalion froze and whispered to each other. Gosta himself merely narrowed his eyes. He took a small tube from his waist, put it to his lips, and piped a single shrill crescendo. The warriors on the beach all cleared away, with Gosta staring unobstructed at Tetsuo.

From the edge of the scrub forest came an inhuman roar. Something ragged and massive erupted into the air, soaring high above the treetops and coming down hard on the sand between Gosta and Tetsuo.

The new arrival was even taller and broader than Gosta, smeared with dirt and dressed in skins. His eyes glowed an unholy green beneath hair and beard so wild and unkempt that Tor could barely determine that the figure was human. He growled like an animal and hefted his two-headed battle-axe with both oaken arms, muscles bulging and rippling under his furry cape. He wore huge spiked gauntlets of silver that covered his forearm from his elbow all the way down to his wrist. A matching sword and scabbard hung at his waist.

"Kasimir," Gosta said, and the wild man spun at the sound of his name. With his sword, Gosta pointed to Tetsuo. "The emperor has sent his champion to talk to us. The free people of Kusho say it is too late for talk. Be our champion, Kasimir. Kill the invaders."

Kasimir grunted at the mention of the emperor and slowly turned to face Tetsuo. The wild man's breath sucked strands of gray hair in and out of his mouth as the two warriors stared at each other.

Tor heard his master's sharp intake of air and the soft, mournful word he spoke under his breath. "You," Tetsuo said, much as Gosta had earlier when he spotted Tor. The archer had no chance to ponder Tetsuo's flash of recognition.

Kasimir's eyes snapped wide open behind his bushy eyebrows. "Umezawa," he growled. Kasimir repeated his bestial roar and raised his axe high overhead.

"Hold your fire," Tetsuo spoke without turning, his eyes fixed on the wild man.

Tor nodded and reoriented his arrow on Gosta, standing tall behind Kasimir. They held this position, four battle-hardened warriors with weapons at the ready. Kasimir let out a rumbling growl that rose in intensity, growing louder and rougher until it became a scream.

All at once, Kasimir brought the axe down, Tetsuo drew his blade, and Gosta cried, "Forward!"

The last thing Tor saw before he let the arrow fly was a blinding flash of white light as the beach between Tetsuo and Kasimir exploded.

* * * * *

Lord Dark's diligence was barely halfway back to his castle keep when the ambush struck. It was an excellent attack, he noted, well planned and flawlessly executed. He expected no less from a kentsu officer.

The carriage had been approaching yet another pass carved through the foothills when his steeds suddenly reared and whinnied. The diligence lurched to a halt.

Devilboon picked himself up off the carriage floor and straightened his hood. "What's happening, my lord?"

Dark peered through the slot that allowed him to see the road ahead. The horses skittered and danced nervously, but they would not advance. "We are being immobilized," he said. "Probably as a prelude to being murdered." Devilboon yelped as Dark grabbed him by the hood and hauled him forward.

"Make one of your little friends," Dark hissed. "Send it out on the road ahead." He released his minion.

Devilboon nodded nervously. "Of course, my lord."

The little man planted his staff on the floor of the coach and spoke very softly. His eyes rolled back in his head, and his free hand clenched into a tight fist. His forehead lolled, and the dark stone in the staff's head emitted a reddish glow.

Lips moving, Devilboon snapped his head up to reveal eyes that glowed with the same dread light as his staff. Smoke poured from his mouth, and he extended his staff forward as he let out a cry. A loud implosion drowned out Devilboon's voice, and Dark heard red-hot feet hiss on wet grass.

The light in Devilboon's eyes and staff winked out, and the little man fell once more to the floor of the coach. He remained conscious, however, and panted heavily as he struggled back up onto the cushioned bench.

"My lord," he said, as proudly as his fatigue permitted. He gestured with his staff, and Lord Dark looked out the window at the small humanoid figure now standing on the path.

It was barely three feet tall and featureless, like an unfinished statue of a man. It seemed to be composed entirely of molten rock, angry red in color and spewing streams of black smoke from its head and shoulders. A small fire had broken out on the grass around its feet, and as it turned its head to face the carriage, blackened flakes of carbonized ore and other slag fell from its neck and waist.

"Well?" Dark snapped. "Send it down the road."

"Hsssst!" The figure oriented its faceless head on Devilboon's command. The hooded mage nodded at the pass, and the smoking homunculus obligingly shambled up the path, leaving small burning footprints in its wake.

The little fire demon walked five paces past the lead stallion and promptly disappeared. Dark had been watching its progress carefully. One moment it was marching steadily forward, and in the next the ground seemingly swallowed it whole.

"It's gone," he said. "Are you still controlling it?"

Devilboon stared hard into the space directly before him. "Yes, my lord." His eyes had ceased glowing, but he was clearly seeing something beyond normal sight. "My friend is both intact and still conscious. Someone has dug a pit in the road and covered it with an illusion."

Dark smiled. "Excellent. So it is an ambush, after all." He concentrated, drawing up memories of his keep and the dangerous marsh around it. The fens were rife with black mana, and by visiting them in his mind, Dark created a link between their supply of arcane energy and his demand for power.

Outside, a single flaming arrow rose from within the pass and buried itself in the ground in front of the imperial steeds. Marshal Hage stepped out of the shadows, his war hammer ready.

"Assassin," he called. "General Elsdragon is too good a soldier to question his orders, even when he receives none. I know you are scheming . . . against him, against the kentsu, against the empire itself. I accuse you of treason, and you will answer for it."

"Marshal," Lord Dark's voice echoed inside the carriage before reaching Hage. "You are a fool. Is it treason or insult that brings you here? Go back to your campground, little soldier. Running the empire is a task for grown men with thick skins, not hot-headed children."

Devilboon gasped and took hold of Dark's sleeve.

Dark snatched it away. "Oaf. Have you lost your mind?"

"My lord," Devilboon whispered. "My little friend is . . . gone. There are men in that pit, many men."

Outside, Marshal Hage raised his hammer and bellowed. From the pass, from the pit, from the tall grass by the side of the road, they came: elite kentsu guards in bruise-colored armor and common soldiers bearing pikes and wicker shields. They came from all sides, surrounding the diligence and advancing on it, the containment circle growing ever smaller. Archers waited in the grass outside the circle, arrows ready but not yet burning or aimed.

"What shall we do?" Devilboon's voice was tight with panic. "What do we do?"

"You, dear Boris, shall sleep until I have a use for you." Dark waved his hand in front of Devilboon's face, and the little man swooned. He did not fall but remained upright, rigid and entranced behind closed eyelids.

"While I—" Dark clenched both fists as he surveyed the approaching squadron—"shall spring the trap I have so carefully laid for the marshal." He whistled to the horses, a low, trilling sound, and they each froze in place as their bodies became like stone. They would remain immobile and unharmed until their master released them.

Lord Dark swung open the carriage door and stepped out onto the road, rising to his full height and spreading his arms wide.

"Come on, then," his huge voice boomed across the cold road. "You'll never get a better chance."

Hage slapped the head of his hammer hard into his open palm. "Forward, lads," he said. "Don't leave any pieces big enough to bury."

The squadron closed tighter around their target, and Lord Dark laughed.

CHAPTER 13

Tetsuo's sword was a blur. All around the champion, sand and stones whistled past as if driven by hurricane winds. The flashing blade kept Tetsuo and Tor safe, however, creating a conical barrier that deflected the brunt of Kasimir's attack.

As he kept the sword in motion, Tetsuo turned his head slightly to face Tor. "Fight your way to the trees," he said. "Get Ayesha and Kei to safety."

Tor looked back to the armorer and her student crouched low in the surf. Ayesha nodded and helped Kei to his feet. Tor loaded and fired another grapeshot arrow in the direction he wanted to go. Kusho's defenders took cover from the exploding cluster bomb, and in the wake of the blast Tor charged into the empty space.

With a normal arrow nocked and ready, Tor was able to cover half the distance to the trees in a single charge. The Kushans had seen his skill with the bow, and they were unwilling to face him. He fired two explosive arrows, one at a turtle woman sealed tight within her shell, and the other halfway between him and the tree line. The explosion thinned their foes' ranks, and Tor gestured frantically for Ayesha and Kei.

Luckily, Ayesha was ready and Kei's legs were long, so it took them almost no time to reach Tor. The Kushans were sufficiently cowed that Tor did not need to fire again, but he kept his last explosive arrow half-drawn and glowing as he led his teammates off the beach. Once Kei and Ayesha safely reached the trees, Tor turned to watch the battle on the beach and to help his master if the chance arose.

Weapons drawn, Tetsuo and Kasimir circled each other. The wild man spat curses and tossed blow after blow at the champion, wielding the heavy axe like a child's baton. He swung the large head in wide sweeps that Tetsuo easily avoided, but Kasimir's shorter, faster chops with the small head prevented the champion from mounting any offense. Kasimir directed a steady stream of unfamiliar language at Tetsuo, and the glow from his eyes reflected on the twin heads of his axe. As the battle continued, the light grew more intense, changing from a sickly yellow-green to a dazzling white.

Tetsuo caught Kasimir's axe on his sword and stepped in close to his opponent. Though far larger, Kasimir was unable to force Tetsuo back, and they faced each other with only a few inches between their eyes. Kasimir's muscles bulged as he strained, but Tetsuo would not be moved.

"I don't wish to harm you," Tetsuo said, the force of his own efforts making his voice louder than usual.

"Bah!" Kasimir roared, and the head of his axe let out another burst of light and force.

Tetsuo fell back a step, but instead of pressing forward, Kasimir stepped back, crouched, and sprang high into the air.

A spear sailed at Tetsuo from one of the knots of chelonian warriors, and Tor quickly aimed and fired. The arrow glanced off the spearhead and sent the missile off course so that it landed in the sand, short and to the left of the champion. Tetsuo spared one brief, inscrutable glance at Tor then returned his eyes to Kasimir at the apex of a thirty-foot vertical leap.

Tor mentally kicked himself. Of course Tetsuo could have dodged the spear. He was the one who taught Tor to be aware of poaching spectators during a duel. Tor could have easily distracted the champion or, worse, shot him by mistake.

Kasimir seemed to float for a moment high above the sand and then brought his axe down with both hands. The axe left a trail of greenish-white energy behind it. A body-sized bolt of the same energy bloomed from the weapon and roared down on Tetsuo.

Tetsuo's eyes remained fixed on the incoming bolt as he drew his sword. He spun the blade over his hand and stabbed the point upward. A blue jag of electricity jumped from the end of Tetsuo's sword and hit the incoming bolt head on, creating another multicolored flash and a muffled explosion a few yards above the champion's head.

Kasimir finally began to fall, and he spun the axe handle between his hands. The spinning axe heads became a blur until the wild man released his weapon from ten feet above the beach. Kasimir cast both arms forward on either side of the rotating axe, and the weapon leaped at Tetsuo like a thing alive.

Tetsuo stayed calm and still until the axe was a mere arm's length away then lunged forward with his sword, sinking the tip into the silver spike jutting over the axe blades. The spike's tempered metal caught on the end of Tetsuo's blade. Tetsuo stood for a moment, holding the still-spinning axe at bay with the point of his sword, then he stepped forward.

Despite its size and weight, Kasimir's axe was a delicately balanced weapon, and the spike was more than mere ornament. As the tip of Tetsuo's blade split the tip of the silver spike, Kasimir's magic lost its hold on the weapon. Without that energy and Kasimir's direction, the axe slowed. Tetsuo merely had to stand firm and wait while the axe quickly ground to a halt and fell to the sand.

Kasimir roared in frustration and drew his sword, a long, curved, vicious-looking blade. He kept it low by his side as he tossed his cape back off his shoulders and charged across the sand.

The champion shook his head. "Enough." He held his own sword out to his right and tossed it spinning across his body to his waiting left hand. As Kasimir bore down on him, he made a large loop with the sword and tossed it back to his right hand. He carved another large loop and bent his elbow to block Kasimir's first overhand swing. Tetsuo spun out from under Kasimir's arms and elbowed the wild man in the ribs. He whirled in place as Kasimir stumbled forward and landed another elbow on the back of Kasimir's head.

Kasimir staggered, and Tetsuo brought his sword up and pointed the tip. The wild man turned, struggling to regain his balance. Tetsuo struck.

A sparking blue ball formed at the end of Tetsuo's sword and flew at the wild man. Kasimir neatly intercepted the ball with his own sword, but doing so released all the energy Tetsuo had placed inside. The explosion knocked the sword from Kasimir's hand and sent the wild man hurtling away from the battle. Kasimir sailed up and landed just shy of Tor. The impact kicked up a huge cloud of sand. The giant warrior did not rise, though he was still breathing.

Tetsuo was not finished. He turned and fired another blue ball at the largest cluster of Kushan defenders, and they scattered before the explosion could hurl them through the air. The champion fired a third ball at Gosta Dirk, and the bearded man literally dropped his sword and crouched behind his wooden shield. Tetsuo's attack exploded against this meager defense, and Gosta was thrown onto his rear.

Before Gosta could rise, Tetsuo's sword was at his throat. "Yield," the champion said. "I am not here to kill you, and none of my colleagues ever attacked your village. I am here on official as well as unofficial business, and you will listen to me now." He kept the sword touching Gosta and raised his voice to the assembled warriors. "Yield," he repeated, "or none of you will leave this beach alive."

From his sitting position in the sand, Gosta looked from Tetsuo to Kasimir's fallen form. He slowly extended his smoking shield out at arm's length and dropped it to the sand.

"We yield," he said. "Nine hells take you all."

* * * * *

One of the imperial guard stepped ahead of his fellows and hurled his spear at Lord Dark.

The assassin smiled as the razor-tipped javelin flew. He raised his clenched fists straight out to either side then folded his elbows. He opened his hands palms-out against his chest so that the ends of his fingers touched, and as the spear struck him dead center in the breastbone, he spoke a single word. There was a loud pop and a puff of smoke, which the wind immediately carried away.

Lord Dark stood unharmed on the road, his arms still folded.

The guard who had thrown the spear fell to knees and grasped feebly at the weapon, now lodged deep in his own chest. The guard gurgled once behind his visor and slumped onto his side.

"Idiots!" Hage yelled. "Stay in formation!" The remaining kentsu soldiers resumed their advance.

Dark broke his folded-arm pose and made a show of counting his attackers as they approached. ". . . ten, eleven . . . and the dead man makes twelve." He theatrically placed his hand alongside his mouth and called, "An even dozen in the first wave, Marshal? Plus four archers and yourself. Is this the most you could sneak past Elsdragon? Does he even know you're here?"

The advancing circle of soldiers was now twenty-five feet away and closing. Dark reached out with his mind to the carriage behind him, where Devilboon slept.

"I asked you a question, Marshal." Hage did not answer, and his soldiers were now mere yards from Dark. "Very well," the assassin said.

"Boris," Dark intoned, and a burst of purple light flashed from his eyes. He uncrossed one of his arms to display his open hand, which he held up for all to see. Very slowly and with obvious strain on the bulging muscles in his forearm, Dark clenched his fist and rotated the knuckles until they faced Marshal Hage. "Produce."

A pained scream pealed from inside the carriage, and Dark caught a whiff of sulfur. Flame flared from the ground in front of the closest imperial guard, then again before the guard to his right. The advancing soldiers all stopped as small geysers of fire erupted in their paths. Each eruption brought a new cry from the carriage.

An imperial guard tried to step over the plume of flame, but the column exploded. Two of Devilboon's lava puppets appeared and latched onto the guard's armor. Their tiny fists left deep, scorched dents in the soldier's protective gear, and the guards screamed.

In sequence, all ten remaining flame geysers produced two of Devilboon's friends. The advance on Dark disintegrated as each kentsu warrior, soldier, and elite guard grappled with the demons. Swords and spears broke on rock-hard heads, shields burst into flame under the pounding of red-hot fists, and every time searing stone touched flesh, soldiers screamed. The tightly organized assault quickly became an ugly, confused skirmish, with Lord Dark smiling unmolested at its center.

"Archers!" Hage screamed. He raised his hand. "On my signal . . ."

Lord Dark quickly scanned the quartet of archers: two women and two men. Each had the intense look of concentration Dark associated with marksmen, their eyes alert but totally focused on the target at hand.

They're staring so hard at me, Dark thought. They should have something more interesting to stare at.

Dark summoned another surge of black mana and held it. The mystic energy churned inside his mind and body, but he waited for Hage's command. The time to strike was just as the archers let their quarrels fly.

Hage brought his hand down. "Fire!"

The archers shot their deadly bolts, but in the time between fingers releasing strings and arrows leaving bows, Lord Dark disappeared from the road.

Most of the arrows soared through the empty space Dark had just occupied. One went wild as the archer tried to stop a wasted shot. The archers quickly glanced at each other, and as one they turned their eyes to Marshal Hage for instructions.

Lord Dark stood behind the officer, smiling.

"What are you staring at?" Hage roared. "Reload! He has to be somewhere."

Behind the marshal, Dark placed two fingers over his own eyes and slowly dragged his hand across his face. Hage went rigid, convulsed, and fell foaming to the grass. Dark cocked his head, and a wave of visual distortion flowed off his body in all directions, enveloping Hage.

Devilboon's fire demons were slowly getting the best of the initial assault, so those soldiers posed no threat. All four archers had loaded new arrows, but the churning bubble around Dark and Hage would baffle any attempt to aim. One female archer even lowered her bow and shook her head to clear it, and one male choked on nausea as he stared into the rippling sphere.

Lord Dark concentrated and cast another spell. "A difficult shot," he said from behind the leftmost archer.

The nauseated man tried to turn, aim, and call his peers all at once. Before he could complete any of these actions, Lord Dark hit him hard in the forehead. His fist stamped the snake seal of his signet ring deep into the archer's face.

The other three archers turned to see what had happened. Their comrade stood alone, slack-jawed and drooling, with a smoking snake symbol burned into his skull.

Behind them, the distortion field around Marshal Hage vanished, revealing the officer on hands and knees and Lord Dark standing smugly over him.

"Slave," the assassin called. "Here are your targets. Fire at will." He reached down and hauled Hage up to his knees by his long red hair. "Pay attention, brute. It's important you see this."

Three archers immediately aimed at Dark and bent their bows. Before the first arrow could fly, the fourth let out an ear-splitting shriek and threw himself onto his cohorts. His eyes had gone jet black, flecked with bright yellow spots. He flailed, gouging eyes with his fingernails and sinking teeth into soft flesh.

The madman grabbed one of the female archers by the hair and the chin, and they fell in the cold wet grass. He twisted her head with a brutal jerk, and her neck snapped loudly.

The other female archer buried a shaft deep in the possessed man's torso. The skewered man grunted and fell on top of her, pinning her to the ground.

Hage struggled, weak and shuddering from the seizure Dark had inflicted on him. Dark extended his hand palm-down, and waved a careful U-shaped pattern in the air so that his palm ended facing up.

While the two live archers tried to untangle themselves from the dead, the woman with the broken neck responded to Dark's gesture. Her head lolled grotesquely as she stood, clumsily took an arrow from her quiver, and shot it deep into her living comrade's spine. The man gasped and fell.

The archer Dark had branded stood up, an arrow lodged in his chest. The woman who shot him grunted as she clawed her way out from under the body and tried to scramble away on her hands and knees. She made it only a few feet before the reanimated bodies of her squad caught her. They gouged and beat her. Ghostly images of the snake seal glowed on their foreheads, casting sickly purple light on their blank, dead expressions.

Dark roughly rolled Hage onto his back, absently kicking the soldier's war hammer aside. As the last archer's screams rang out across the foothills, Dark glanced at the carnage around his diligence.

Devilboon's friends had done well for themselves: None of the soldiers were left standing, but nine of the twenty-two lava puppets survived. Dead and dying kentsu soldiers littered the road, and Devilboon's homunculi walked in aimless circles among the bodies. If a human so much as twitched, the little demons pounced, smashing in skulls and burning off faces.

For a moment more, Dark watched them work, then he reached out to Devilboon in the carriage. Each of the little lava men slowed, hardened, and crumbled to dust.

"Now then, Marshal."

Through paralysis and rage, Hage stared with murderous fury at Dark. His lips moved, but he could not form any words.

"Normally, I would turn you over to the vivisectionists in my castle so that your last year of life could be as painful as possible, but you present an interesting problem." He walked around Hage and stood near the officer's head.

"I need the kentsu," Dark continued. "I need a man like Elsdragon in command, for the time being, and I need him compliant. The loss of your personal death squad is unlikely to turn him against me, but if you were to disappear, he might make inquiries. He might even connect your pathetic little raid to me." Dark scowled, but then broke into a smile. "A quick comment, Marshal, if you don't mind a little professional criticism: Never try to kill someone until you know all his strengths and weaknesses. Brute force and careful deployment may work on the battlefield where there are a thousand targets. If you're trying to be precise, you'd best leave it to the experts.

"It further occurs," Dark reached down and grabbed hold of Hage's hair once more, "that a man like you could be extremely useful in the right circumstances. Your only real shortcoming is your reckless pride and the illusion of freedom you take from it. Let me show you how things really work in this empire of ours."

Dark yanked Hage's head forward so that the man's chin touched his chest. The assassin raised his fist, and his signet ring glowed high in the night sky. Dark's mind went once more to the swamps near his home, to the reeking, bubbling source of his most subtle and powerful magics.

Dark's fist slammed into the base of Hage's skull. The officer screamed incoherently, and his body convulsed anew. Dark held the ring tight against Hage's flesh, whispering silently and focusing more black mana into the helpless man.

At last Dark stood and let Hage's head fall back to the ground. He dusted off his hands and walked around the supine form. He paused at the officer's feet, in full view of eyes steeped in hatred.

"You are mine, now," Dark said evenly. "You'll notice a few changes, but only a few. You will be stronger, for one thing, faster and more coordinated. You will be more durable, better able to resist injury, and less prone to fatigue. Before you try to leap up and brain me with your hammer, hear this: You may never act against me in any way, ever again. Simply touching your hammer's handle while looking at a picture of me will induce seizures ten times worse than the one that put you on the ground just now. I am very careful about whom I recruit, Marshal, and even more so how I bind them to my service.

"For all intents and purposes, I am your new commanding officer. When I say 'jump', you say, 'how high?' When I say, 'kill,' you say, 'whom and when?' When I say 'die,' you say, 'with pleasure, my lord.' These are facts I am telling you, not predictions. This is not an oath that you have sworn voluntarily or a bargain on which you can renege. It is what I am taking in lieu of your life for assaulting me."

Hage growled. To Dark's surprise, the downed officer actually pulled his head to one side and torturously pulled it back to the other side.

"Never," he spat.

Dark smiled. He crouched and patted Hage on the head.

"Keep telling yourself that. Beyond the physical enhancements I have bestowed and your inability to resist me, you may not even notice your new allegiance. In fact, it would be quite acceptable if you forgot this little incident ever took place." From his crouching position, Dark leaned over Hage's face. The assassin's eyes had gone jet black, his pupils a metallic blue.

Under Lord Dark's penetrating stare, Hage's face relaxed. His teeth unclenched, and his eyes slowly drifted shut.

"Forget, my new servant. No one, not even you, will know whom you truly serve until the time is right. Maintain your appearance and your habits and your illusion of free will, but take heart. I am not abandoning you, I am merely saving you for the future. When and if I ever need you, you will be there."

Dark walked away from Hage without looking back. He picked his way through the fallen kentsu soldiers and arrived at the coach.

Devilboon opened his eyes and rubbed them drowsily. "What happened, my lord?" He started to climb down, but noticed the scorched and broken bodies. "Did my friends do all that?"

"Get back in the coach," Dark said. He fought off the irritation that Boris always caused him, focusing instead on his triumph. "I got what we came for."

He whistled again to wake the horses, and the carriage was soon on its way.

CHAPTER 14

With his bow in hand, Tor followed Gosta Dirk as the island leader dismissed his fighters. They glared and blustered at the archer, but Gosta cleared them all from the beach without major incident.

As Kusho's defenders made their angry way back under the sea or into the scrub forest, a small procession of unarmed citizens came to the battleground. Under a flag of truce, they marched out of the ruins, and many of them carried medicine bags similar to Kei's.

Tor counted fewer than a dozen in all, and they followed a man who looked enough like Gosta to be his younger brother. He was blond and nowhere near as towering as Gosta but was tall and broad, with a thick beard and long, braided hair. He wore brass bands across his biceps and brass bracelets around his forearms, each with a colored gem lodged in its center. His face was stern but open as he scanned the beach where the wounded were being gathered.

"Ragnar," Gosta said, standing between Tetsuo and Tor, a makeshift bandage over his shoulder.

The blond man motioned for the procession to wait then approached. He pressed his palms together and bowed, never taking his cold eyes off of Tetsuo.

"This is Ragnar, my healer," Gosta said. "With your permission, he and his staff will begin treating the wounded."

"No fatalities?" Ragnar's voice was deep and loud, as if he were used to making himself heard.

"Not this time." Gosta glanced at Tetsuo. "With your permission," he prompted.

Tetsuo nodded at Tor, and the archer sprinted off to find Kei. "I will give more than permission," Tetsuo began.

Tor missed the rest, but he ran quickly in the hopes that nothing too interesting would be said while he was away. He jogged across the beach, stepping over and around the injured until he spotted Kei treating a Kushan's burned face and burst eardrum.

"The local healer's here," he said. "Come on. The champion wants you to help."

Kei handed his patient a poultice, and the two young men quickly made their way back to Gosta and Tetsuo.

Tetsuo nodded to Tor and Kei but continued to speak: ". . . sent here to kill you. I believe the attack on your village was a prelude to an attack on you personally."

Gosta frowned and shook his head. "Killing me would accomplish nothing. Kusho is a loose collective of radically different tribes and species. There is no one ruler. They listen to me only because of Kasimir, and they follow me only when they need protection." He gritted his teeth. "Does your emperor give his death warrants any thought before he issues them, or does he simply toss them off at random?"

Tetsuo's face remained blank, but Tor knew he gave Gosta's words serious consideration. The champion waved Kei forward. "This is Kei Takahashi, a healer-in-training. I would like him to observe and assist with the treatment of the one you called Kasimir."

Gosta glanced at Ragnar, who was eyeing Kei critically. "As long as he stays out of my way," the blond man said. Gosta nodded.

"Kasimir needs you the most right now." Gosta looked hard at Tetsuo and then pointed to a shaded spot. "He's over there."

Ragnar immediately followed the direction of Gosta's finger, waving for his staff to follow. He paused for a moment, measuring Kei once more with his eyes, then gestured for the white-faced youth to come along.

"Champion," Gosta said. "Kasimir is more than Kusho's best warrior. He is my friend. May I watch Ragnar's work?"

Tetsuo nodded. "We are all interested in Kasimir's recovery. Tor?"

"Master?"

"Accompany us. And you, Gosta Dirk—tell me more about the assault on your village."

Tetsuo and Gosta walked after Ragnar, and Tor fell in behind them. Gosta spoke stiffly, sneaking repeated glances at Tetsuo as if he expected the champion to draw and behead him at any time.

"She came out of a sigil burned into a rock," Gosta said. "I would show it to you, but we destroyed it to keep her from returning."

"That was sound but unnecessary. The demon has a powerful master, and she can go anywhere he sends her. Describe the creature that attacked the village."

"Huge," Gosta said, "fifty feet tall at least. Flaming eyes, bald head. She was dressed in blue metal robes." He scowled. "Robes bearing your standard."

"A deception," Tetsuo said. "Your enemies are my enemies. They would rather have us fight each other while they stalk us both. Have you seen any eumidians in the past few days?"

Gosta shook his head. "I don't know what that is."

"A wasp-woman—a humanoid insect with wings. It's important that we find her as quickly as possible."

They approached Ragnar's assistants, who stood in a semicircle with their heads bowed. They were chanting.

Gosta tapped two of the robed assistants on the shoulder, and they separated to allow him, Tetsuo, and Tor to pass.

Gosta turned to the champion. "You said you were here on imperial business—a response to a declaration of war."

"I am," Tetsuo said, "but I am also seeking the eumidian. Have you seen her?"

"No," Gosta said. "Just that giant roaring bitch and her tar."

Tetsuo fell silent. Tor peeked over the larger men's shoulders and saw Kasimir lying unconscious on his back, his head propped on a pillow of dry leaves and sand. Ragnar knelt beside him, waving his hand over the fallen giant's face.

"He is in no danger," the blond healer called, "but only because he is a tough, tough man. I expect all he really needs is two days' sleep and a table full of roasted meat."

Tetsuo nodded. "How soon before he can speak?"

"Not before tomorrow morning. As I said, he needs—"

"Can you heal him, restore his vigor, now?

Ragnar glanced at Gosta, who nodded urgently. The blond man took one last look at the sleeping warrior. "Yes."

"Then for pity's sake, do so."

Ragnar shook his head. "He won't be fully restored until he rests. He won't be able to fight. You there," Ragnar said to Kei, "what methods are you trained in?"

Kei hesitated, and then spoke clearly, almost proudly. "I am fluent in local herbs and preventive magic. I also—"

Ragnar grunted. "Bah, another pseudo-Samite. Anticipating injury is all well and good, but eventually you have to face reality. You can't prepare for everything. Take our sleeping friend here. What would you do for him, now that the damage is already done?"

Kei actually glowered. "The burns can be treated with the juice from a number of local succulents." The healer spoke mechanically, a student grudgingly reciting his lessons. "The neck should be hot-massaged before sundown to prevent stiffness tomorrow. And this—" he produced a pearl-textured vial from his pouch—"will cure his strains and bruises while also restoring his strength. In an hour, it will be as if the injury never happened."

Tor grinned behind Tetsuo and Gosta, and even Ragnar smiled.

"Very good," he said, "but that seems like a lot of steps and a lot of medicine when I can achieve the same result with my bare hands. Stand back, all of you, and watch me work."

The gems on Ragnar's arms sparkled. A wind kicked up, seemingly from beneath his feet and spread his long braided hair up and around his face like a frame. Ragnar recited a measured series of phrases in a language Tor didn't understand, though the name of the nature goddess Gaea ended every line.

Ragnar stopped rubbing his hands and held them aloft. His assistants in the semicircle took up the chant, repeating the phrases and Gaea's name at a steady, droning volume.

Ragnar cried, "Ho!" and fell forward, slapping his palms into Kasimir's chest. The wild man's entire body shone with uncanny green light that spread out and enveloped both patient and healer. The assistants finished their chant with a collective shout of Gaea's name, and the green light around Kasimir and Ragnar flared then died out.

Both Kasimir and Ragnar's bodies were smoking. The healer fell back and buried his hands in the sand behind him. He drew great, ragged breaths.

"He was worse off than I thought," Ragnar panted, "but

fine now. Whew, he soaks up a lot of healing, doesn't he?"

Kei held out the pearl-colored vial to Ragnar. "Maybe this will help."

Ragnar's eyes narrowed, but he smiled again. "All right, whitey. Take your potions and your smart mouth and get to work."

Ragnar pointed to the injured warriors that his assistants had lined up nearby. Kei turned to Tetsuo, and the champion nodded.

As Kei went off with Ragnar's students, Tetsuo helped Ragnar to his feet. Kasimir groaned and struggled to open his eyes.

"Find Ayesha," Tetsuo said to Tor. "Tell her we will be leaving shortly."

Tor saw his own confusion echoed in the faces of Gosta and Ragnar. "But I thought—"

"We were misled. *I* was misled." Tetsuo bowed his head to Gosta. "Forgive me. I—"

"An imperial apology," Gosta marveled. "There haven't been too many of those over the years, have there?"

Tetsuo's expression and tone hardened. "I am apologizing for myself only. The assault on your village was a ruse, carried out only to draw you into conflict with me. Likewise, I was led into an orchestrated conflict with you. None of this should have happened."

Gosta eyed Tetsuo suspiciously. "But it has, Champion."

"So it has. Make no mistake, Gosta Dirk. If the emperor desires your island, he will have it. But if he desires it," Tetsuo placed his hand on his sword, "he shall have it honorably. Through force of arms, if need be, but in open warfare, not clandestine murder. You may yet die by the emperor's order, but you will at least see your enemies declared before they strike."

"Well spoken, Champion, but I have no choice but to accept you at your word." Gosta crossed his arms. "I do not think the rest of your empire is as concerned with honor as you are. Your nation wants to rule our little island collective. We will resist you with every ounce of strength we have. If you return to Kusho, you will be treated as the enemy."

Tetsuo stared at Gosta, unblinking. "I am your enemy." He turned to Tor. "Find the armorer. As soon as all the wounded have been seen to, we sail for Argenti.

"We will fight another day, Gosta Dirk. Consider this fair warning: Caleria of Argenti has attacked the empire. She will answer for it, as will any who ally with her."

Tetsuo turned to Tor. "Prepare the boat for our departure. I would speak with Kasimir. Alone."

* * * * *

Lord Dark stepped out of his carriage and onto the footman's cushioned stool. The master of the house climbed the steps leading to his front door, where the majordomo stood waiting.

"Welcome home, my lord."

"Is the vault prepared?"

"Yes, my lord. It will—"

"Run ahead and clear the halls," Dark snapped. "I am going directly to the vault then to my study. I do not wish to be disturbed by anyone. I will send for you when I have further instructions."

Dark turned back to the carriage and snapped his fingers loudly. "Wake up, cretin."

Devilboon groaned, and the little man stuck his head out, rubbing his eyes. "Are we home, my lord?"

"I am home. You are dismissed. Get out of my coach and begone. I will summon you when I want you."

Lord Dark swept into his castle and made excellent progress down the empty halls. When he came to the passageway's dead end, he paused and listened closely, straining to detect anyone or anything spying on him. Satisfied that he was alone, Lord Dark whispered a password known only to himself and his majordomo then touched a loose brick in the wall. The dead end silently dropped into the floor, and Lord Dark continued down the newly revealed staircase.

At the bottom of the torch-lit stairs was a long, curved hallway without any illumination whatsoever. Dark moved expertly along the corridor, mentally noting all the lethal defenses built or warded into the walls and floor. Like the servants, the building itself recognized and feared its master. As he passed, poisoned spikes sat dormant in their hidden chambers, caustic vapors stayed safely inside their fragile glass bottles, and inflammable liquid remained inert in ceiling reservoirs. Dark pressed his back against the northern wall and carefully inched his way past the camouflaged pit at the center of the corridor.

He turned a corner to face another dead end, this one lit by two bright torches. The wall beyond the torches bore a mosaic of black and royal blue tiles that formed an image of a monstrous, muscular figure whose legs trailed off into smoke. Dark walked right up to the mosaic and stared directly into the tile efreet's glaring eyes.

"Stand aside or face your master," Dark said.

The image of the efreet began to move. Mosaic tiles shifted across the surface of the red stone wall. The tile efreet squinted at Dark and bowed and stepped aside. As soon as there was a space big enough, Dark walked past the efreet and through the wall without resistance.

Efreets made excellent sentries, provided they had been properly bound into service and sufficiently cowed into obedience. As it was, anyone but Lord Dark would have been torn to shreds by the mosaic efreet and smeared across the red stone wall.

Dark paused inside the vault until his eyes adjusted to the gloom. He had been collecting objects of mystical power and monetary worth for the better part of twenty years. Stretched out before him in the gloom lay his most important treasures and most valuable hidden assets. He was the only living person ever to set foot in this part of the castle, and he knew every piece and its location as intimately as a miser knows the contents of his wallet.

Though tempted to stop at each item and revel in his ownership, he pressed on. Dark moved past vast shelves stocked with scrolls, racks loaded with weapons and armor, long wooden tables crammed with ivory boxes, sculpted metal totems, and tiny crystalline skulls. When he was halfway through the collection, he stopped alongside a carved stone pedestal and smiled.

"Glorious," he whispered. The pedestal held a strange metal device about the size of a horse's saddle. It had a heavy cylindrical base studded with yellow gems and a wide funnel tube that twisted toward the ceiling like a huge, malformed ear. Though the device had been untended for years, it still gave off a faint hum, and the gems glowed softly in the gloom.

Dark placed his hands gently on the device, and the cool pewterlike metal quickly warmed under his touch. The device was clearly operational. All he needed to do was alter its ignition sequence and deliver it to his operatives in the Edemis.

My lord. Xira's inner voice brought an involuntary wince to Dark's face. He had gotten used to Xira's strangely musical vocalizations years ago, but something about her enunciation grated on Dark's nerves.

I am here. Dark spitefully raised his own inner voice, hoping to pain Xira as much as she annoyed him. *You may speak freely.*

My lord, I have arrived, and I am in position, but I fear we have a problem.

Dark felt the rush of a carefully researched hunch bearing fruit. *Continue.*

Xira spoke two short sentences, her voice uncharacteristically tense. She obviously didn't see the larger picture and was nervous about how her report would be received. . . .

So, you see, she concluded, *I think we have a problem.*

Dark remembered the words of Devilboon's proclamation, and he fought the urge to smirk even though Xira could not actually see his face. He also avoided looking at the pewter device and cleared it from his mind before he replied.

On the contrary, my dear, he thought. *I think you have just given me a solution.*

CHAPTER 15

When the sampan left the shores of Kusho, she was in better shape than when she had arrived. The main mast had been repaired, the traveling spell recast, and all of the cargo and crew were intact. In exchange for the safe release of all who surrendered, Gosta vowed not to direct the wind or the waves against the champion's vessel again until it had safely returned to imperial territory. Tetsuo took Gosta at his word, and the bearded man shook his head as the sampan pushed off from the makeshift dock.

"You are a noble enemy, Tetsuo Umezawa." Gosta shouted as the boat drifted away, "but your emperor is a beast. Even you cannot defend honor that does not exist." The afternoon sun cast long shadows behind Gosta and Ragnar. Before them, a squadron of chelonians waded into the sea to follow the sampan and report back if it altered course.

Tetsuo stared so intently at the cliffs above the dock that he didn't seem to hear Gosta's words. Tor followed Tetsuo's gaze to a massive figure crouching among the vines. Tetsuo and the shaggy figure stared at each other until Kasimir's perch faded into the distance. Then Tetsuo turned and went below decks to, as he put it, "prepare."

Tor could tell by the weight of his quiver and the tension on the bow that he was as prepared as he was going to get. He glanced around the sampan and saw Ayesha busy with her barrow. Kei sat cross-legged nearby and breathed evenly, his eyes closed. Ahead, the skies darkened with the coming evening. Behind, a hundred feet of sea mist and fog had swallowed up Kusho.

Nothing to look at, nothing to do, and no one to talk to. Tor had never regretted his choice of the warrior's path. In many ways it was simpler than the healer's or the maker's—and especially the champion's.

As he dejectedly slumped down onto the deck, Tor realized that simpler is not always easier. He vowed that before he went on another boat ride, he would ask Tetsuo about incorporating some form of meditation into his regimen.

The sampan pitched, and Tor held tightly to the rail until the waves settled down.

Preferably, one that would alleviate seasickness.

* * * * *

"Argenti Island ahead!" Ayesha's voice cut through Tor's head like a dagger. She shook his shoulder roughly. "Get to the fore. We need you to spot."

Tor crawled out from behind the nest of crates he had made to keep from being pitched into the sea while he slept. He was instantly alert, but he walked gingerly on a cramped foot.

"What's going on? What am I looking for?"

Ayesha directed his eyes beyond the prow. They had sailed all night and most of the next day, so the sun was just about to disappear over the horizon.

"I see it," he said. "Large island dead ahead. Lots of evergreen trees. Not many places to land." He squinted. "What's that covering it?"

"It looks like mist," Ayesha said, "but it's too uniform.

Look at the shape, the consistency. I think someone's cast a very large spell."

In the fading light, Tor concentrated on the approaching shore. Argenti was an island of massive evergreens, the oldest and largest trees towering high over the rest of the forest. Even they were contained by the inverted bowl of mist that rested over Argenti from one end to the other. The mist itself was thick and white, but it flowed and moved without breaking its half-shell form. It refracted any light and provided an eerie illumination to shapes visible inside.

Tor realized that Ayesha was waiting for his input. "Looks like a spell to me," he said. "What do you think it does?"

Ayesha shrugged angrily.

The two of them stood at the bow as Kei and Tetsuo approached. Tor stepped aside, and Tetsuo took his place, leaning out over the water on the driftwood figurehead.

"Argenti?" Tetsuo kept his hands cupped around his eyes.

"Argenti protected by white magic," Ayesha said. "Which could mean anything from an intruder alert to a barrier that kills uninvited guests. I'd like to know more before we sail into it."

"Agreed." Tetsuo turned from the figurehead. "Tor? Opinions?"

Tor felt his face flush. "White isn't my strong suit," he said. "If Ayesha hadn't pointed it out to me, I would have steered us right through it."

The barest twinge of exasperation showed on Tetsuo's face as he turned it to Kei. "Healer?"

Kei stood behind Tetsuo and Tor, tall enough to see over their heads. He closed his eyes, inhaled and exhaled deeply, then opened them again. "It's a field, one that cancels or reduces the impact of violent acts. Most likely the rulers of Argenti can invoke the spell's protection whenever they need it. They may even be able to apply it selectively. So long as they see the harm coming, they can blunt it." Kei caught Tor's impressed expression and shrugged. "I have some experience with mystically avoiding injury," he added blandly.

"Kei—" Ayesha's voice squelched the faint stirring of a smile on the healer's lips—"is probably right. It's a defensive spell, a preventive. It probably leaves the locals alone and works on nonresidents only. Or even imperial subjects. What do you say, Champion? After our reception on Kusho, do we dare land here when in all likelihood we won't be able to defend ourselves?"

Tetsuo slowly nodded his head. "We have to, but thankfully, we are no longer in such a rush."

Ayesha glanced at Kei and said, "Why not? How can you say that? Kei is still—" She caught herself and regained her temper. "What do you mean, Tetsuo?"

"The protection spell," Tor said. When Tetsuo nodded, he continued, "It's there to keep people from doing harm. If it works on us, it will work on Xira also."

"And Orca." Kei's eyes went cold and blank.

Tetsuo turned back to the view of Argenti, growing ever larger as they approached. "Argenti is a declared hostile, and I fully expect us to be met by armed troops. We must treat this like Kusho: land and obtain an audience with the leaders without seriously harming any natives. I see no reason we shouldn't land and announce ourselves openly."

Tor started to speak but changed his mind. The armorer was not so cautious.

"No reason except that we'll be fighting again," Ayesha said. "And no closer to finding Xira."

Tetsuo spoke calmly. "Xira is here. She has come to kill Caleria, or Magnus, or both. We need to be there when she strikes and stop her."

Tetsuo raised his voice. "Thank you for your opinions. Proceed as I have outlined." He went back to the rudder. "We will land at the first available spot."

* * * * *

They sailed the sampan up to a thin strip of muddy beach and camouflaged the boat with layers of moss and branches. Unlike the white sand beach at Kusho, Argenti's shore was a rich brown, littered with discarded pine cones. Waves rose less than a foot before they broke. The thick forest began mere feet from the sea, and some of the trees stretched over three hundred feet into the sky.

There was no sign of any sentient thing on the narrow strip of mud or in the forest beyond. Tor scouted around the landing site, but he found nothing of concern.

Things were not so calm back at the boat. As Tor came out of the forest, he heard Tetsuo discouraging Ayesha from forcing the bearers to carry her barrow. The armorer obstinately insisted that if they didn't know what they were about to face, they needed all the tools and equipment they could carry.

From beside Ayesha, Kei spoke up. "All that I can carry, you mean."

Tor stifled a laugh, but his mirth quickly evaporated.

As astonished as his master's face was, Kei's was even more so. He seemed pained at the sound of his own voice, and he all but clapped his hand over his mouth as he fell to his knees. "Forgive me, Teacher. I don't know why I said that."

"We do," Tetsuo said. He stared gravely at Ayesha until the armorer nodded.

"Tor," she called. "Help Kei and the others get my barrow off the boat."

Tor offered the healer a hand up while Tetsuo and Ayesha had a quiet discussion farther down the beach.

"I'm not trying to be funny, Kei," Tor said, "but I have to ask: What's gotten *into* you? I've heard she kills her students for eating with the wrong utensil. What's she going to do to you for cracking wise like that?"

Anguish flooded Kei's face and voice. "I don't know," he said miserably. "My stomach hurts constantly. I'm having trouble concentrating." Kei rubbed his temples. "My head throbs for hours at a time. And I can't see clearly." He pinched the bridge of his nose. "I feel like I'm half in a dream, like I'm watching my life instead of living it."

"Kei, you don't have a life. You're Ayesha's student." Tor grinned, but Kei didn't. The darker implications of his joke immediately sank in, and Tor forced out a dry chuckle. "Sorry."

Kei waved him off. "Never mind." The healer started past Tor, en route to the sampan, but the archer stopped him and peered into his eyes.

"Is something wrong?" Kei asked.

Tor shook his head. "Your eyes are bloodshot," he said. "And, uh, kind of yellow."

"Yellow? Nine hells!" Kei angrily kicked the makeshift ramp that connected the sampan to the shore, and the board splashed into the water. "I'll probably grow wings and an extra set of arms before we leave here."

"Take it easy, Kei."

Kei snarled as he waded after the ramp. "*You* take it easy. I've got a parasite in my guts that's turning my eyes yellow as it kills me."

Tor fell silent as Kei struggled with the wet board. The healer's voice was growing rougher and more pained as the trip wore on, as if he choked on the words he spoke. The

169

bearers waited nervously on the deck, their eyes darting between Kei, Ayesha, and the forest.

Kei propped the board up between the boat and the mud, but he was rushed and clumsy, and it fell right back into the water. He hissed a curse straight out of Ayesha's forge room and stomped on the floating board, forcing it under. Kei stood with all his weight on the board, snarling.

"Kei," Tor stepped forward. "Stop that and let me help—"

With an earsplitting crack, the top half of a nearby evergreen suddenly snapped off and toppled straight for Kei. Tor dived into him, shoving the healer back into the water, away from the heavy segment of trunk.

Tor surfaced with Kei still in his grasp, both of them coughing and spitting and coated with needles.

"What's wrong with you?" Kei yelled. "Why do you keep pushing me into the water?"

Tor held up his hands to calm the healer down. "The tree fell," he said. "It was heading right for you."

Kei grumbled and clawed at the mud to haul himself up onto the shore. The two men stood side by side.

When Kei's hand touched the base of a tree, the moss growing there reacted. A thin green tendril snaked out and latched onto Kei's hand. The healer spat out another curse and tried to draw his hand back, but a second tendril caught his palm. Then a third and fourth lashed out and attached themselves to his fingertips. Kei yanked, but the moss held him fast.

"Tor. . . ." He turned as he spoke, but before he could say more, the moss launched itself at him. Like a colony of green ants, the soft plant circled Kei's arm, thin spirals growing thicker and shaggier as they covered his flesh from wrist to elbow.

"Master! Ayesha!" Tor's arrow severed the tendrils connecting Kei to the base of the tree. "We are under attack!"

Cutting the link had no effect on the moss already on Kei's body. It continued to spread up his arm, colonizing and coating all the skin it touched. The healer let out an anguished cry as the moss flowed over his shoulder and up the side of his throat. Tor watched helplessly as the moss grew over Kei's mouth and one of his eyes. The healer's breathed frantically through his nostrils, and his visible eye was wide and pleading as he clawed at the moss.

One of the bearers muttered a blessing, and another leaped into the water to help Tor push Kei completely onto the shore.

The moss now covered Kei's nose and quickly moved over his remaining eye. After a moment's hesitation, Tor plunged the tip of an arrow through the moss covering Kei's mouth.

"No! Archer!" Ayesha was suddenly beside him. "What are you doing?" She stopped when she saw the green mass engulfing Kei and heard the desperate breaths wheezing through the hole Tor had made. She pulled a razor-sharp utility knife from her tool belt and nodded as Tor lifted an arrowhead in his hand.

"Try not to scrape off too much skin." Ayesha could only put the slightest hint of hope in her voice. "On three. One, two—"

"Stand back from the healer." Tetsuo stood with his hand on his sword, his muscles tensed and ready. Tor stepped aside immediately, but Ayesha lingered to give Kei's flailing hand one last comforting squeeze. Then she too moved away.

Tetsuo narrowed one eye at the thrashing figure, now almost completely encased in green. The champion drew his sword and slashed the air in front of his own face. In one continuous motion, he bent his arm, brought the hilt of the blade up to his own chin, and pointed the tip at Kei. Tetsuo thrust the sword forward, and as both of his elbows locked, a withering blast of black heat gathered on the tip of his blade. The smoky mass grew as wide as a melon and burst to engulf healer and moss alike.

As the black smoke touched it, the green mass covering Kei's body slowed its advance. It drew the smoke into itself, and within seconds it withered and turned brown. The moss dried and hardened around him, and Kei stood as motionless as a scarecrow on the shore.

"Call him," Tetsuo said. "He must move."

Ayesha wasted no time: "Kei, to me."

The healer's head turned, and Tor watched the coating on his skull and neck burst into a thousand powdery fragments. Most of Kei's face paint was gone, and his tears washed away what was left. He coughed dust and dried moss from his lungs.

Ayesha went to his side and supported him as he struggled to regain his breath.

Tetsuo repeated the maneuver twice more. Each complete form created a fresh black cloud. Tetsuo sent the first into a small willow tree whose whiplike branches were reaching for the sampan, and the other into a thorny shrub that oriented its glistening spikes on the bearers.

The armorer tore handfuls of dead moss off Kei's torso, and Tor stepped forward to help her. Ayesha's voice was sharp and exasperated. "What was that?"

Tor grinned. "Herbicide."

Tetsuo sheathed his sword. "That is an adequate description."

Ayesha transferred Kei's weight onto Tor and approached Tetsuo.

"I meant the moss," she said, "and the trees and everything else that hasn't lashed out at us yet." Ayesha angrily crossed her arms into her sleeves. "I think I've spotted another flaw in your plan, Champion. We can't make any honorable declarations or chat with the locals if they never show up."

"Kei's all right," Tor called. He pretended to be totally occupied with helping Kei stand on his own. "Still sucking wind, but that'll pass." Tor risked turning and facing the two masters.

Ayesha flushed, and her face twisted with frustration, but her stance was firm and steady. Tetsuo looked as he always looked, as if he had just returned from a long, thoughtful walk.

"Magnus is supposed to be deep into forest magic," Ayesha said, "and there's plenty of forest for him to work with. How do we cross Argenti if the whole island is trying to kill us?"

Tetsuo saw the answer on his master's face before Tetsuo ever spoke. The champion had answered a hundred of Tor's first-year questions with that very expression and a short phrase that signaled the end of any discussion.

"We work hard," Tetsuo said.

*   *   *   *   *   *

They quickly loaded everything they needed from the sampan and struck out into the forest. With an arrow at the ready, Tor led the procession, watching the barely visible path ahead and protecting the champion's standard-bearer. Ayesha and Kei were next, followed by her barrow and the other bearers. Tetsuo guarded the rear.

They had been hiking for hours, and despite Ayesha's dour predictions, they did not have to fight every step of the way. Some of the dangers seemed like everyday obstacles:

impassable deadfalls, hidden sinkholes, the odd carnivorous plant. . . . What had Tor edgy and battle ready were the unusual obstacles. Each new acre brought hostile and decidedly focused reactions from the landscape. Trees fell at them, as if the trunks decided to snap off and hurl their weight at the visitors. Vines lurked like rabbit snares, biting into unsuspecting ankles. A swarm of fist-sized dragonflies rushed out of a hollow log and painfully stung nearly every member of the party. A hot spring erupted under Ayesha's barrow, knocking it over and scalding one of the bearers. Most recently, the standard-bearer almost fell into a field of foot-high bamboo spikes that shot up before him as he hiked.

They had covered only about five miles, and the trip had taken its toll. There were cuts and bruises all around, with two of the four bearers limping. Another came around a thick tree trunk too quickly and found himself noosed and hanged, his feet kicking helplessly until Tetsuo cut him down. Tor broke a finger on his bow hand when a rock he stepped on suddenly pitched him off. Even Ayesha suffered a deep gash on her cheek when a huge yellow flower snapped at her face as she passed.

Of them all, Tetsuo had it the best, and Kei had it the worst. The champion had so far avoided all of the direct attacks launched by flora and fauna and had otherwise suffered only minor scrapes and a few stings. The healer, on the other hand, carried pain in his head and stomach, and his lungs were still clogged with bits of moss. He had to pause every so often to steady himself on a handy tree to weather yet another coughing fit.

Tetsuo said they were bound for the castle near the center of the island. All they had to do was pass through the forest and cover several miles of farm country. They would then come to Lady Caleria's castle and the thriving city that had sprung up around it. No one in the empire was sure if Lord Magnus had his own castle in the forest or any permanent home anywhere, so their only option was to press on and find Caleria.

In the meantime, as the armorer reminded Tetsuo, they had to face all the bugs and plants and rocks and water Argenti had to throw at them.

Tor stepped up to a clearing, waved the standard-bearer to a halt, and jumped up on a protruding tree root for a slightly higher view. The misty glen ahead seemed tranquil enough, but that made him suspicious, and he wanted to avoid it. With no other choices, Tor beckoned to the standard-bearer.

Ayesha and Kei were passing under his perch when Tor felt an implacable band surround his chest and squeeze the air from his lungs. He gasped and struggled to raise his weapon, but whatever had grabbed him had also pinned his arms to his sides.

The evergreen treefolk was an immature sapling, barely thirty feet tall and not much thicker than the sampan's mainmast. Its arms and hands were extremely powerful, however, and the force exerted by each yard-long finger made the living wood feel more like forged iron. Through the pressure building up in his ears, Tor heard Ayesha shouting.

Something whipped through the air behind Tor's head, and he felt the shock of a blow travel along the treefolk's fingers into his own body. He dropped, still bound but no longer suspended. The landing drove Tor's knees up into his chest, and he grunted loudly as he fell onto his side.

Tetsuo stood between Tor and the treefolk, his blade out and his expression severe. "Enough," he said.

The treefolk flexed its head forward as much as its stiff and streamlined body allowed. It held up the cleanly severed stumps it had in place of hands and screamed a high, keening wail of agony.

Tetsuo waved his sword, and a blue blast of light slammed into the middle of the treefolk's body. The force tore it loose from the soil and sent it crashing through the nearby branches and out of sight.

Tetsuo looked at the thin wooden hands still clutching him, and he worked his shoulders and arms to spread their grip apart. He quickly snapped off four of the fingers, and the rest of the clenched fist fell off behind him.

Tor turned to hail Tetsuo, but the champion still stood with his sword drawn. Tor held his tongue. His master didn't seem angry but was close to it, and Tor decided to keep silent.

"Magnus!" Tetsuo raised his voice and his sword. His words echoed across the glen and were swallowed up by countless trees on the other side. "Kusho has been attacked. Sekana has been attacked. Now we have been attacked. If there is to be war between the empire and the Edemis, at least let it be an open one.

"I am Tetsuo Umezawa, imperial champion of Madara. I have come to accept the challenge issued by Caleria. I have not come to fight, but I will to defend myself and my colleagues. What say you, rulers of Argenti? Is there still time for an audience with Caleria to seek out an honorable resolution? Or shall we simply start killing each other until only one side remains?"

There was no immediate answer except the lonely call of some far-off bird. Then, after a long pause, something growled.

It was a deep, powerful growl that Tor normally would have associated with a wild boar or grizzly bear . . . except that neither bears nor boars growled from forty feet up in the trees. Something else howled from ground level, but Tor could not even hazard a guess as to what kind of creature could make such a chilling sound.

On the far side of the glen, a robed figure stepped out of the trees. He wore heavy robes with druid markings and a green domed hood. A thin live tree branch stretched across his collarbone to anchor his cape, and he held a live wooden staff studded with inch-long brass ringlets. The visible part of the man's face was an angry red. He called out to Tetsuo, who was clearly visible on his elevated mound of dirt.

"An 'honorable' resolution, Champion?" The druid's voice was warm and melodious. "How strange that word sounds on the lips of an imperial. I am Lord Magnus." The figure threw his hands out wide and thumped his live walking stick on the ground. "You should not have come here."

From the tall trees behind Magnus, huge bestial figures emerged. A squat reptilian, as broad and heavy as a hippo, lumbered out and stood hissing beside its master. With disarming speed and grace, a giant six-legged sloth scurried down the trunk of a tree and roared at the imperials from the lowest branch. A gargantuan man-thing with pointed ears and bluish-green fur grinned with needle-sharp teeth. As Tor and the rest watched and waited, a legless wurm slithered up and coiled around Magnus's feet, winding around the druid five times. There were more figures lurking and snorting in the wood behind Magnus, larger and louder brutes that did not come forward to display their size or ferocity.

Tor didn't think they needed to. Magnus had made his point.

The druid stamped his staff again, and greenish flame erupted from the top end, illuminating the glen in an otherworldly glow. The flame did not consume Magnus's stick but hovered several inches above it.

"Tor," Tetsuo whispered coolly, "target Magnus's right shoulder. If any of his creatures attack, I want his staff on the ground before the fighting goes too far."

"Got him," Tor said. He hadn't drawn or aimed the arrow, but Tetsuo had trained him and knew his skills well. If Magnus or his familiars struck, the red-faced druid would find that for Tor the difference between targeting and firing was a matter of split seconds.

"This is your final warning, Imperials. Leave our island. If you won't be discouraged, then you shall be compelled."

"We are already compelled to stay," Tetsuo said.

Magnus lowered his flaming staff. "So be it." He took the living wood in both hands and drove it deep into the ground. The flame flared up to twice its original size, and the beasts all around Magnus reared, ready to leap forward.

Tetsuo nodded at Magnus across the glen. "So be it."

Magnus howled, and his menagerie sprang forward with teeth and claws bared.

CHAPTER 16

"Wait!" Ayesha cried, but Tor's arrow was already on its way.

The robed druid moved with amazing speed, ducking away from the incoming bolt. Even so, the shot would have scored somewhere on his body if the wurm hadn't undulated one of its coils out to intercept the shaft.

The sloth raced back up the tree trunk and disappeared among the needles. The ground-bound reptilian and the needle-toothed shambler both hurtled out into the glen, screeching and roaring as they charged. Hidden monsters on either side of the clearing approached Tetsuo and the others from the cover of the woods.

"I said, wait!" The armorer stood up from her barrow and drew her hand back to throw. She hesitated for the briefest moment until Tetsuo made eye contact, scanned the object in her hand, and nodded. Ayesha spat the words to a shrill incantation and heaved something high over the glen.

The opaque crystal globe shattered at the apex of its trajectory and released a blinding flash. The shambler screamed and fell, covering its face, but the reptilian's eyes were better protected. With heavy lids shut tight, it surged forward and tasted the ground as it ran.

Ayesha's device was not finished. After the initial flash, a ball of sparking white energy hung in the air, whirling and crackling above the forest floor. The sphere drew both matter and energy into it. Dead needles, dried twigs, and spent pine cones all succumbed to its mystical gravity and spiraled into its center. Even Magnus's green flame leaned into the vortex, stretching and thinning as its master fought a losing battle to keep it in place.

The reptilian creature rolled under the white sphere and resumed its charge.

Tor sank a shaft into the creature's upper thigh, and it went down in a tangle of mulch and flailing limbs.

Ayesha's sphere finally sucked Magnus's flame completely off his staff. The druid howled again, this time in anger, then every living thing in the glen dived for cover as lightning struck the sphere from above. Jag after jag of explosive energy slammed into its center. It took Tor a moment to realize that this was part of the sphere's nature, that it was in fact calling fire from the sky.

"Tetsuo?" Ayesha's voice rose over the noise in the glen.

"Ready."

Ayesha drew back another, smaller globe for a second toss. She held her hand behind her ear and said, "Go."

Tetsuo's sword appeared in his hand, and Ayesha hurled the second sphere directly at the champion. Tetsuo stood perfectly still until the sphere was upon him, then he split it in two with a blow from his sword.

Halving the sphere released another cascade of energy, this one liquid rather than light. The bluish plasma splashed over Tetsuo's body, and for a brief moment a Tetsuo-shaped figure glowed and crackled at the top of the dirt mound.

The white energy in the first sphere reached out to the blue energy surrounding Tetsuo, and there was another blinding flash. A violent stream of harsh white light blasted across the glen and sank into Tetsuo's veil. A final burst of light ignited the trees directly behind the champion. Tor had to blink repeatedly before he could see again, and when he could, he gasped.

On the edge of the clearing stood Tetsuo—twenty feet tall and covered in crackling blue-white energy. His sword was a bolt of lightning, and his eyes were angry stars. He stepped into the glen and thrust his sword at Magnus. Galvanic energy leaped from the tip into the trees behind the forest lord.

Magnus dived once more to avoid the explosion and the hail of dirt that followed.

The six-legged sloth pounced on the back of giant Tetsuo's neck, but its paws burst into flame where it touched him, and it fell back screaming. Tetsuo directed another bolt at Magnus, and the wurm that had been guarding him slithered quickly off into the forest. Unobstructed, surrounded by pan-icked hoots and screeches from the treetops, Tetsuo strode across the glen and raised his sword above Magnus's crouching form.

"I ask again," the champion's voice boomed like thunder. "Is it too late for an honorable resolution?"

Magnus peered up at Tetsuo towering over him. He glanced around the glen, where his beasts either cowered, fled, or lay wounded. Slowly, Lord Magnus stood to his full height and let his staff fall to the ground.

"I yield, Champion," he said. "Kill me, if that is your goal. If you truly seek an audience with Caleria, however, there is no way she will allow you anywhere near the city without my recommendation."

The huge crackling form of Tetsuo suddenly exploded, sending streams of light and blasts of force radiating up and away from the glen. When the glare and the smoke had cleared, Tor relaxed the arrow he had drawn.

Tetsuo stood at his true size, his sword pointed at Magnus. "Then you shall be our guide and escort." Tetsuo's sword disappeared back into its sheath. He offered his hand to Magnus, but the druid rose without aid.

"I will be your hostage, you mean." Magnus flinched as Tetsuo knelt and retrieved the forest mage's staff.

"Not at all." Tetsuo offered Magnus the staff, which still had smoke rising from its top. "We have enemies in common, Lord Magnus. If we are to kill each other, let us at least do so for our own reasons."

Magnus took his staff and stared in naked confusion at Tetsuo. He glanced past the champion and locked eyes with Ayesha, Kei, and Tor, each in turn then he bowed his head slightly and pointed with his staff.

"This way," he said. "I will take you to Caleria."

* * * * *

Magnus proved to be the most sullen and tight-lipped tour guide Tor had ever met. They made excellent time through Argenti's forest, however, and the woodlands seemed to create paths for Magnus that had not been there for the champion's party. In every possible way, following the forest lord was far better than being squeezed by a tree.

Magnus's beasts never strayed far from the procession. The forest was thick, but eyes leered and horns flashed from every gap in the trees.

Kei grew steadily worse. He had reapplied his face paint, but the rest of his skin was pale and sallow. He sweated profusely. Kei's strides seemed oddly stronger than before, but the healer's glassy eyes were only half-open, and it was difficult for him to form words. When he staggered it was not because of weak legs but due to a loss of balance. He had fallen twice since they met Magnus, but he waved off any help. He kept one hand on his medicine bag and the other over his eyes to shield them from the few bright beams of sunlight that stabbed through the canopy overhead.

As far as Tor could tell, they were no closer to finding Xira or a cure.

Tetsuo recounted for Magnus their arrival on Kusho. The forest lord was clearly dubious of Tetsuo's version of events, but Tor knew his master had to present a true account of things even if Magnus wasn't listening.

Through the trees, Tor caught a glimpse of a human face, and he hiked up alongside Tetsuo. "There's a druid up ahead, the first I've seen," Tor muttered. "Could be an ambush."

"Thank you," Tetsuo said simply. "I don't think we have anything to fear, but stay alert." The champion raised his voice to Magnus, hiking ahead. "What is that great stand of trees to the west?"

Magnus reacted as if stung. He jerked his head and snapped, "This is a very dangerous part of the forest. We have to move faster." The druid actually began to jog, and the path and the beasts and the forest itself struggled to keep pace around him.

"Stop here." Tetsuo held up his hand, and all but Magnus fell still. "My lord," Tetsuo called to the retreating figure, "you are our guide, but you are also our prisoner. If you leave us behind, our agreement becomes void."

Magnus stopped but did not turn. "We must keep moving, Champion. It is not safe here."

"Safe for us or for you?" Kei's head was still bowed, and his hand covered his eyes, but his voice came sharp and strident.

Magnus remained still, with his back to them all, but Tor could see his ears flush even redder.

"He's hiding something," Kei hissed, and his breath grew short. "That grove, those trees." Kei panted like a winded dog. He clenched his fists and forced himself to take a deep breath. "I can feel it."

"Is it danger, Kei?" Ayesha stood beside her student but did not offer a supportive hand. He had brushed off far too many lately.

Kei started shivering. He clamped both hands around his sides and knelt on the ground as a wave of cramps knotted his stomach. "Not danger," he husked. "Bigger. More important." He nodded toward the towering throng of trees. "In there. Older and greener than any tree.

"Druids teach," Kei continued, "a thousand years of lore. Lessons lived and handed down for generations." He curled up tighter and fell onto his side, moaning softly. "Herb and root, flower and fruit. Knowledge hoarded, hidden, lost, and forgotten." His teeth chattered, and he shivered, spattering the fern leaves around him with cold fever sweat.

Tetsuo's voice rang out sharply. "Magnus. What does he mean?"

Magnus turned. His expression was part anguish and part sympathy. "This is a dangerous area," he said numbly. "We must move on. Especially if your boy is sick."

Ayesha stepped up to Tor and Tetsuo. "He's right. We need to reach Caleria's castle and get a line on Xira's whereabouts. The forest is a mystery for another day."

Tetsuo nodded. Ayesha and Tor knelt, lifted Kei to his feet, and held him up until his shivering abated.

"It's all there," Kei said. "Past, present—" he stared at Magnus's clenched jaw—"and future." Kei swooned again, but Ayesha and Tor both caught him and guided him back onto his feet.

"Thank you, Teacher." Kei's voice was weak, but at least it

was his voice and not a death rattle. He turned to face Tor. "And you, archer."

Tor looked into Kei's swollen, red-rimmed eyes. The healer's brown pupils had turned a pale, mottled green. The rest of Kei's eyeball was a ghastly, bilious slug-yellow.

"Anytime," Tor said, but he felt a desperate urge to release Kei's arm and wash his hands in the nearest stream.

Ashamed, Tor walked alongside the healer until the bearers got the barrow up and moving again. Then he resumed his position beside Tetsuo and ignored all but the forest directly before his feet.

* * * * *

Magnus led them out of the woods into the setting sun. Unlike the terrain they had just covered, this part of Argenti was a wide, relatively flat expanse of farmland and gently rolling hills. Clear of the trees, Tor could see the ocean, distant in the west, and a trio of white stone turrets rising farther to the north.

"We will enter the capital city of Lisu within the hour." Magnus had stopped them and sullenly delivered this information. He gestured with his staff at the standard-bearer's flag. "I will ask you to strike that banner for the time being. After the recent attacks on Kusho, imperial emblems will only frighten and anger the citizens."

The standard-bearer looked to Tetsuo, and the champion shook his head. "We are here on imperial business," he said, "and your people have nothing to fear from us. Assassins and thieves hide their true colors." He turned to the bearer. "Hold the standard and your head high, Hatoki."

The road into town was smooth and even. Well-kept roads were a rarity in the empire, but perhaps the fewer roads were easier to maintain. The fields on either side of the paving stones were empty, the final harvest having taken place weeks ago. There were no crops, no domestic or draft animals, and no people. Either Argenti's farms had already shut down for the approaching winter, or the farmers were more frightened of imperials than Tor had imagined.

They saw their first Lisu citizen on the edge of the city itself. A dark-skinned man with a small girl on his shoulders walked around a large wooden building. When he spotted the approaching party, he quickly turned and disappeared around the corner.

There were no walls around Lisu, but the entire city lay in the shadow of Caleria's castle fortress. It was a familiar feudal arrangement, wherein the landowner lived in a large, fortified structure and the merchants and artisans built their homes and shops as close to the castle's protection as they could. If trouble came, the castle doors opened for all the citizens to take refuge inside then shut tight until the danger had passed. Even the farms that bordered the forest were close enough for the farmers to retreat inside the walls, especially if the invading force had to slog through Magnus's forest.

The densely packed buildings clearly indicated the strength and duration of Caleria's reign. The people of Argenti had had a stable ruler long enough to build hundreds of permanent houses and a complicated series of roads and alleys all within easy running distance of the castle. Though the streets were currently empty and every building in town had its doors and shutters barred, Tor guessed that Lisu had a population that rivaled even the largest cities in the empire.

Caleria's castle was also deceptively large. It looked massive from the main road in Lisu, but it seemed to grow even bigger the closer Tor got. The defensive exterior wall had been assembled from huge blocks of precisely cut white granite. It rose fifty feet above the ground and was crenellated along the top for sentries, archers, and spearmen to take their positions. The main gateway was large enough for a full-sized catapult to pass through, and the gate itself was a combination of bleached hardwood and gleaming steel.

The gate was closed, but the castle turrets loomed high above it and were composed of the same white granite as the walls. The center tower was the tallest, and it was crowned by a snow-white winged gargoyle crouching on its pointed roof.

Magnus held up a hand and bade them wait. He walked up to the glittering gate and thumped on it with his staff.

An armored sentry leaned out from the top of the wall. "Greetings, my lord. Your pardon, but our orders are that all visitors must stand fast and identify themselves."

"Lord Magnus, with urgent business for our lady. Tell her I have brought imperial visitors who wish to parley."

The sentry jerked his head back, and the party waited for several long minutes. Tor watched Magnus idly twirling the brass ringlets around on his staff, and the archer wondered if their guide was more nervous than his guests.

A loud boom and a sharp crack signaled the gate's interior bar being shot back, and the huge wood-and-metal door swung open. A phalanx of twelve armed soldiers armored in spotless shining silver marched forward with pikes on their shoulders. Beside them stood a tall, dark-skinned man with his broadsword drawn. His visor was open, and he wore a long white feather fixed to the top of his helmet.

"Surrender your weapons," the plumed soldier said. The other soldiers spread out into a semicircle, their pikes pointed at the imperials. Magnus quietly stepped aside, but he waited with a look of genuine anguish.

Tetsuo stepped up to the plumed soldier, who seemed to be in charge. "I am Tetsuo Umezawa," he said, "imperial champion. I am here as an official of the Madara Empire to discuss matters of state with Lord Magnus and Lady Caleria. These," he indicated the rest of the party, "are my colleagues. We are here as envoys, not as warriors. We expect to be treated as such."

The lead soldier eyed Tetsuo and licked his lips nervously. "Surrender your weapons," he repeated.

Tetsuo stepped forward so that his face was a hand width away from the soldier's. "No."

"It's all right, Lieutenant," Magnus said. Tetsuo maintained his fierce gaze, and the plumed soldier seized the opportunity to look away.

"My lord, our lady's orders were—"

"Umezawa," Magnus said, "is an honorable man. So far, I have seen nothing to indicate that he will betray that honor to strike at our lady. Let them keep their weapons. I will vouch for their behavior."

Magnus held the lieutenant's eyes for a second longer, and the armored officer nodded. "Escort party," he barked. "About face." The pike squad shouldered their weapons and turned.

"Left and right flank . . . take your positions." The soldiers split up into two groups of six and formed an honor guard on either side of the gate.

"My lord," the lieutenant said. Magnus took a step, the lieutenant fell in next to him, and they passed through the gauntlet of soldiers and the open gate.

Tor started to follow them, but Tetsuo stopped him with a hand on the shoulder. "I should go first now," he said. "Stay back and be ready for anything. Don't leave Kei unattended." The champion turned back to Ayesha. "Stay with your tools and the bearers," he said. "This is delicate business. No one is to speak to Caleria or Magnus but I. The wrong word at the wrong time could plunge us all into a fight for our lives and our nations into full-scale war. Tread lightly and follow my lead." He motioned Hatoki the standard-bearer back near the other bearers and then walked forward.

The champion filed past the guards and into the courtyard. As soon as the last imperial passed through the gates, the phalanx of guards turned and marched in after them, keeping a safe and respectable distance.

The castle itself was a magnificent piece of architecture and engineering, with domineering walls, soaring towers, and a gleaming white veneer. Two huge deer statues, a hart and a hind, guarded the marble steps that led up into the building. Each of the two shorter towers also had the hart-and-hind standard flying over them.

Magnus and Caleria's lieutenant led them up the stairs and through the entranceway, while the armored guards kept pace behind. They crossed a great trophy room hung with the heads of all kinds of wild beasts and came upon a pair of ornate doors inlaid with silver, gold, and animal horns. Either Caleria or one of her ancestors had been an accomplished hunter.

As Magnus approached, the sentries on either side of the doors stepped up and opened them for the party to pass through. Tor wondered why all Caleria's troops were so crisp and somber. They were either very well disciplined by Caleria, or very frightened of Tetsuo.

The ornate doors led to a large and dim great hall. Candles glowed on evenly spaced wall sconces, but the windows were shuttered and the torches unlit. Tor could barely determine another squad of armored soldiers standing against the far wall, lined up around a large throne. Above it were bolted the biggest pair of deer antlers he had ever seen.

"Tetsuo Umezawa," a woman's voice called. The echo in the great hall was considerable, but Tor knew the voice came from the throne even if he couldn't clearly see the person sitting there.

The woman in the throne continued, "Imperial champion. The Edemis have had more than their share of imperial visitations in the past few days, haven't they, Magnus?"

"Indeed, Lady. They have."

"None of them has been welcome. Speak, Champion. What are you doing here?"

Tetsuo bowed. "I am here to answer officially a declaration made by one of your creatures on the shores of Sekana, to discuss a threat to these islands that could ruin us all, and to seek your help in capturing a dangerous assassin who assaulted my healer. These are all matters of honor, my lady. Will you speak with me?"

"I have spoken to imperials before. There is very little value in anything said by the emperor or his lackeys."

"With respect, milady, this is an official visit. I ask that you declare yourself."

The woman chuckled. "Very well." She snapped her fingers, and hidden servants came out of cubby holes to light the torches and throw back the shutters. In an instant, the room went from candle-lit gloom to midday brightness.

A dark-skinned woman with braided white hair and an antlered headdress sat on the bleached wooden throne. She wore ceremonial skins around her shoulders and a large diamond medallion around her neck. Two servants flanked her, one bearing a huge wooden longbow and the other a quiver stocked with white-feathered arrows.

"I am Lady Ohabi Caleria, caller of the hunt and ruler of Argenti." She casually raised a hand to the left of her throne. "And I believe you know our other visitor? In the past few days, she has told me so much about you."

A tall, thin figure stepped out of the throne's shadow. She was dressed in silver and white metallic cloth with a subtle antler motif stitched across her shoulders. Her translucent wings vibrated excitedly, and the effect of the sudden bright light on her clothes and skin was almost hypnotic.

Tor froze, waiting for Tetsuo to react. Kei cried out and fell back. Behind him, Ayesha snarled and drew her short blade.

"Champion," Xira Arien chimed, snapping her sharp mouth shut twice. "How fares your healer?"

PART  THREE:

IMPERIAL HONOR

CHAPTER 17

Ayesha stopped short of Tetsuo's outstretched arm. She had almost acted on the immediate urge to chop off Xira's wings and kick her until she told them how to cure Kei, but there were a dozen or more of Caleria's soldiers between the armorer and her target. She had also sworn to follow Tetsuo's lead and so would trust him to bring Xira to her as quickly as possible. With her eyes fixed on Xira, the armorer slowly sheathed her sword and crossed her arms into her sleeves.

The eumidian laughed merrily, floating six inches from the floor.

"My apologies, Lady," Ayesha said. "I have a personal matter to discuss with your . . . other guest. I forgot myself."

Caleria stuck two fingers in her mouth and whistled. From the side doors two more phalanxes of armored troops marched in and stood ready, their pikes pointed into the room.

"You may have forgotten yourself, imperial, but I have not forgotten the threat you pose." Caleria's voice was dry and weathered, a deep, throaty croak.

"You see, my lady," Xira's voice chimed musically, and she came to the floor in front of Caleria's throne. "They have come bearing weapons. They intend to kill you, as I said they would."

"That creature is a liar," Tetsuo said. "We have come in pursuit of her, to seek treatment for an injury she inflicted."

Tetsuo pressed his palms together and bowed lightly. "Also, we would discuss with wise Caleria the imperial attack on Kusho and her retaliatory strike on Sekana."

"Your beast invaded the Edemis. We merely responded in kind."

"A beast wearing the champion's standard," Xira added. She snapped her jaws at Ayesha, and the armorer smiled coldly.

Tetsuo had been correct: Dark and his minions treated this as some kind of game. The more Xira taunted and capered, the more certain Ayesha became that the eumidian would overplay her hand.

"Ask her what standard she wears," Ayesha called. "She is no friend to you, Lady. She is a spy and an assassin, notorious in Madara."

Caleria's sneered. "She said exactly the same about you. Everything else Xira has told me has so far proven true."

"My lady." Tetsuo bowed again. "I fear we have all been manipulated."

Caleria nodded, unimpressed. "Then your emperor has no interest in annexing our islands?"

Tetsuo paused. "The emperor," he said evenly, "has legitimate claim to the Edemis."

"Only if a decade of exploitation and martial law now grants legitimacy."

"My lady," Tetsuo said, "I am not a diplomat, and I have not come to settle our differences. I am here to tell you Xira Arien must come with me. Also, I appeal to you: Withdraw your declaration, and send no more beasts to Madara. We need not go to war to satisfy the emperor's honor."

"Beware, my lady," Xira cackled. "He speaks of honor as a pretext to convince you to relax your guard. I told you they would come and strike here as they did on Kusho." Her wings lifted her off the floor, and she cupped her hands around her mouth. "Where is your giantess, Champion? Is she lying in wait for another surprise massacre?"

"Lady Xira," Caleria snapped. "Please."

Xira curtsied and then settled on the floor.

"You did say they would come here," Caleria said, "but their purpose still remains unclear." She came down the steps from her throne as she spoke, the longbow in her hand.

"Champion," she said to Tetsuo across fifty feet of open floor, "Gosta says you had him at your mercy, and that you defeated Kasimir the hermit."

Tetsuo merely held his stoic expression, and Caleria went on.

"Magnus tells me that you also spared him, though you were poised and able to take his life."

Ayesha glanced at Magnus, who shifted uncomfortably from foot to foot. The druid had been with them since they defeated him in the forest. When did he have time to report to Caleria?

"So I wonder . . ." Caleria took another step closer to Tetsuo, and six gleaming guards assembled on either side of her. "Are you here to kill someone specific? Is it only me you're interested in putting to the imperial sword or my entire kingdom?"

"Go no closer," Xira chattered. "He is studied in the art of sudden and lethal strikes."

Caleria paused, and her lip curled in annoyance. She turned to Xira, and the soldiers on her right side turned with her.

"Be silent, insect. I have tolerated your presence because you are harmless here and even when you lie, you reveal the intentions of your masters. But the Imperial Champion himself stands before me, so I have no further need of your flattery and your lies. Keep silent, or I will have you gagged."

Xira gasped. "My lady," she said, "I must protest."

Caleria drew and shot without another word. The Argenti noble aimed slightly high in case Xira took to the air again, but the eumidian was not caught. She kept both feet on the ground and lunged to her left so that the arrow sailed harmlessly over her.

The bow shot was also a signal, however, and the soldiers nearest Xira sprang forward with pikes at the ready. Magnus waved his staff, and Caleria barked orders as she trained another arrow on Xira.

Xira ducked away from Caleria's first arrow and found herself facing the points of three oncoming spears. She ignored the closest, allowing it to punch right through her borrowed robes without touching her flesh at all. The nimble assassin shoved a second spear into the stone floor. With her other hand, she grabbed the third shaft just behind spearhead and snapped it off, twirling it so that the oncoming soldier rushed onto the point of his own weapon. The eumidian swung the broken shaft into another oncoming soldier then sprang on the man who had punctured her outfit. In a heartbeat Xira's horrid stinger slipped out of her wrist and drove deep into the armored man's chest.

Ayesha's hand twitched to her blade, and Tor reached behind him for an arrow. Tetsuo still extended his hand, however, holding them back. Caleria's soldiers trained arrows and spears on them, and Ayesha forced herself to stand still.

When the time is right for action, she thought, the champion will take it.

The skewered soldier did not cry out or clutch at his chest. Instead, he backhanded the insect assassin with an armored glove and stretched her out onto the floor.

All around the her, soldiers who had been stabbed and cuffed and beaten aside regained their feet and closed in once more. None of them showed the slightest sign of injury.

Xira chittered angrily and rubbed her chin. She leapt up and planted a solid kick beside a soldier's kneecap. Again, there was no reaction from the soldier, though Ayesha saw a brief white light flash at the point of contact.

Unharmed, the soldier slashed at Xira with his sword.

She danced back. Off-balance and confused, Xira unleashed a hail of blows on the man, striking his head and shoulders with both clenched fists. Each time she touched his body, a white flash absorbed the impact.

Ayesha looked to Caleria and noticed that the huntress's eyes flashed the same bright white with each defused blow. Xira screeched angrily at Caleria and soared straight up into the air.

Caleria's next arrow narrowly missed Xira's torso.

As she flew, the eumidian quickly shucked off the courtly Argenti robes and elegant shoes. She wore her blue bodysuit underneath, and she used the metallic robe as a bullfighter's cape to snare several more arrows aimed her way.

She could have slipped through the floor-to-ceiling doorway or gone directly out through one of the large open windows high on the wall. Instead, Xira circled the room, dodging spears and arrows and chittering madly to taunt the soldiers below. Even Caleria missed another shot before Xira finally escaped into the cold evening air.

"Magnus!" Caleria's throaty voice carried over the noise of armored feet and soldiers' swearing. "Find her. Take twelve of my men along with whatever you need from your own fief. Track her down and bring her here."

Magnus nodded. "It will be done."

"I don't care if she's alive or dead, I want her back before dawn tomorrow." Magnus was already on his way, tapping armored soldiers, who fell into step behind him.

Magnus and his twelve marched off, leaving Caleria and the rest to attend the imperials. The Argenti leader climbed back up the stairs to her throne and sat heavily while her soldiers kept their weapons trained on the visitors. She handed her bow back to the attendant but kept the quiver looped over her shoulder.

"Well, Champion," she said. "Our nations have traded blows. I have made my formal declaration, and now you have asked me to withdraw it. Before I answer you . . . answer me something first.

"Is this all a sham? Did your emperor kill chelonians on Kusho and plant spies in my castle to put me in danger or to put you in danger? There are simpler ways of carrying out an assassination or a purge."

"Whatever it is, Lady," Tetsuo said, "it must wait. Right now, there is another life-and-death matter I must address."

Caleria rose angrily. "Let me spell things out for you, Tetsuo Umezawa. Matters of life and death are far more immediate than you think. You are all helpless before me. My comrades are currently hunting down your spy, and even with your sword and your servants you can do nothing."

Caleria snapped her fingers, and a soldier brought her a burning torch. "Here on Argenti the meekest child is more dangerous than you." Caleria shoved her hand into the torch flame, and her eyes flashed white. She pulled her hand out, and displayed it unharmed for all to see.

"Do you see this? Did you see the effect the insect's blows had? None! Red mana, black mana, the colors of fire and decay. They are impotent on Argenti. Just like you and all imperials, all of you steeped in those colors."

Not all of us, Ayesha thought, but she said nothing and waited for Caleria to pause for breath.

"This is white magic country," the huntress raved on, "and my entire island is protected by it. While I live, you can literally do no harm."

Tetsuo folded his arms into his sleeves. "Xira is not my spy. These people are not my servants. I say again, the eumidian infected my healer-in-training. I need her to determine his cure. I only ask your permission to join Magnus on the hunt and the chance to save an innocent life."

Caleria glowered. "None of you are innocent, and Magnus doesn't need your help. He is the finest tracker I have ever seen, and more, he is the undisputed lord of the wilds here. Even if every living thing in the forest hadn't already sworn allegiance to him, he knows this island down to the last pine cone. If so much as a single needle is out of place, he will notice."

"A tracker needs tracks," Tetsuo said. "Xira leaves none. The only cones and needles she disturbs will be fifty feet up."

"Then the trees themselves will betray her," Caleria said. "By the light, enough! I have no idea what's wrong with your lad or how to cure him." She turned to Kei. "I'm sorry, boy, but there's no help for you here.

"Warriors of Argenti!" Caleria stood and raised her arm.

A room full of armored soldiers stood waiting for her orders.

Caleria's arm fell. "Take them."

* * * * *

Lord Dark and his majordomo stood by the main gate as the rest of the staff filed out. The majordomo, a rigid little man in his sixties, held a tablet on which he scribbled with each servant's departure.

"That's the lot, my lord." The majordomo made one last notation on his pad. "All staff and retainers accounted for. Except for your noble self and some of the keep's more . . . dangerous guardians, the castle and grounds are now empty."

Dark watched the last servant in line retreat down the marsh road. "You are still here."

The majordomo flushed. "Of course, my lord. I shall be gone soon."

"You will be gone now." With a rough shove, Dark ushered the man through the gate. The majordomo sputtered feeble protests as Dark leveled his hand and brought the heavy iron gate down with a wet thud. The master assassin then turned and climbed the path back to his home.

Inside the wide front door, he paused and smiled. He preferred the huge keep when it was silent and deserted, but it had been years since he had last enjoyed it that way. There were too many details for Dark to manage, and most of them were far beneath a man of his position. His previous attempts with zombies, faeries, and other magical servants proved even more trouble than humans, so Dark resigned himself to the lax and grubby little attentions of local peasants and learned to make the most out of his infrequent brushes with complete solitude.

Dark made excellent progress through the empty halls, even if he was loaded with equipment like a draft animal. He made three trips between his private study and the exterior courtyard then one back down to the hidden vault. As he walked and worked, his thoughts whirled with the details of the ritual and the necessity of exquisite timing.

Dark lit and positioned a ring of nine torches in a circle

and placed a small bleached skull in the center. He stretched out a dried snakeskin under the skull and scattered black rose petals around the grisly pile. From a covered wicker cage he drew out a terrified, struggling owlet and with a savage twist snapped its neck.

Lord Dark separated the bird's head from its body, holding both pieces so that the falling blood would spatter across the array of bones and roses. Smoke rose from the skull and the snakeskin where the owl blood touched them, and Lord Dark whispered a short incantation.

The blood hissed as it boiled away, and Dark cast the owl's body into the cloud of steam and debris. A foul fog coalesced, thickening and contracting until it had taken the shape of a small winged humanoid. The smoke-figure flexed its wings and bowed its tiny smoke-head before Dark. Dark nodded and pronounced one final syllable to transform the smoke monster into one of flesh and bone.

It was as large as a chimpanzee, with an ape's long arms and grasping feet. It was covered in black and gray feathers, and though it had a long canine snout, the rest of its skull was rounded and squat like an owl's. It flapped its wings silently, hooted a chilling little song, and hopped up and down in place. Throughout its performance, it never took its eyes off Dark's.

Dark whipped a concealing cloth off of the strange pewter machine he had collected from his vault. Without a word, he took the device up in both hands and carried it to the ragged imp that capered on the ground beside him. He held the device out to the imp, and the little monster took it with two long arms.

Dark held onto the machine as the imp tugged and stared excitedly at its master. Dark reached into the thing's mind, making sure it understood the simple task he was giving it.

The imp's mind was a chaotic place, full of clamor and noise. Dark waited for the chorus of howls, hoots, and chattering to die down. When it didn't, he drowned them all out with a single withering word that exploded inside the imp's brain like a bomb.

Silence! The imp cowered and released its hold on the device. Dark patiently presented the object to the imp again, and this time the imp gently took the machine, hugged it tightly to its chest, and nodded over and over again, chittering excitedly. It understood its instructions now and what would happen if it failed. Dark held on a moment more then released the device.

"Go," he said aloud, and the imp leaped high into the air. With arms and legs wrapped around the device, the imp started flapping its wings madly and soon disappeared into the night sky.

Xira, Dark thought. *I am sending you a package.*

My lord, came Xira's reply, *now is not the best time.*

Only for you. For me, this is the perfect time. Look to the skies over Caleria's palace, starting at midnight tomorrow.

My lord, Xira half-pleaded, *leave me be for another few hours, and your precious package won't even be necessary.*

Of course it will, Dark snapped. *Don't think, Xira. Just do as you are told. Now, confirm your instructions.*

Xira's reply was delayed, but only for a moment. *Meet your courier over the palace. Midnight tomorrow. Confirmed.*

Lord Dark extinguished the torches, snuffing each flame with a word and stepping to the next one. He left the smoking brands and the empty wicker cage for the servants to clear away when they returned, and reentered the castle. He had more spells to prepare for this night, more rituals to perform. The forces he was about to conjure and manipulate could easily level the keep and turn the surrounding wetlands into a smoking hole.

As Dark ascended the winding staircase that led all the way up to the top of the western tower, he enjoyed a last few minutes of solitude and silence before he took the world by the throat and made it scream.

CHAPTER 18

"Tor," Tetsuo flicked his eyes across the two plumed officers and Caleria as the Argenti forces moved in. "All three. When I say."

"Got them."

The champion drew his blade. "Stay with Ayesha and Kei," Tetsuo said, "and keep yourselves clear and ready to follow me out."

"We will be ready." Tetsuo glanced at Tor and smiled thinly. "Shall we, Second?"

"Do so, Mas—"

Tetsuo unleashed his loudest cry and lunged forward with his blade aglow.

Tor fired three quick bolts at Caleria and her two lieutenants. The first struck a white flash off of Caleria's breastplate and fell harmlessly to the floor. Caleria's eyes flashed twice more, and Tor's other shots sparked in midair and fell straight down. He swore to himself and had to duck under a pike thrust. Tor tripped the charging soldier and bolted back to Ayesha and Kei, where the armorer kept the encroaching soldiers at bay with her short sword

Tetsuo meanwhile occupied the bulk of Caleria's forces. The champion dodged arrow after arrow and took glancing blows from armored fists and wooden batons. Every return stroke of his sword, every blow of his hardened hands, was negated by Caleria's flashing eyes.

She stood once more on the steps to her throne, watching Tetsuo twist and strike. Her eyes carefully negated each potential injury her armored warriors received.

Tor looped his bow over his shoulder and prepared to defend himself without striking back. He stood and focused as he had been taught, eyes and ears alert, hands open and ready.

Tetsuo had almost completely disappeared behind a cascade of bright white flashes. He himself was little more than a blur as he batted soldiers and their weapons aside. He let out another loud battle cry and sprang straight into the air, knocking arrows and pikes aside. He landed with his sword sheathed, facing the throne.

"Tor," he called. "Go now." The champion drew his sword and held it point-down with both clenched fists in front of his face, as if the blade were far too heavy to lift.

Tor turned and grabbed hold of Kei. "Time to go."

Tetsuo pointed his sword directly at the oncoming horde and whispered. Black light sparked on the edge of his blade, and dense smoke wafted from the tip.

Ayesha scooped Kei off of the archer's arm, and they bulled their way through the confusion. Tor kicked the legs out from under any soldier who came near, and thus he managed to keep his party moving even if he didn't do any actual harm.

With one final cry, Tetsuo raised his sword, and the entire room went black. The darkness in the great hall wasn't an absence of light; it was a presence all its own.

Tor felt it resisting him as he hustled Kei and Ayesha out the door. It stuck to his skin and held him back like a strong breeze. He had been trained to fight in the dark, but the magical shroud blinded them all completely.

Tor heard the champion sheathe his blade as the crush of

soldiers shouted and fumbled. Is this it? he thought crazily. We close our eyes and sneak off?

Next came the telltale whistle of an incoming shaft, and something bumped into Tor's rib cage. Reflexively, his hand jumped to the sensation. He expected to feel half an arrow sticking out of his chest, but instead he batted the entire arrow away. Somehow, the point had struck him without penetrating.

The sounds behind them indicated that the soldiers had located the champion and were once more flailing at him with sword, spear, and fist. Tor heard grunts and the clang of steel but not the sound of steel on flesh.

A hand settled gently on Tor's shoulder, and the archer jumped.

"We can go now, Tor," said Tetsuo, suddenly beside him. "Take hold of Kei, put your hand on my shoulder, and follow me."

"Enough!" Caleria voice came from atop her throne. "Stand down! Get some light in here before you all kill each other."

Tetsuo's voice rang out through the darkness. "My lady," he called. "There may yet be war between us, but today, I hunt the eumidian."

Within minutes, all four of them were out of Caleria's castle and through the main gate, heading straight for the forest.

* * * * *

Lord Dark brought the last of the materials he needed to the top of the western tower. The room's only window was carved into the rock facing westward. There was a round stone pedestal set in the center of the room and a wide trench cut into the stone floor around the pedestal. Lord

Dark took off his cape, stepped over the moatlike trench, and sat cross-legged on the pedestal. He stared at the western horizon, particularly the thin ribbon of water just below the darkening sky. He closed his eyes and imagined the sea beyond and the Edemi chain beyond that.

Dark chanted. With the merest thought, he opened four gold and purple jewelry boxes he had placed at the four points of the compass along the round room's wall. The first box released an invisible waft of briny air and the second a puff of oily smoke. The third produced a whirling column of wind, but the fourth merely opened and sat idle.

The salt air, the smoke, and the cyclone all drifted over to the pedestal and hovered there, waiting. Dark rose, still chanting, and crossed the room to retrieve the last box. Holding it reverently between both hands, he approached the miniature moat carved around the pedestal. He spoke a final few lilting syllables and upended the box.

Foamy seawater poured into the trench and filled it to its rim. The water was brackish and opaque, with fish swimming it. Dark shook the container, and a few nuggets of coral and a rope of green seaweed also fell into the trench. He cast the box aside and stepped back onto his pedestal. Then he crossed his legs and sat once more, safe and surrounded by his miniature moat.

Lord Dark concentrated as he settled back into his meditative state. The water in the fourth box came from the Argenti coast, as did the live specimens it contained. Living things were essential to this kind of spell—indeed, to every spell. Unlike heat or light, mana was living energy, and it often required a living conduit before it could be shaped and employed. In this case, only living things from the target ecosystem would resonate properly for his magic to work, and Dark couldn't afford for a spell of this size to go awry.

He continued to chant. He focused all his thoughts on the ocean, on the waves he could see and the vast distances and depths he could not. There was such power in the tide, power that drove seawater against the rocks of Madara's shores and carried ships to and from the emperor's domain. Waves traveled up Madara's rivers like impulses up a nerve, where they joined with the dark forces already bubbling in Lord Dark's marshy home.

The seas were both barrier and conduit between Madara and her neighbors. The life-giving liquid that irrigated her fields also stagnated and bred diseases in her swamps. There was so much water and motion that the portion Lord Dark redirected to his own ends made only a ripple.

The water in the moat around Dark churned and slapped the sides of the trench. Above his head, cyclone, smoke, and sea spray all twisted together like the braids in a child's hair. Dark heard the roar of the ocean in his ears and felt the pounding of the tide in his head. He opened his eyes.

Instead of the western tower's magnificent view, he found himself looking at the coast of Argenti from directly overhead. Dark beat back a surge of vertigo as his heart pounded. He grinned in pure exhilaration and continued to chant. The noise in his head rose in pitch and intensity.

Dark reached out, feeling the force of the tides as they pushed and pulled the Argenti coastline. His view of the wooded isle remained static, but Dark's mind shot out farther into the open sea, pressing his perception all the way down to the ocean floor.

He passed brutes larger than leviathans and found forces more powerful than waves. The ocean was a vast and complex system of action and reaction, with tidal forces vying against planetary ones and the constant cycle of warm water rising as cold water sank. When all of these forces were properly aligned, they could create a river within the larger body of water, a powerful current with its own direction and life span. These rapidly moving inter-tidal streams could grow to hundreds, even thousands of feet in width. Dark sought not a wide current, though, but a powerful one.

Several days' journey from Argenti and a thousand feet below the surface, he found what he was looking for. The river tide was just over a hundred feet wide, but it moved fast enough to founder an armada. Dark mentally completed the connection between himself, the tide, and the coast of Argenti. His body went rigid, and his eyes glowed royal blue as the water around him boiled, killing fish, coral, and seaweed alike.

Miles away from Argenti, a small but powerful river tide ceased to exist. In his mind's eye Dark watched the coastal sea begin to swirl. He stood and raised his hands into the mass of wind and smoke above his head. He touched the braided air and screamed in ecstatic joy. Unholy light flooded the tower, and blue sparks leaped from his hair.

A dark cloud formed above the shallows near Argenti. The thunderhead rolled in and settled over the island's southern tip, its heavy black mass dipping almost to the ocean surface. Dark's tidal jet surged up to meet the descending cloud, and a full-fledged waterspout formed. Once the swirling shape was complete, the thin end of the funnel detached from the water and skipped madly across the waves. As the tail of the waterspout zigzagged closer to shore, Lord Dark clenched his fists and crossed them over his chest.

He spared the waterspout just enough of his attention to keep it intact. The rest of his mind focused on the funnel's wider end. The muscles in Dark's massive arms bunched and squeezed as he forced carefully structured black mana into the spout's hollow center.

The funnel's tail skipped off of the waves and onto the shore. The misty, bowl-shaped barrier around Argenti flashed brighter, resisting the intrusive force.

Dark relaxed his shoulders and arms and cleared his mind, his breath becoming slow and even. In his mind and on Argenti, the raging funnel balanced impossibly on the protective dome's convex surface, spinning in place like a child's toy.

Dark suddenly and smoothly lowered himself back down onto the pedestal. As he slipped into his cross-legged position, the funnel likewise slipped past the protective barrier and dug into the muddy soil of Argenti. The waterspout began to chew up the landscape, but Dark concentrated and stopped its advance. Instead, as easily as squeezing juice from a lemon, Dark squeezed the black mana he had camouflaged inside the waterspout through the spout's tube and past Caleria's barrier. The raw magical energy manifested as a dusky gray cloud, and it hovered in the air until Dark had extracted every last iota of black mana from the funnel. Then the waterspout collapsed into a brief but heavy rain of seawater and dirt.

Dark reached out, took hold of the gray energy, and converted it into a thinner, distorting haze. The shimmering cloud looked exactly like a great heat mirage on a distant desert mound, then it faded into nothing.

Dark opened his eyes. The physical view of western Madara showed through the huge window before him, but Dark still saw a ghostly view of Argenti. The inverted bowl of icy white mist that covered the island was now a sickly pale yellow, like the winter sky before a storm. Dark focused on the scene for a moment to determine that everything was as he wished it. The protective dome had been successfully breached, and all of his spells had gone off as intended.

Dark stood up, painfully flexing his stiff joints and aching muscles. The water in the trench had boiled away, leaving only the bones of a single fish and a few nuggets of coral.

Dark stretched his neck to the left then to the right. He retrieved his cape and stepped off of the stone pedestal.

Lady Orca, he thought. Dark knew better than to wait for the siege demon to reply. She could hear him, and she would be eager to carry out her instructions.

Dark felt another wave of exhilaration, and this time he didn't even try to fight it off.

Lady Orca, he repeated. *Rise.*

CHAPTER 19

 On a mossy stone at the edge of Lord Magnus's forest home, a small wisp of smoke rose. A coal-black scorch mark formed under the wet green moss and crawled across the face of the rock like a frenzied insect. Soon the black trails completed a rough, smoking sigil. The forest remained still and silent but for the hiss of burning plants. Overhead, the noon sky had a sickly yellow tint, and the sunlight was diffuse and muted.

The mossy stone suddenly exploded, and a huge plume of black tar jetted up to the canopy. At seventy feet, the jet burst into blue flame. When the flames faded, Lady Orca stepped onto the soil of Argenti, and the impact of her first step shook birds and branches from the surrounding trees.

The giantess quickly surveyed her surroundings and twisted her face into a malevolent smile. She did not know the forest behind her or the countryside ahead, but she recognized the site of her latest assignment.

She turned and took an absent swipe at the tallest tree behind her. The lazy blow snapped the huge pine off at its center, and its bark and needles burst into flame under Orca's fist. She bent and lifted the top half of the tree with both hands, further igniting it. Drawing it back like a giant dart, she heaved the entire flaming mass into the depths of the forest.

Lord Dark's instructions had been quite clear, but Orca

had learned to relish the small bursts of freedom he allowed. She had not been human for quite a long time, decades before Dark had found her and pressed her into service. Some of her original personality had survived the transformation from battle mage to siege demon, however. That part of her warped, chaotic mind reveled in the opportunity to unleash her fury on a new and untested enemy. She eyed the level road that stretched out to Caleria's distant castle, and the glowing coals in her sockets popped and spat out a stream of gleeful sparks.

Fresh meat, she thought.

Orca raised her arms high and shrieked an awful battle cry. She could smell the sweet, acrid scent of burning pine resin and hear the panicked screams of forest denizens as the fire spread. Ahead lay the fat and tempting target of a fortified castle. In between . . .

Orca cast her arm out and launched a flaming ball of pitch into the center of the empty field. The ball splattered on the cold, dry ground and spread flames across the furrows.

Annoyed, Orca spat fire. The impact had been satisfying, but there was nothing in the field worth burning. She took a few steps and scanned the acreage ahead until she spotted something more promising: a two-story barn with a hayloft and animal pens. Orca quickened her pace, red-hot feet searing into smooth paving stones, and prepared another flaming mass. Within range of the barn, there was even a farmer with a female child in tow.

Orca hissed happily and sent a thousand pounds of viscous black death hurtling at the barn.

The tiny human scooped up the child and started to run, but he was already in the shadow of the descending ball. He would never get clear in time.

A stream of green pine needles suddenly erupted from the forest behind Orca and plowed straight into the flaming ball of tar. They burst into flame as they struck her missile, but there were millions of them, and they flew with the force of a hurricane. The flow of needles curved under and around the ball, all the while peppering it with miniature darts and magical energy to slow its descent. The column of needles slowly assumed the shape of a human hand that clutched the giant ball of tar, holding it in place just above the spire on the farmer's barn.

Orca swiped at the column where it passed close to her, but the stream merely flowed around her fist and reformed when she drew her hand back. Then the great green hand turned and cast Orca's fireball into the same burning field she had already ruined.

"You are the beast that attacked Kusho." The deep, melodious voice came from the edge of the forest. "I am Magnus, defender of this forest."

Orca shrieked in fury as she turned to the red-faced druid who stood below the stream of needles. He held up a wooden staff with green flames shooting out the top. The druid dropped his arm, and the stream of pine needles fell to the ground.

"You killed three score of our chelonian allies. Their spirits cry out for vengeance," the druid said. "I shall answer them." From the trees behind him came a chorus of snarls, growls, and other bestial warnings. Dozens of eyes shone in the shadows, and the druid raised his staff over his head with both hands.

Without waiting to see what the forest mage would conjure, Orca roared with laughter and lashed out.

* * * * *

Tetsuo, Tor, Ayesha, and Kei had spent the night in scrub lands east of Caleria's castle. Pursuit was active and constant, but they were well concealed by Tetsuo's spellcraft. The party slept in a dry creek bed, and by morning there was no sign of Caleria's soldiers. The dawn had a sulfurous tint that made Tor edgy and fatigued at the same time.

Under that yellow sky, they broke out the last of the provisions for their morning meal. Kei remained feverish and incoherent, but Ayesha did her best to keep him comfortable and quiet.

"We will make for the stand of tall trees near the center of the forest, the one that agitated Kei," Tetsuo announced quietly as the others ate. He clearly had been devising the plan all night, though he seemed dissatisfied as he outlined it for them. "Kei said the stand contains knowledge, and he is the only one among us with an affinity for nature magic. Also, Magnus's refusal to discuss the grove or linger nearby speaks of its importance. We will investigate the site then take possession of it in order to bargain for Xira," Tetsuo blinked in thought. "If we are fortunate, Magnus's attention will be focused on capturing the eumidian, and we won't have to fight our way through."

Tor and Ayesha were not thrilled with the plan, but they had few alternatives. They could return to Caleria and face her soldiers or make for the sampan and try to sail on. Neither option seemed likely to help Kei or stop Dark's operatives, so they resigned themselves at least to taking the initiative.

Ayesha prepared Kei for the trek, and Tor rooted around for branches to use as a stretcher.

The champion suddenly drew his sword, and for the first time since Tor had known him, the blade wavered. "Something is happening," Tetsuo said. He stared due west, the direction of Caleria's castle. "Something has been happening since this morning." The champion's eyes drifted eastward, to the ocean and Madara beyond.

There was a faint and muffled boom in the distance, and a thick curl of smoke rose over a hill on the horizon.

Tor dropped the load of branches. "Something we need to take part in?"

"I fear so." Tetsuo sheathed his sword and turned inland. "Tor, you go on ahead and see what just exploded. Stay out of sight." Tetsuo knelt and lifted Kei onto his shoulders. "We will follow as quickly as we can."

"What if I'm seen? Should I defend myself or run?"

Tetsuo stood, his eyes grim and fixed on the distant spires of Caleria's castle. "Don't be seen," he said.

* * * * *

Lady Orca's fist smashed down into the space where the druid stood, but she could tell right away there was nothing human beneath her knuckles. She raised her hand slightly and saw a scorched tangle of wood, grass, and dirt. Perhaps the tree-hugger had been an illusion or a construct of animated branches and mulch.

A saber-toothed sloth pounced on Orca's shoulder and barked its fangs on her steely robe. The giantess brutally slammed her head and shoulder together, crushing the sloth into a bloody smear.

She pivoted and scattered a hail of tiny flaming pellets into the forest, and the trees began to burn.

Something massive plowed into her right shin, and Orca teetered. On the ground, a gigantic rhinolike biped had its horn buried in Orca's leg, and it shoved against her with all its might. Round feet dug deep into the ground, and thick back muscles rolled as it tried to force her leg out from under her.

Orca spat a gout of flaming tar down into the rhino-man's face. The brute was too thick-skinned to feel any pain, but it broke off its attack and clawed at its face, blinded and unable to breathe.

"Back, my children," came the druid's melodious voice, now strained with fury and choked by soot and smoke. He stepped out of the forest to Orca's left, and several beasts slunk back or stepped aside before him.

Magnus stamped his staff into the turf, and the ground behind him erupted. The flaming trees tore from the soil, trailing roots and loose dirt behind them. They flew at Orca, who easily batted them aside.

From her height, she could see huge evergreen treefolk moving among the flames, uprooting the stricken trees and hurling them at her. Orca sneered as she slapped another missile away. The tree-spears were doing more damage to the treefolk than to her.

The red-faced druid cried out, and a huge bolt of green force bloomed from his staff. It caught Orca in the sternum and actually knocked her off her feet, carrying her backward dozens of yards before dropping her heavily onto the road.

Furious, she snatched up a broken chunk of paving stone and slung it like a discus at the forest mage.

The druid swept his flaming staff in a wide circle, and a cylinder of green light formed around him. The chunk of road burst into smaller rocks and pieces against Magnus's shield. The forest lord stamped his staff again and produced a killing gust of wind that send the stone fragments hurtling back at Orca.

Orca allowed the stone shrapnel to pass right through her. She was taking too much time here at the forest's edge, drawing too much attention. If her main targets were on the island, they surely knew by now she was here. Orca sprang back to her feet and roared in frustration.

In reply, the druid raised his staff again and slowly leveled it at Orca. From the cracked and broken road, small green shoots formed and climbed Orca's leg like ivy up a drain pipe. The new plant growth resisted the ever-increasing heat of her skin. Though the leaves blackened and curled where they touched her, the vines kept growing, encircling her ankles, shins, and knees.

A horn blared from the top of Caleria's wall, then came the sound of dozens, perhaps hundreds of marching feet.

At the forest's edge, the beasts inched closer, eager to watch Orca fall but hesitant to be in her path when she did. The druid continued to point his staff flame-first at her, the vines kept growing, and the soldiers marched nearer.

Orca stretched her arms overhead and howled. A bright spark flew off the tips of her fingers, and orange flame flowed down her body like water. Soon she was only a semi-human shape enveloped in fire.

With a wail, the burning figure erupted and shot countless streamers of smoldering tar high into the air. They disappeared among the darkening clouds. The deadly geyser continued until Orca was completely gone and only a tangle of smoking vines cast in the shape of giant feet remained on the road.

Bestial roars and howls of victory pealed out from the trees, but Magnus was more cautious. He stepped alongside the hollow heap of vines, his staff at the ready.

High above, Orca watched and waited. It was extremely difficult for her to maintain control over her body, spread out as far as it was. She fumbled, confused by her disembodied perspective, but then reclaimed all of her mass from suspension in the clouds. She howled an attack cry and was rewarded by looks of shock and terror on the upturned faces of the forest assembly.

Orca brayed a cruel, raucous laugh as she rained down on them—a hundred million droplets of burning, boiling tar.

* * * * *

Tor peered over the crest of the hill he had just climbed, out toward the forest's edge. He gasped.

The entire area was either on fire or had recently burned out. Blackened trees lined the road, and indiscriminate shapes lay scattered all around. Even the ground itself was covered with scorch marks and dirty haze. The killing field reminded Tor of the beach at Kusho. Whatever had struck there had arrived on Argenti. The smoke and haze combined with the pale yellow of the sky to create a gloomy shroud.

Tor spotted Caleria at the top of a distant hill, mounted on a furry steed that had a long neck and the massive back legs of a hare. She looked down into the carnage and waved her arm. Two columns of thirty soldiers each quickly streamed past her on either side, spreading out to the edge of the flaming ruins and encircling them.

Tor lay down on his belly, though in the smoke and the gloom he was certain he had not been spotted.

The last lingering flames all burnt out at once, and plumes of black smoke drifted across the ruined stretch of ground. Caleria barked an order to her troops, and each soldier readied his pike.

A harsh, grating roar fell from the sky, and each soldier tightened his grip on his weapon. A thousand smoking bits of tar leaped straight down and rushed together with a sickening slap. More dabs of hot tar continued to rush into the central mass, which was quickly taking the shape of a giant humanoid.

Caleria waved her arm, and from beside her a squadron of ten archers all loosed their shafts at the emerging figure. The arrows struck but had no effect, and were quickly drawn into the expanding heap of tar.

There was a flash of ignition, and the black tower transformed into a steel-skinned woman of tremendous size.

"Lady Orca," Tor whispered. He recognized her only from descriptions he had heard from Tetsuo and Kei.

Orca spotted Caleria, pointed at the mounted ruler, and hissed. "You're next." The same pointing finger released a thick stream of boiling hot, clinging tar.

Caleria's eyes flashed as the stuff splashed across an armored soldier's chest. There was no answering flash at the point of contact, and the hot sludge burned into and through the soldier's metal breastplate. Caleria's eyes flashed again, but the man fell.

The island ruler wailed as her eyes flashed and her soldiers dropped. "Fall back!" she hollered. "This can't be happening! Fall back!"

Orca turned back to Caleria and showed her a mouthful of black and broken teeth.

"No need to rush off," Orca screeched. "You'll all be dead soon enough." She howled her battle cry.

Tor nocked an arrow and targeted Orca's glowing eyes.

"Hold, my archer." Tor had never been so happy to hear the champion's voice. He rolled over in the wet grass and saw Tetsuo stooping to let Kei slide off his back. Ayesha stood by them, supporting Kei as the champion stepped forward. The healer's head lolled, and he caught sight of Orca towering over her victims. Kei's face tightened, and he let out a sound that was halfway between a groan and a growl.

"I will not abandon him," Tetsuo told Ayesha, "but this is the other reason we've come to Argenti." Ayesha nodded, and Tetsuo drew his sword.

"Come, Second." Tetsuo strolled past the spot where Tor lay and ascended to the top of the hill. Tor jumped up, nodded at Ayesha and Kei, then fell in alongside the champion.

Below, Orca pounded the Argenti soldiers with boulder-sized blobs of fire and pitch.

Tor felt a whisper of motion as Tetsuo maneuvered his sword. A blue bolt of energy lashed out of it, soaring straight into Orca's face.

The giantess staggered back a step and oriented on her new enemy.

"Servant of the empire!" Tetsuo's voice rolled down the hill like thunder. "I am Tetsuo Umezawa, Imperial Champion. I order you to cease this attack at once."

Orca's face was still reforming after Tetsuo's blow. Before she finished, a vicious grin formed on her distorted lips.

"Champion," she rasped. "At last." Orca's eyes remained fixed on Tetsuo while her arm jerked out straight toward Caleria, hurling another flaming payload into the midst of the soldiers. Then she turned away from Caleria and completely ignored both the Argenti noble and her army.

Tetsuo had sprung forward as soon as Orca's arm moved. By the time she released her throw, the champion was halfway down the hill and closing fast. Tor kept his arrow at the ready and followed his master into battle.

Orca shrieked with glee and strode forward to meet them, flames and tar building up in the palms of her giant hands.

CHAPTER 20

Xira Arien bypassed most of the guards by soaring over the west wall, which overlooked an impassible valley with an almost vertical slope. She throttled the first sentry she came across, then because the castle was so empty and still she ambushed and killed three more in succession as they made their rounds past her hiding place.

When a full hour had passed and no more sentries came sniffing down her hallway, Xira picked up her burden and crept silently along the empty corridor. Lord Dark's courier had been both punctual and efficient, and the cylindrical device with the misshapen funnel on top was no heavier than the average adolescent human. She had had no trouble transporting it or hiding it while she eluded Magnus's hunting party.

Now it was time to carry out the rest of Lord Dark's orders: Conceal the device somewhere inside Caleria's castle, somewhere neither servants nor searchers would stumble across it. She soon found the perfect place, tucked into a corner of the ceiling over a stone doorway.

Outside the castle, she heard the sounds of marching feet and the moans of wounded people. Irritated, she realized that she was missing all the real fun and hurried to place the finishing touches on her work.

Xira wedged the device between the door frame and the white stone ceiling. She concentrated, imparting to the device some of the enchantment that Lord Dark had bestowed on her so long ago. The metal box and funnel shimmered in the shadows then disappeared completely.

Xira exhaled. The device had no moving parts, and her ambush camouflage was nearly perfect as long as the hidden subject remained still. There was virtually no way anyone would find it here. Even if there were direct sunlight from the nearby window, the device would remain hidden . . . and today the sunlight was feeble and wan, far more like dusk than midday.

Xira. Dark's voice sounded in her ears. She wondered if he knew how much his booming voice rattled the bones in her head. *Is everything ready?*

Yes, my lord. The device is secure and ready for activation.

Excellent. And my flight enhancement? You are still able to fly past the limits of your own wings?

Yes, my lord.

Then return here as soon as the device goes off. Your work on Argenti is nearly complete.

But, my lord—

Don't make me repeat myself, Xira.

My lord, Xira persisted, *I had hoped to witness the champion's demise.*

And the emergence of your offspring from the healer. Dark paused, and Xira could almost feel the drag on her master's attention, as if something else were occupying his thoughts even as he called on her.

Very well, he grumbled. *Suit yourself, but stay out of sight. No matter what else happens, I expect to see you bowing before me in three days at the very most.*

Count on that, my lord. Xira took one final look at the hidden machine then climbed straight up the stone wall and crawled upside-down along the ceiling.

Xira had left the hive long, long ago, but the hive-mind was still very much a part of her. She could feel a presence that was very close to that of her own kind and not too far away. Since she herself had planted the egg in Kei, she merely had to follow the call of her kin to find the healer and the precious cargo he carried. And then . . .

Xira snapped her mouth shut excitedly but made sure to minimize the noise.

And then she would have a eumidian slave of her own. She wondered if Lord Dark would be able to control two of her kind. Together she and her offspring might be able to use force or guile to free her from Lord Dark's service once and for all.

Xira licked a spot of congealing blood off her fingers. She hoped it would require force.

*   *   *   *   *

Under gloomy skies, Tetsuo and Lady Orca charged each other. Orca's eyes were aflame, and Tetsuo's blade carried a nimbus of force around it as the champion ran.

Tor stayed behind him, careful not to be caught in any attack the champion made. This was not a formal duel, so Tor was free to assist Tetsuo as he saw fit.

Orca hammered a crushing blow down on Tetsuo, but the champion stood his ground and held his sword overhead. Orca's fist met the nimbus around Tetsuo's blade and split like water before the prow of a ship. Her arm followed her fist while Tetsuo stood firm in the middle of the forking stream of hot tar.

The giantess was unharmed by the cleft in her arm, but she hissed in outrage and tried to reverse her momentum. Tetsuo stepped forward, pressing his blade deeper into Orca as he went. The nimbus of energy around the champion's blade streamed up Orca's arm and across her neck and shoulders, sundering the viscous demon in two.

The top quarter of Orca's torso, including her head, separated and dropped to the ground. Tetsuo spun his sword and body, and a low-frequency hum vibrated from the blade. The champion dashed to the spot where Orca's head and shoulders would land and waved his sword in a wide, slashing arc.

But Orca's one-armed body caught its own falling head before Tetsuo could unleash his next attack. Orca manually turned her face down at Tetsuo and snarled, then she kicked, and the champion had to jump out of range.

Orca slapped her head and shoulders back in place, and the hot tar quickly sealed itself. Even her severed arm healed. She laughed mockingly and brought her hands together with a deafening blast of noise. As her hands met, they disappeared, and Orca jetted a double stream of flaming darkness at the champion.

Tetsuo's sword flew around him faster than Tor could follow, and by the time the stream of tar hit, he was safely inside a translucent sphere of purple crystal. Orca's attack splattered harmlessly off the amethyst bubble and onto the cold ground.

Tetsuo threw himself forward and started the sphere rolling. The giantess re-formed her hands and reached out, hoping to snatch up the champion like a child's toy, but Tetsuo leaped, and the sphere followed him. The amethyst bubble bounced over Orca's grasping hand, with Tetsuo spinning end over end inside.

Orca made another grab for her foe, and as Tetsuo tumbled back to a standing position, he thrust his sword through the crystal barrier. Like a lightning rod, the blade drew in the amethyst until the sphere was gone and the metal had taken on a purple tinge. Tetsuo slashed at Orca and released a violet-blue stream of energy.

The stream connected Tetsuo's sword to Orca's chest. The champion drew his short sword and touched the tips of both blades together. Blue-white energy crackled from his hands through his weapons and into the arc of energy.

The jagged bolt slammed in Orca's chest, and she thrashed at the far end of the beam. The siege demon screamed. A tremendous wave of cold flowed from the light, and the fires in Orca's eyes sputtered.

Tetsuo poured more blue mana into his maneuver.

Condensation formed on Orca's skin. The giantess screamed again and grabbed the shaft that sapped her strength, but her hands froze helplessly around it. The condensation began to freeze, and the fires around Orca faltered.

Tetsuo's eyes were fixed on the struggling Orca. "Tor, target her face. Dead center. Standard arrow."

Tor bent his bow and stared at the hateful coal eyes of his enemy. "Got her."

Tetsuo's teeth clenched as the effort of freezing Orca began to take its toll. "Fire."

The arrow sailed straight into the bridge of Orca's nose. The killer's head did not shatter to pieces as Tor had hoped, but it did crack and split like a mirror in a frame. Orca's face became even more monstrous as her eyes looked around independently of one another and her sneering lips on the right side failed to align with those on the left.

Tetsuo opened his grip and spun each sword over the backs of his hands. The line of energy winked out. Orca staggered forward onto one knee, a hand on her face to keep it in place. The champion crossed his blades over his chest and leaped once more at his opponent.

Orca saw him coming but could do nothing to avoid him. Instead, she opened her mouth wide and prepared to swallow Tetsuo whole.

When he was mere feet from Orca's hideous black teeth, Tetsuo uncrossed his swords. The edges scraped along each other, and a rounded bolt of pure force slammed into Orca's open mouth.

Orca's eyes widened, and her head exploded into nauseous black mist.

Tetsuo sailed right through the empty space over Orca's shoulders and landed gracefully behind the giantess. He crossed his swords again as he pivoted, and unleashed another bolt into the crouching, headless figure.

Orca's body also exploded, but not as efficiently as her head had. Huge smoking chunks of her flew in every direction, but they were cool and almost completely solid.

Tetsuo stood with his swords stretched out on either side of him until the last piece hit the ground. He slowly crossed his arms again and returned his swords to their sheaths.

A cheer went up from the nearby hillside where the last platoon of Caleria's troops retreated. It was now so gloomy that Tor could barely count the number of Argenti troopers, but he could see Caleria herself. She sat atop her bizarre steed and wore a cold and furious expression. Without taking her eyes off Tetsuo, she ordered her soldiers to be silent.

Tor ran to the champion. "Well done, Master."

Tetsuo looked at Tor as if he were surprised to see the archer, and then he grimly shook his head.

Tor pointed at a steaming chunk of tar nearby. "You mean she isn't dead?"

Tetsuo shook his head again. "Orca is a creature of will

and malice. Her body is mere housing for her bloodlust, a weapon she employs. It takes more than physical force to kill her."

Indeed, even as they spoke, Tor could see the smaller pieces of the giantess' body undulating across the dirt, crawling like legless insects to one another. Each time two pieces met, they would melt together, form a single ball, and start undulating to the next nearest piece.

Tor swallowed uneasily. "How much more?"

* * * * *

Lord Dark sat cross-legged in his private study, meditating. Though the majority of his spellcraft was complete, he had not summoned the servants back to the keep. They would distract him from the spell that baffled Caleria's protective field. Even now he rocked back and forth, chanting softly as he pumped black mana into the hex that enshrouded Argenti in a dismal veil.

His meditations were almost interrupted by a scream of pain from Lady Orca. He did not have the same high degree of discourse with Orca as he did with Xira. The giantess's mind was too twisted and angry. He was in contact with her, however, as he was with all his operatives, and from her single incoherent shout, he knew something had gone wrong.

Dark continued to chant and monitor his spell, but he also turned a portion of his attention to Orca.

Of course, he thought. Umezawa.

Lord Dark whispered to Orca in his mind. *Rise again. Finish what you have started. I will protect you.*

Orca's reply was diffuse and scattered, but she tried to obey. Carefully continuing the maintenance of his other spell, Lord Dark sent a small stream of black mana out to Orca on Argenti. Just as he had enhanced Xira's wings and Boris's creation of lava golems, he had enhanced Orca's combat effectiveness.

Umezawa was unbeatable in a fair fight, but in Dark's world there was no such thing.

* * * * *

"Stand behind me, Tor." Tetsuo squared his stance and faced the growing mass of tar.

Tor quietly backpedaled until he was twenty feet away from his master.

Orca's body had reclaimed most of its substance from the surrounding area, but she was slow to complete the process and take humanoid shape. Tor guessed it was because her head had been so completely destroyed, but he was wrong.

When the mound of tar was roughly two-thirds as large as Lady Orca had been mere moments ago, it burst into blue flame. A smaller version of the giantess sprang free: She hadn't been waiting for her head to be complete; she had been lulling her enemies into thinking they had more time than they did. Now only fifty feet tall, Orca was wild and terrible to behold. She flung herself at Tetsuo.

The champion had not been lulled. When the blue flame ignited, he drew his sword and slashed it over his right shoulder and behind him. As the giantess erupted out of the flaming mound, Tetsuo quickly brought his arm forward and slashed the blade through the air at chest level.

Tor had seen the champion perform this maneuver in dozens of battle situations. The practiced series of movements were a physical mantra he recited before unleashing his ultimate attack. After these movements, Tetsuo's blade could produce waves of fire that could reduce an entire warship to splinters and ash. It could form cutting arcs of energy like the one that had killed the land wurm back in Sekana, or bolts of force strong enough to level mountains. This time, a black scythe of light flew out of Tetsuo's blade.

The jagged energy spun end over end and flew into Orca's chest. The impact stopped her forward charge and even carried her back a step.

Tetsuo sheathed his sword.

Orca's eyes widened, and her mouth opened and closed wordlessly. The attack had buried itself in her body without leaving a mark, but she clutched clumsily at her chest where it had landed. The giantess staggered back a step, and then forward. She looked down at Tetsuo standing calmly below her, and a dumb, lazy expression crossed her wicked features.

Orca fell heavily to both knees and pitched facedown in the dirt.

Tor looked to the hill where Caleria waited. This time her troops did not cheer. The armored soldiers were returning to the battleground, but their leader kept them clear of the action. Tor turned back to his master, who stared hard at Orca's motionless form.

Black light crackled over Orca's back and spread across her body. The huge figure rose several feet into the air, surrounded by a cocoon of sparking energy.

"Master?" Tor called.

Tetsuo shook his head in disbelief. "That was a death blow. She is being repaired from without." He drew his sword again, raising it high over his right shoulder.

The crackling field around Orca faded, and the giantess rose to one foot. She seemed smaller again, only forty feet tall. The hate in her eyes had returned, as focused and dangerous as before.

Tetsuo completed the mantra for his killing stroke and sent another twirling scythe of energy into Orca's body. Once more the giantess screamed, swooned, and fell motionless. Her wide, staring eyes fixed on the hazy sky above.

Tetsuo sheathed his sword and, to Tor's horror, faltered. He did not fall, but his legs seemed unable to hold him steady.

Black energy crackled anew across Orca's supine body. Tor called his master's name and carefully approached.

"Are you all right?"

Tetsuo let his hand drop to his side. "I only hope it's taking as much out of Orca."

"What can I do?"

Tetsuo stared hard at his second. "Stand clear. Stay alive. Find a cure for Kei." Tor nodded and stepped back.

Orca was very nearly on her feet again.

Tetsuo grabbed Tor's arm. "Tor," he whispered. "If Kei cannot be cured, he must be set free. Do you understand?"

"What? Master, I don't think I—"

Tetsuo pulled him close. "Set him free, Tor. If that egg hatches, he won't be Kei anymore. He'll be something else. Something that needs killing. Swear to it."

"I—"

Orca roared, smaller than ever but still five times taller than her foes.

"Swear it!"

"I swear, Master." Tetsuo nodded, and Tor scurried back.

Tetsuo drew his sword, completed the forms, and blasted Orca again. The giantess grunted and fell lifelessly onto her side. This time Tetsuo also fell, though the champion quickly got back to his feet.

Tor stole a glance back at Ayesha and Kei on one hill then Lady Caleria and her soldiers on the other.

Black energy crackled around Orca's fallen form. She rose to kneel inside her energy cocoon.

Tetsuo drew his sword, positioned his feet, and visibly summoned the wherewithal to keep fighting.

Tor realized for the first time that Tetsuo might actually fall here on Argenti. His second, his armorer, and his healer-in-training would surely follow.

* * * * *

In his private study, Dark fumed. Whatever was happening on Argenti, it was not going well for Orca. He had revived her four times in the past few minutes, but she kept requiring more. If she didn't achieve victory soon, he would have to tap into his personal reserves of black mana in order to keep her going.

Caleria also vexed him. She refused to accept the limitations his spell had placed on her protective barrier and kept trying to activate it. Eventually, she would figure out what he had done and how to get around it. And if Orca hadn't finished Tetsuo by then . . .

Dark hesitated, something he rarely did. His primary scheme was slowly coming unraveled, but he had secondary and tertiary plans ready for implementation. How likely was Orca to succeed at this point? How much would it cost him even if she did?

The master assassin reached his decision. Imperial politics was a great game, and a great player doesn't put all his faith in a single roll of the dice. It was time to lose a battle in order to win the war.

With a twinge of regret, Dark abandoned the interference

he had created. Within minutes, Argenti's protective field would reassert itself, and all black or red mana attacks could be negated with the barest shrug of Caleria's shoulders.

Orca, he thought. *Return.*

* * * * *

After the tenth killing stroke, blood trickled from Tetsuo's nose and ears. Orca had dwindled down to a mere twelve feet, but her ferocity was unabated.

Tor had never been so miserable in his life. His master was tearing himself to shreds against an unkillable foe while Tor himself prepared to cut down a friend.

The crackling energy around Orca suddenly changed color, becoming red and then orange. It also seemed to be shrinking.

Orca's face forced its way out of the cocoon and snarled at Tetsuo. The champion drew his sword and waited.

Orca's lips moved, but Tor could hear no words. Her entire diminished body collapsed in on itself, and the energy around her imploded with a dry pop.

Tor paused in the sudden silence. There was smoking debris and ruined ground all around them, but no tar. Orca, at last, was gone. Tetsuo sheathed his swords and sank down into the cross-legged meditation position.

"Master," Tor turned. "I think that did it. She's—"

Blood ran from Tetsuo's lips, and he smiled a weak but encouraging smile, then the champion slumped silently to the ground and lay still.

The archer was at his side in a flash, rolling Tetsuo onto his back. He called for Kei but remembered the healer was in no shape to perform his function. Tor heard armored feet approach and the heavy tread of Caleria's freakish mount.

"When your master awakes," Caleria said, "he shall be rewarded."

Tor nodded.

"But our nations are still at war." Caleria's troops stepped forward, surrounding Tor and the unconscious Tetsuo with a ring of pikes. "You all are my prisoners."

CHAPTER 21

Caleria's soldiers rounded up Kei and Ayesha and forced them to kneel beside Tor at the lady's feet. She had their weapons taken and their hands tied, but she did not otherwise abuse them.

Tetsuo remained insensate. He was carefully bound and handed over to a small throng of druids in green and white robes. Kei was not coherent enough to offer an opinion, but perhaps these were healers. Caleria would probably want Tetsuo standing under his own power when she had him beheaded.

Tor shifted uncomfortably on his knees. He wondered glumly if beheading was the standard form of execution on Argenti. Perhaps Caleria would hunt them with her long bow, and they would wind up as trophies on her wall.

The rough hemp rope bit into his wrists, and his shoulders ached. Beside him, Kei finally lost consciousness and pitched forward onto the ground. Ayesha struggled to the healer's side, but the soldiers pushed her away and pulled Kei back onto his knees.

Most of the Kei's white paint was gone, and now half his face was smeared with dirt. His eyelids fluttered as he swooned again, but he managed to keep himself upright. His tongue lolled out, and he shook his head rapidly from side to side, straightening his spine.

"Kei?" Ayesha's voice was softer and more tender than

Tor had ever heard. "Kei, look at me." The feverish youth jerked his head away from Tor and turned to his teacher. Ayesha looked at Kei for a long, slow moment then swore softly. Tor could see Kei's jaw working, but he didn't hear the healer's voice. Ayesha's impassive face began to crack, and she heaved a weary sigh.

"What is it?" Tor could not keep his voice at a proper whisper. "Ayesha? What's wrong?"

Kei turned at the sound of Tor's voice, and the archer flinched.

Kei's lips were moving silently, all chapped and blistered and flecked with foam. His eyes were open wide, his eyeballs a toxic yellow. His pupils were tiny dots of brilliant red on separate patches of shabby green.

Kei's lips kept moving as he tried to speak, but Tor concentrated on his friend's pupils. The archer counted softly to himself as he stared. He raised his head and saw Ayesha watching them anxiously.

"Eight," he said. Kei had four tiny pupils in each eye, four specks of red on green that seemed to crowd his eye sockets and change the shape of his skull. The pupils nearest the center were in the process of dividing again, pinching half of themselves off to add yet another facet to the strange and terrible jewels growing in Kei's head.

"Kill me," the healer said. His voice had a musical quality to it, like someone striking a silver chime. "Kill me."

Caleria turned away from the forest and faced her prisoners. "Your fates have not been—" She stopped when she saw Kei then turned to the druids in green and white robes. "Hoy, here! Come here at once!"

The druids hurried over and swarmed around Kei. They lifted him and pitched him onto the rough wood of a prisoner's cart. He was tied to the cart's slats, an armed guard standing on either side. Ayesha was likewise loaded and trussed up.

As the soldiers carted Ayesha and Kei over the hill, Tor stared after them but could see only a ring of green robes. He was next.

* * * * *

Ayesha and Tor were taken to Caleria's great hall. Their hands were cut free, and they were allowed to stand but were still very much prisoners. In case they had forgotten, armored soldiers lined every inch of the room's interior walls.

"Think they'll kill us?" Tor rubbed his wrist while Ayesha scanned the room's ceiling.

"They'd better." The armorer's eyes followed the line of the roof to the main support beam on the western wall. "If Kei dies and I don't, I'll come back to hunt these bastards." She lowered her head and looked at Tor. "This is a well-built room. It looks strong enough to withstand a full catapult barrage, even without magical enhancement, and I'm pretty sure it's got enhancements."

"That's terrific," Tor said. "Maybe they can hang us all at once without breaking the beam."

Ayesha's eyes narrowed. "Watch your tongue, boy."

"Or you'll do what? Kill me?" Tor fought the hysteria rising in him. "That'd be a real setback at this point, wouldn't it?"

The tension seemed to be getting to Ayesha as well, because Tor was almost certain she had started to smile. The first stirring of a grin became a sour expression of disappointment. "I thought you warriors were supposed to be brave. And I know Tetsuo taught you respect for your betters."

Tor started to answer, but then Caleria and three plumed lieutenants swept into the room.

"We *will* pick this up later," Ayesha whispered. "Remember, we aren't dead yet."

Tor sighed and nodded. He hoped the armorer had an escape plan, because the only thing he had was a headache.

Caleria climbed the stairs to the throne and waved her hand.

"Bring forth the prisoners."

The guards prodded Tor and Ayesha, who exchanged a quick glance before walking to the throne. The guards stayed a single step behind them, and more armored figures came around the throne.

"Imperials," Caleria said, "you represent a state that makes war on Argenti. Your emperor sends assassins and monsters alike against my allies, against my people, and against me. These are acts of war, by every definition.

"But I understand how things get done in your empire, how power is concentrated in a few individuals, and used to keep the rest of your population subservient. Though it is clear that the emperor had ordered my death, it is not clear how willingly you came to do his bidding."

"What's she getting at?" Tor whispered.

"Pay attention, warrior. This is politics."

"Silence!" snapped one of the lieutenants.

"Tetsuo Umezawa," Caleria continued, "is an imperial official, the emperor's hand-picked champion. He came here to represent the empire, and so he shall. I hereby renew my declaration of war on Madara. As a representative of our hostile enemy, Umezawa dies tomorrow, and his head shall be shipped back to your god-king. I continue to defy your emperor, as I have defied the killers he sent."

Caleria paused, and Tor wondered if she expected them

to beg or bluster. She would wait a long time. Ayesha was too centered for such behavior, and Tor had no idea what to say.

"Your servants are in the tower. Your stricken healer is being attended by Magnus's druids. So I am left with the question of you two. You serve the champion, who serves the emperor, so I have the right to your lives, but I know how things get done in your empire. I know there is a difference between a disciple, a servant, and a slave.

"Tor Wauki," she snapped. "You are the champion's second. You also fought with honor and restraint against the forces of Kusho. I ask you now, would you have fought at all if the champion had not forced you to?"

Tor blinked. "What?"

"She's giving you a chance to change sides," Ayesha said.

Tor understood the words Ayesha spoke, but they still seemed alien and strange to him. "Change sides?"

"Archer," Caleria's throaty voice was low and menacing. "Do you wish to stay by the champion's side, or will you renounce the emperor and swear fealty to me? Speak carefully. Life and death literally hang on your answer."

"I stand with the champion," Tor said instantly. "I am more than his second, Lady, I am his student, and I have much yet to learn from him." He glanced over at Ayesha. "My oath was not to the emperor, but to the champion himself." Tor crossed his arms and planted his feet. "I go where he goes."

Caleria regarded him coolly for a moment. "So be it. I admire your loyalty, archer, but I despair at your naïveté." She clapped her hands, and another armored soldier came into the room with Ayesha's barrow.

The man pushing the barrow was completely encased in shining metal that fit him like a second skin. He was tall and lanky, with the strong features common to Caleria's tribe. Tor could make out each silver-coated hair on the man's curly head and beard and each metallic fold and pleat in his clothing. Tor might have believed him to be a golem or animated statue, but the man's posture and body language were human. The silver man rolled the barrow up to the throne and stood silently beside it.

"Ayesha Tanaka," Caleria said. "The champion's armorer. This is Mudai, my own chief smithy." She gestured toward the silver man, who nodded respectfully. "Mudai is fairly awed by your collection of materials and tools. I've never seen him so excited. He would be most interested in speaking to you about its contents, and even more interested in working alongside the woman who uses them all." Caleria's voice softened. "I myself would welcome you to our community. Will you ply your skills as a maker for Argenti, or will they die alongside Umezawa?"

"Lady," Ayesha said, "with respect, I am a breaker, not a maker. But allow me to save us all some time. I have sworn an oath to the empire and the champion, but I am also master to the youth your druids seek to help."

"The stricken boy is your student?"

"Yes, Lady. As of now, my responsibility to him takes precedence over all. Help him, and I will gladly serve you."

"Hey!" Tor yelled, but the soldiers behind him quickly pinned his arms and dragged him back.

Caleria stroked her chin thoughtfully. "An interesting proposition . . . one we should discuss further." She looked up at the guards holding Tor and jerked her head to the door. The guards manhandled the struggling archer out of the room.

The last thing Tor heard before he was swept out of earshot was Caleria's voice saying, "Tell me about your student's illness. . . ."

Minutes later, Tor was alone in a small stone cell halfway up the central tower. He paced around the cell for a while, tried to force himself out the tiny window, then sat cross-legged on the straw mat.

After a long and fruitless attempt at meditation, Tor slumped with his back against the stone wall and waited. He didn't know which would happen first, but he was sure that before too much longer, either Tetsuo would come to rescue him or armored guards would come to kill him.

As had been the case in Sekana not two weeks earlier, the situation in Argenti had passed far beyond the mental and physical abilities of the champion's second.

CHAPTER 22

Tetsuo walked alone on his path. The way was rough and uneven, mostly uphill. He had no sandals. He had no weapons. He had only his robes and his skills as he pressed onward.

The journey had become very dark for Tetsuo, but the skies overhead were at last starting to lighten. He couldn't clearly see the landscape around him, and he didn't recognize what he saw. Nonetheless, he knew he was far from his goal and he had to keep moving if he ever wanted to get there.

A sick and spindly tree rose out of the beige road ahead, in the direct center of the path. The tree had no leaves, and a huge wasp's nest occupied most of its upper branches. Tetsuo walked straight up to the buzzing hive, ignoring the angry insects that flew at his face and circled his head. He reached for his sword, but his hand closed on the empty scabbard. Tetsuo paused a moment then plunged his bare hands through the papery nest and opened it up like a huge oyster.

The wasps inside swarmed up Tetsuo's arms and viciously stung him repeatedly from fingers to biceps. The pain was bad, but he ignored it. Tetsuo leaned forward and peered into the nest.

At the center of the vibrating mass of insects sat a lone queen, far larger than her subjects and bound in place by her own ponderous bulk. The entire hive was constructed around her, the center of the hive's little universe. Tetsuo brushed stinging wasps from his face and stared closely at the queen, who had golden skin and a humanoid body from the waist up.

From her tiny throne in the center of the hive, Xira Arien buzzed angrily at Tetsuo.

The champion's eyes darted to the countless wasps encircling him. They all had similar human body structures, and each angry insect face was snow-white. Tetsuo's stomach went cold as he looked at the dozens of crushed wasps on his robes and on the ground, tiny insect Keis now broken and twisted. Their ichor coated his hands and face.

Tetsuo stepped around the scrawny tree and walked on. Soon the buzzing of the wasps had died away behind him, and the pain from the stings started to fade.

Another tree materialized on the path, this one large and sturdy. It was twisted and black like the first tree, stripped of all leaves, blooms, and buds. A man hung nailed to the tree through both hands and both feet. Scavengers had been at the body, birds and vermin alike, and most of the exposed skin on the arms and around the face was torn and stripped away. There was a red headband around the nearly naked skull, and the figure wore a leather breastplate with red leather gloves. Wedged into the branches above the body was Tetsuo's own bow.

"Tor," Tetsuo whispered. He reached out to touch his student's cheek. Before his fingers made contact, the ravaged head twitched and opened its eyes.

"Ready for action, Master." Tor's eye sockets were filled with blood, which ran down his ravaged cheeks like tears. "You've led me this far. Where to next?" Tor threw his head back, smacking it hard into the trunk of the tree, and laughed insanely.

Shaken, Tetsuo gently took the bow down and turned away. Soon Tor's laughter became so faint the champion couldn't hear it, and he did not look back.

Tetsuo walked on until he heard the gentle burbling of a stream. Up ahead he saw a simple wooden bridge made of lashed logs. The bridge spanned a fast-moving brook, and a burly, broad-shouldered figure loitered on the far side.

"What a mess, eh?" Lord Dark walked to the center of the log bridge. "A bow with no quarrels, a sheath with no sword. The children who rely on you tortured, murdered, transformed." The assassin smiled. "Don't let me keep you. By all means, stay on your path."

Tetsuo stepped up to the little bridge but did not set foot on it.

"Where have you been, Champion? I've been waiting for a very long time. What else do you think has happened while you've been away?"

Tetsuo did not answer, but he took a single step onto the log bridge. Dark's smile held, but he took a surreptitious step back.

"Let's not get excited now," Dark said. "I'm merely a schemer. Certainly no threat to a warrior like you."

Tetsuo held his ground. "There are graveyards in Madara full of great warriors who thought you were 'merely a schemer.' "

Dark smiled winningly. "Was that a compliment?"

Tetsuo slowly shook his head. "I will listen to no more of this. Stand aside or fight me."

"Oh, I'll stand aside, by all means. I told you I didn't want to keep you."

"And I told you to stand aside." Tetsuo took a step forward, and Dark took another step back.

"Very well, but I did want to warn you about what you'll see on the road ahead." He nodded his head at the path behind Tetsuo. "The wasps and the crucified child? Just the beginning. Ahead, things get much, much worse."

Tetsuo took another step, but this time Dark held his ground. They were now a single pace from each other, Tetsuo on the edge of the bridge and Dark on the stony path.

"I won't lie to you, Champion." Dark's smile hardened, and the look of malevolent glee in his eyes became something far darker. "I'm here to watch you suffer. You have lost, you know. Soon your second will be dead and your healer-in-training will work for me. That's not even the best part. The people you tried to spare? Caleria, Magnus, and Gosta? All will be dead within a day, and you, their would-be savior, will take the blame.

"You'll be dead by then, too, of course, but your name and reputation will live on forever, a defender of the emperor's honor who couldn't even defend himself. A champion who fell in battle, betrayed those he had sworn to protect, and led his followers into useless, ugly, and painful death." All the humor had drained out of Dark's tone, and he now spat the words at Tetsuo.

"Your failure is complete. Your life, your status, your very honor will be stripped from you and dragged through the sewer. You will travel the road to death and ignominy knowing that it was your own stubborn pride and bad judgment that led you there."

Tetsuo maintained his outer appearance of calm, but he crossed the last foot of space between himself and Lord Dark and drove the heel of his hand into the master assassin's nose. The hand passed through Dark without resistance. Tetsuo blinked, and when he opened his eyes, his target was gone.

"Always looking for a fight." Dark's voice boomed from the air around Tetsuo. "That's the real difference between us, isn't it? Assassins try to avoid conflicts before they start. You provoke them everywhere you go."

Tetsuo ignored Dark and stepped completely off the bridge. After a dozen paces, the sound of the stream fell away.

"Remember what I told you," Dark's voice began to fade, too. "Up ahead, it only gets worse."

Tetsuo walked on. The path remained featureless for quite some time, and the champion lost himself in the rhythm of his stride. Left, right, left, right. The bow bounced slightly on his shoulder, and the empty scabbard mocked him.

Tetsuo came on a room without walls. It was set up alongside the path ahead, with torches, benches, tapestries, and people, but no walls or ceilings. There was a tall throne at the far end, and Tetsuo recognized it as Caleria's. The entire area was a close approximation of Caleria's great hall, right down to the armored guards standing along what should have been a white stone wall.

Caleria herself stood halfway down the steps leading to her throne. She watched the animated discussion between a silver-skinned man and a dark-haired woman in imperial robes. They were rooting around in a great wheeled cart, removing strange items from inside, examining them, and putting them back. Tetsuo recognized Ayesha but not the stranger with whom she catalogued the contents of her barrow.

"As a girl, I was apprenticed to a Hyperion blacksmith," the armorer was saying. She held up a strange object that looked like a miniature temple with a glass ball at its center and frosted white gems over each stone column. "When I constructed this as my masterpiece, he acknowledged that he had no more to teach me."

Tetsuo had heard of the Hyperion smiths before, mostly

from Ayesha herself. They underwent a ritual that permanently encased them in an organic form of heat-resistant steel. This allowed them to work the forge in conditions that would kill a normal person. The champion moved closer to the open-air room, going to the very edge of the road.

"Remarkable," the silver man said. He turned the boxlike contraption over in his hands, then gently set it back in the barrow. "Not many artificers study the ways of Hyperion anymore." To Caleria, he added, "His way was to test things by subjecting them to the most extreme use conditions, and then rebuild them to withstand those conditions."

"I am a breaker, as I said." Ayesha gently closed the barrow. "You can't armor the champion unless you know exactly how much punishment his equipment can take. And dish out.

"On to my proposal." Ayesha turned to Caleria standing above. "I need a cure for my stricken student. If you can provide a cure, then we can come to an arrangement."

Caleria shrugged. "As I said, I know of no way to help your boy."

"Magnus might," Ayesha said, "and Kei said there was knowledge hidden in the forest. Perhaps we can look there?"

Caleria looked decidedly uncomfortable as Ayesha mentioned the forest, but she kept her voice neutral. "We will have to ask Lord Magnus about that."

Ayesha smiled. "So, you don't believe he died, either. I wondered why you weren't grieving or at least searching for his body."

Caleria remained silent, offering nothing.

Ayesha offered her wrists to the Argenti ruler. "You should bind me and put me in a cell, Lady. At least until we hear from Lord Magnus. I will join you, and renounce the empire, but not until I have done right by my student."

Tetsuo's heart fell at Ayesha's words. From behind him a wind puffed along the stony ground, but to the champion it sounded like laughter from the lips of the master assassin.

Caleria waved Ayesha's wrists away. "There's no need for that. Stay and talk shop with my smithy. When Magnus returns, he will come here." A flicker of suspicion crossed Caleria's face, and she added, "You have no regrets about abandoning Tetsuo and the archer?"

"The champion has led us into one death trap after another," Ayesha said, cold anger coloring her words. "And his second follows him like an eager dog, never questioning. I will not allow my student or me to suffer anymore on account of Tetsuo's peculiar brand of honor."

The laughing wind grew stronger, and the open-air room receded into the haze. Tetsuo watched it fade for a few moments then angrily turned and resumed his trek.

"I did warn you," Dark's voice was on the wind, hissing, mocking, sneering in Tetsuo's ears. "You've been working with the armorer for what, eight years? And she turns on you simply because you doomed her student and repeatedly led her into mortal danger. There's no pleasing some people." Dark's voice clicked suspiciously. "She seems to have become awfully friendly with that blacksmith in an awfully short time, doesn't she?"

In the distance, Tetsuo saw the sky brighten as if the sun were just rising over the horizon. He maintained his steady pace, striding purposefully to the light.

"If only you had your weapons," Dark's voice went on. "Surely an army of well-trained soldiers and savage beasts poses no problems for the emperor's champion."

The sky grew brighter. It was not the sun that chased away the haze but something on the road itself. A huge ball of light sat at the top of the next rise.

Dark raved on. "I'd bet that you can defeat the whole lot even without your sword. So what if Caleria has a protection spell? You're the most dangerous man in the empire! You haven't lost so much as a coin toss since you earned your position. The champion always prevails; even I know that. There is no middle ground for a man like you. It's either honorable victory or honorable death. That's one of the things I like so much about you, Tetsuo. You make everything so simple."

Tetsuo approached the edge of the mass of light. He could not see into it, but he felt it pulling him in. All he had to do was step forward. . . .

Instead, the champion turned and looked back along the road. Slowly, he lifted the bow he had taken and let it clatter to the ground. Then he retied the sash of his robe so that the phoenix standard was clearly visible over his right breast. He raised his head to the sky.

"When this is over," Tetsuo's voice thundered out of his chest, filling the air with sound, "I will come for you, Lord Dark. As you have lived, so shall you die: disgraced and alone."

Without waiting for a reply, Tetsuo turned and plunged into the light.

* * * * *

Tor heard the ruckus on the tower stairs and leaped up from his mat. He went to the small window cut into his cell door and wedged his face into it, but all he could see was an empty hall.

Voices rose in pain and called for assistance. Wood splintered, and steel scraped on stone. A burning smell wafted in the air, and the hairs on his neck stood up.

There was a final, panicked yelp, and the wooden door leading to Tor's level of the tower exploded inward in a great flash of yellow flames and red light.

Tetsuo Umezawa came through the doorway, his hands empty but wreathed in arcane energy. The champion's green eyes glowed intensely, his expression severe. The lone sentry guarding Tor drew his short sword and charged Tetsuo. The champion ignored the downward flashing blade and drove his glowing fist into the man's chest.

With his face wedged in the window, Tor could not follow the flight of the sentry as Tetsuo's blow hurled him backward the length of the hallway. The champion stormed up to Tor's cell, his eyes still gleaming, and he nodded at his second.

"Stand back," he said. Tor popped his face clear and dropped into a crouch alongside the doorway. There was another burst of light and flames. The heavy cell door flew off its hinges and slammed into the far wall of the cell.

Standing above, Tetsuo offered Tor a glowing hand. Tor took it, and the champion pulled him to his feet.

"I'm awake now," Tetsuo said. "The armorer has bought us some time." He was already looking back at the staircase. "Let's not waste it."

Tor's voice caught in his throat, and he struggled to work it free. He could hear dozens of running armored feet and the shouts of soldiers being deployed. Tetsuo bore neither sword nor scabbard. It would be the two of them, alone and unarmed against all of Caleria's castle guards, with a major protection spell potentially canceling their every blow.

Tor grinned and cracked his knuckles. "Ready when you are, Master."

CHAPTER 23

23 Invisible behind her magical camouflage, Xira Arien clung patiently to the exterior of the castle and waited. Below her in the courtyard, a platoon of armored soldiers marched double time into the prison tower where the champion and his second were being held. This was the second platoon to pile into the tower.

Shortly after the first had entered, Xira heard the sounds of battle, then all had gone eerily quiet. The second wave of expendables tramped up the stairs toward a similar defeat.

None of the soldiers had even looked up as they crossed the courtyard, but Xira still waited until the last man had gone inside before she moved. In short, choppy bursts of motion, she skittered headfirst down the smooth stone wall, constantly pausing to make sure she remained unnoticed. When she was roughly halfway down, she stopped to listen. Two pairs of sandaled feet were quietly rushing down the stairs inside. Xira froze and faded back into invisibility against the tower.

Tetsuo and Tor ran out into the courtyard. The archer scanned the courtyard and the battlements, but the champion barely paused at all before tearing up the stairs to the castle's main entrance. A cry of alarm sounded from the sentries on the exterior wall, and the archer turned and disappeared inside after his master.

Xira paused. It would be extremely dangerous for her inside the castle, or she would have grabbed the two-legged cocoon that housed her offspring and made off with him. She could feel the larva developing, calling to her, eager to be reunited with its dam. Xira wanted to be there when it burst forth, all wet and new and eager to imprint on a mature mother figure.

She cursed Tetsuo's stubbornness. If the champion had simply accepted his defeat, Xira would have had no worries. As it was, he seemed determined to get himself and his entire entourage killed in the most inconvenient time and place possible.

My lord, she thought, *I am reporting from Argenti. The champion has escaped, and he is in the process of rescuing his people. What is your will?*

After a brief pause, Dark's angry tone rang in Xira's ears. *I know the champion has escaped. Who do you think goaded him into it? I'm more concerned about your interference spoiling my plans.*

I don't understand, my lord. You said—

I said you could suit yourself as long as you stayed out of sight and were here when I expected you.

But—

Do nothing but observe. Nothing. Dark's voice left no room for further negotiation. *The champion exhausted himself against Orca. Between Caleria's troops and the surprise we have in store, there is no way he can survive the next few hours. You must learn when to step back and trust my leadership, Xira. I have prepared for everything. Now . . . have I made myself clear?*

I understand, my lord.

Confirm your instructions.

Continue to observe. Do nothing else. Confirmed.

Xira waited several moments then cursed Lord Dark. He liked to pretend that he had everything under control, and the irritating fact was that he often did.

There was a small explosion from inside the castle. Xira scanned the courtyard below with her multiple eyes before skittering back up the tower.

She could do as Lord Dark commanded: observe as Tetsuo challenged Caleria and fell. At some point before, during, or after his demise, there would surely be an opportunity to collect her property and hide it away from Lord Dark until she needed it.

* * * * *

Tor finally caught up to Tetsuo after the champion battered down the doors to Caleria's great hall. The archer had taken a bow and quiver off of a fallen soldier, and he quickly loaded another arrow as he came up alongside the champion.

Tetsuo was still empty-handed but perhaps was more dangerous unarmed. Instead of graceful, flowing streams of light from his blade, Tetsuo produced short, sharp blasts of fire and brute force from his bare hands. The champion's expression and demeanor had the same smooth composure as always, but he seemed even more intense than usual, more emotional and focused.

The two imperial warriors nodded then swept into the room.

Inside, Ayesha and the silver man were standing over the armorer's barrow at the foot of Caleria's throne. The lady herself stood as she aimed at the escapees.

"You're too late, Champion. Your healer and your armorer have both accepted my offer of employment."

Ayesha and Tetsuo calmly met each other's eyes.

"Stand back!" Caleria cried out to the soldiers approaching Tetsuo. In that moment, Tor fired first, hoping to catch Caleria on the bow arm. The Argenti noble sneered and let her shaft fly, flashing her eyes at the incoming bolt. Tor's arrow struck an irregular circle of white instead of Caleria's shoulder and fell harmlessly to the ground.

Ayesha yelled a warning as Caleria's arrow flew at Tetsuo. Tetsuo held his position for a split second then struck the incoming bolt head-on with the tips of his fingers. The arrowhead exploded on contact, and the wooden shaft fell splintered to the floor.

Tetsuo crossed one arm over his chest and held the other out in front of Tor to keep the archer from firing. "Lady Caleria," he said, "let us end this. Quickly."

"By all means," Caleria said darkly. "You and your second fall down on your knees right now, and I won't have you riddled with spears where you stand."

Tetsuo actually smiled. "I was thinking more along the lines of you and I settling it ourselves." He pulled the jade phoenix talisman from around his neck and sent it skidding across the floor. "I challenge you to a duel, Lady."

"And I refuse. What benefit to me, if I give you a fair fight? I've won a dozen campaigns against whole armies and defeated a hundred foes in personal combat. I did not do so by accepting their rules of engagement. You came to Argenti, and you shall fight by my rules." She flashed her eyes at Tetsuo for emphasis.

Tetsuo replied with a flash of darkness from his own eyes. "I have resources of my own, Lady, as effective as your prevention field. Shall we both cast defensive spells at one another until Lord Dark figures out a way to kill us all at once?"

Caleria shook her head. "I told you before, imperial. Argenti produces white mana, and white mana in turn protects Argenti." She raised another arrow. "I will pit my spells against yours any day. You will exhaust your resources long before I do.

"Lady." Ayesha spoke from the side of the barrow. "It's time for you to decide. Will you help my student and accept my services?"

"Silence." Caleria's eyes didn't even flicker, and she kept the tip of her arrow pointed at Tetsuo.

"I must know your answer."

"By the light, be silent and keep clear! This is not the time for—"

Caleria's words were interrupted by a metallic rasp of razor steel and a strangled yelp from the blacksmith. Tor's eyes darted to the sound, then to Caleria, and back to Tetsuo.

Ayesha had the blacksmith pinned against the barrow, a long, sharp metal tool held against his jugular vein. The silver man's eyes were wide and terrified, and Tor thought he saw a sheen of sweat break out across his silver forehead.

"My barrow is deeper than it appears," Ayesha said calmly, answering the question in Caleria's eyes. "Now, I must tell you, Lady, that if you can't commit to curing Kei, I feel it would be in my student's best interest for us both to stay with Umezawa."

"I approached you in good faith," Caleria hissed. "You're no better than the insect."

Ayesha shrugged. "Not at all. Either the situation has changed, or my mind has. Whichever way you care to see it, I am still placing my students above all else." With the tip of her long metal punch, she prodded the blacksmith's throat.

"You're with me, smithy. Place both hands on the barrow and start moving it slowly toward the champion."

Mudai the blacksmith whimpered. "But we are both students of Hyperion."

Ayesha nodded. "I forgot to mention: I created my Hyperion masterpiece when I was eleven years old. Your school was a fine way for me to begin my training, but I have since moved past it." She prodded the blacksmith again, and they continued to move across the floor.

"Stop."

"Keep moving. This needle is the only master you have right now."

Tor licked his lips as the barrow inched closer. Caleria's facial muscles throbbed under her ebony skin. He did not envy Caleria. With Magnus missing, she was all that stood between the empire and the denizens of Argenti. She had hundreds of armored soldiers, but in these close quarters superior numbers were more of a handicap than an advantage. Tetsuo had defeated both Kasimir and Orca, and for all Caleria knew, the champion had been the one who had interrupted her protection spell earlier.

"Umezawa." When Caleria finally spoke, her voice was low and stern. "Call off your she-wolf. Let us discuss the terms of your duel."

* * * * *

My lord, Xira's voice chimed.

Lord Dark did not look up from his meditation mat in his private study. *Go ahead.*

I stand amazed, my lord. The champion has convinced Caleria to fight him in a duel.

Then she is far more stupid than I thought. Umezawa is invincible in such circumstances.

So I am told. Shall I—

Do nothing, Xira. I shall handle it from here.

But I could—

Sit back, watch closely, and learn. Dark broke the connection and rose to his feet. He considered climbing back to the western tower again but decided it wasn't necessary. Everything he needed was right here.

Lord Dark spread his arms wide, his fists tightly clenched. Once more, his mind turned inward as he called up a lifetime of memories from the swamps around his keep. He drew on his experiences with the Suido River, which flowed south to the imperial shrine. He mentally took hold of each square foot of sodden marshland and salt-crusted shoreline in the northern quadrant of Madara, the whole of his personal dominion. Mana churned within the land and created a sympathetic motion inside Dark's mind. Properly focused, this ocean of energy would create an irresistible wave of power. Dark summoned that wave and held it ready with the power of his will.

Then he reached out to the device Xira had concealed in Caleria's castle. It had many names in many different regions, but ever since Devilboon's proclamation Dark had been thinking of the device by its original name, the serpent generator.

A connection sparked between Dark and the device. The mana Dark had gathered flowed from Madara, through him, to the serpent generator so far away. Once the links were firmly in place and the power flowed smoothly, Dark reached out and with the merest mental nudge, activated the machine.

In a ceiling corner of a white stone hallway, hidden inside

a bubble of invisibility, the device responded. Eerie yellow lights flickered and cast pale shadows on the walls below. The machine whirred softly, and a metallic gray head poked out of the end opposite the earlike funnel. The head was roughly triangular and about two inches across. A forked pink tongue lashed the air, and then the first four-foot snake slithered whole and complete out of the machine. Its tail was scarcely clear of the cylinder before the next head appeared. A third head crowded the second metallic snake before it could slither free, and then came a fourth. And a fifth. Snakes started pouring from the machine into the castle like water into a sinking ship.

In his private study hundreds of miles away, Lord Dark raised his clenched fists high and roared in triumph.

* * * * *

"This is a simple matter," Tetsuo said. "You and I will engage. If you win, we surrender to your judgment. If I win, you grant us safe passage through the forest and back to Madara."

Ayesha stole a glance at Tor, and the archer nodded. "Through the forest" meant that they would go past the secret stand of trees and investigate it.

The champion's voice took on a tone of urgency. "We must hurry," Tetsuo said. He glanced over his shoulder into the depths of the castle and said, "We haven't much time."

Caleria came down from her throne and stopped on the final stair. "I will not be rushed, imperial. Before anything else happens, I demand that you release my smithy."

Ayesha looked to Tetsuo, and the champion nodded. Slowly, the armorer withdrew the metal punch and bowed lightly to the blacksmith. Mudai returned the perfunctory bow and walked back to Caleria.

The champion waited until Ayesha moved beside him then spoke to Caleria. "We can begin anytime."

Caleria's face curled in suspicion. "You don't want your weapons back? Or any weapons at all?"

Tetsuo shook his head. "I am ready."

Caleria slipped her bow over her shoulder. "So it's to be magic, then? And your first spell will be the one that interferes with my protective barrier."

Tetsuo did not change his stance. "I am ready," he repeated.

Caleria smiled. "Done."

Tor leaned closer to the champion. "She's not going to let any of us live," he whispered. "Even if you win, her troops will cut us to pieces."

Tetsuo glanced at the archer. "Stand ready, Second."

Caleria stepped down onto the floor. She waved her hand, and the soldiers nearest the heavy wooden doors swung them shut and bolted them with a heavy beam.

"Begin," she said.

As soon as the word left her mouth, Caleria lunged forward and slammed her wrists together, her palms out and her fingers hooked into claws. A corkscrew beam of energy spiraled out of her hands and streaked across the room at Tetsuo.

The champion watched the beam but did not move away. Instead, he crossed his flattened hands over his chest and took the beam full in the chest.

A cheer rose from the assembled troops as the champion became engulfed in a blinding flash of white light. The cheer turned into startled shouts as the corkscrew beam suddenly reappeared in the air between Tetsuo and Caleria and slammed into the stone floor so hard that the walls shook.

Unharmed, Tetsuo maintained his stance and his position on the floor. Then he lashed out with his right hand, and five small fireballs leaped forward, one from each finger. The fireballs did not fly true but wove and spiraled like frightened birds.

Caleria didn't even try to follow their flight but simply waited until all the balls converged on her. Then her eyes flashed as each one impacted, to no effect.

Caleria drew her hand back, but before she could cast a new spell, Tetsuo released five more fireballs with his left hand then five more with his right. The huntress abandoned her own casting and quickly stopped each of the ten fireballs in midair, one after the other. Caleria loaded her bow and fired, but the champion's eyes blazed, and the arrow burst into flame a foot away his face.

Sparks flew from Tetsuo's hands and feet. These sparks ballooned into fist-sized balls of fire that orbited Tetsuo. They shot forward, each following a different path toward the Argenti noble.

Caleria's hands were poised to extinguish the potential threat, but before they could, twin beams of scintillating blue light stabbed out of Tetsuo's eyes into hers. The fireballs converged on her, exploding. Caleria was not dismembered or even burned by the impacts, but she did scream and convulse.

The blue lines connecting her to Tetsuo did not break. Power churned back and forth along the mystic link between the two warriors. Tetsuo seemed to grow larger, and his body glowed with a bluish-white aura. Caleria's breath and legs both faltered, and the lower she sank, the brighter Tetsuo glowed.

Abruptly, Tetsuo severed the link and let Caleria drop to the floor. The Argenti noble seemed humbled but not defeated, and she spat curses at Tetsuo as she tried to get back to her feet.

Tetsuo called out to his opponent. His body was almost too bright to look at, and his voice sounded very far away, as if he were speaking through a dream. "Your protective barrier is intact," Tetsuo said, "but I have drained away the mana you use to power it."

"Bastard," Caleria husked.

Just then, something heavy crashed into the closed and barred door. The hardwood bulged and creaked so loudly that even Tetsuo turned at the sound. A hairline crack formed in the center of the door, and metal scraped angrily on stone.

"Another of your tricks, Champion?" Caleria's eyes were wild, and she fumbled with her bow.

Tetsuo did not take his eyes off the door. "I fear not," he said, his voice distant and wistful.

The door burst with a deafening crack. The soldiers nearest to it were swatted aside by the thick wooden planks like flies by a horse's tail. Those who remained found themselves buried under an avalanche of squirming metal bodies.

Tor had a split second to register that the new arrival was not a single huge creature but a multitude of gray metal serpents. They poured into the room like a river, and Tor could see them stretching out into the corridor, filling it.

Caleria sputtered and tried to summon the energy to protect herself and her troops. The soldiers spread out to either side of the serpent tide, trying vainly to keep them contained and out of the room. The mechanical snakes raised a cacophony of metallic clinks and terrible, alien hissing.

At the center of the chaos stood Tetsuo Umezawa with an expression of cold determination. "Lord Dark reveals his final card."

The tide of snakes surged and carried Caleria's bravest into the room like petals on a storm-tossed sea.

CHAPTER 24

Tetsuo's face was wreathed in bright light as he confronted the oncoming wall of serpents. The air around him hummed. Tor shared Tetsuo's view of the avalanche headed straight for them.

"Stand behind me, Tor." Tetsuo's voice sounded like a fading echo of itself, but Tor lost no time in responding. He sprang behind Tetsuo and continued to backpedal until he bumped up against Ayesha's barrow.

The champion spread his arms, tensed the muscles in his back and shoulders, and brought his hands together with a sharp clap.

Tor choked as Ayesha's hand snatched him by the collar and hauled him backward over the heavy cart. She pulled him down to the floor behind the barrow, where she herself crouched.

Tor furiously wrestled loose from Ayesha and tried to stand. "I'm the second!" he hissed.

Ayesha merely yanked his collar into his throat again. As Tor's face sank below the top of the barrow, Tetsuo finally drew his hands apart.

There was light between champion's palms, and the wider he spread them, the brighter it got.

Tor realized what was happening and stopped resisting Ayesha. She dragged him down again as the light between Tetsuo's hands exploded and the very air went dazzlingly blue.

Safe in the shadow of the barrow, Tor and Ayesha watched the bright blue light fill the room. After the initial flash, the walls glowed with reflected energy. For a second, everything was frozen stiff and silent, then all the soldiers staggered and fell gracelessly to the floor.

Tor's eyes darted from rattling pikes to rolling helmets as clattering sounds reverberated through the room. Ayesha turned him loose, and he quickly pulled himself up on the barrow and peeked over the top.

Tetsuo stood at the center of a metallic spiral of humans and serpents. He was no longer glowing. Several of the snakes still twitched and wriggled their tails, and farther up the corridor, more snakes pressed over the bodies of the first wave. The only thing left standing near the door was the champion.

The flash of light had gone off in all directions, and most of Caleria's troops lay facedown and helpless throughout the room. Caleria herself and half a dozen of her soldiers had taken refuge on her throne and the steps that led to it. Tor suspected that the chair was enchanted to provide some measure of protection beyond even Caleria's barrier.

Tor quickly ran to Tetsuo and scooped up one of the metallic snakes. It was cold and motionless but not dead. It had never been alive. The snake did not just have metallic scales; it was made entirely out of metal.

"Armorer," he called back to Ayesha by her barrow, "it's some sort of machine." Tor threw the quiescent device into her waiting hands.

Ayesha scanned the snake from head to tail. "Definitely an artifact, but I don't see any rivets or welding."

"Whatever they are," Tetsuo said, and his voice had also returned to normal, "they are not made of colored mana. So they will be unaffected by Caleria's protection spell. Lord Dark has unleashed a weapon that can kill us all, even here." Tetsuo pointed to Ayesha's hands. "And that one is only stunned."

Tor stepped back from the pile of motionless snakes just as the one he had given to Ayesha sailed high over his head to the back of the mound.

"If these are constructs—" Ayesha approached Tetsuo and Tor—"something must be constructing them. Some kind of portal device, or a miniature snake factory. . . . If we back-track along the trail of serpents, we should be able to find this thing and shut it off."

Tetsuo grimaced. "We may have a great deal of trouble shutting it off, even if we can find it and fight our way to it."

"I can do it." Ayesha's voice had the pure, flat confidence of experience. "Easily. It's what I do. I've got things in my barrow that could—"

"We need to go light and fast, armorer. Can you do it with your bare hands?"

Ayesha almost smirked. "Even easier."

"You are not going anywhere, Champion." Caleria had come down off her throne. She had an arrow nocked and all six of her conscious soldiers at her back. "Our duel isn't finished." Caleria looked strained, but her voice was strong, and her hands were steady.

Tetsuo regarded Caleria coolly then glanced back at Tor. "Forgive me, Lady," he said, "but I am unavoidably called away. However," with a sweeping wave of his arm, he presented Tor to Caleria, "my second is right here."

"What?" Tor laughed, but it turned into a strangled choke when saw no one else was even smiling. "Wait. What?"

Tetsuo's voice came low and stern. "You must assume my role against Caleria. If Ayesha and I can't shut off the snake machine, we'll all be dead, and Lord Dark will have his way in the Edemis and Madara alike."

Tor looked into the champion's eyes. Tetsuo was right: This was the essence of his role as second. This was what he had been training for.

"You two go," Tor said. He hooked a thumb over his shoulder at Caleria, wishing his smile didn't feel so weak and panicky. "I'll handle this."

Tetsuo lifted his head. "Ayesha?"

"Ready."

"Champion!" Caleria yelled. "My fight is with you."

Tetsuo pointed at Tor. "Now it is with him." He took off over the mound of motionless snakes, Ayesha following close behind.

Caleria howled in fury and fired. Her arrow shattered and fell, however, as Tor split it in midair with a shot from his own bow.

"I am Tor Wauki," he said, and his voice sounded strong and powerful off the stone walls. He squared his stance, faced the throne, and put the doorway squarely at his back. "I represent the imperial champion." He nocked another arrow onto his bow.

Caleria glared at Tor with cold disdain. She raised two fingers alongside her face and chopped the air beside her.

"Kill him," she said, and all six soldiers drew their swords. "Then find his master and drag him back here to finish what he started."

The soldiers marched forward, and Caleria nocked another arrow onto her bow.

Tor braced himself and prepared to fight. He had seven targets and seven arrows. He fought alone, with only his speed and a thin layer of red leather to protect him from his enemies' swords.

Tor smiled. Tetsuo had never even hesitated. He had turned to Tor and told him to step up, as if it were the most natural thing in the world—as if there were no cause at all for concern.

The Argenti bow he had appropriated felt sturdy in his hands. The archer's song occurred to him again, but he drew back the bow and fired before the tune could get stuck in his head.

No time for songs. He had work to do.

* * * * *

Tetsuo unleashed a blast of fire at the edge of his stun spell's radius, where the mass of stalled serpents ended and a fresh wave of wriggling snakes crested. The flames cleared enough space for Tetsuo and Ayesha to advance another few feet, but then they were right back in the same dire situation: surrounded, tiring, and slowly being overwhelmed.

"This is taking too long," Tetsuo said as he rotated his hands and sent a corrosive jag of black lightning through the mass of mechanical snakes.

Ayesha had seized a curved Argenti sword in either hand and used them to beat the snakes back. "Agreed," she said. "We need to kill more of them faster or find another route."

Tetsuo locked his fingers and aimed a freezing blast of ice onto the serpents before him. He saw a heavy wooden door nearby. "Or another destination," he said.

Tetsuo stunned a tangle of snakes with a smaller version of the spell he had cast in the throne room. He motioned for Ayesha to follow, and the two of them quickly forced their way through the door and slammed it shut behind them.

"Okay, we're safe for the short term." Ayesha had shot the bolts and placed the bar across the door, and now she inspected them for signs of weakness. "But what are we doing here? I need to know where the device is before I can neutralize it."

Tetsuo nodded thoughtfully. "Do you need to see it?"

"No. If I knew it was on the other side of this door, for example, I could affect it."

"Good." Tetsuo closed his eyes, and as he gracefully folded his legs beneath him, he reached out and took the sword from Ayesha's hand. He dropped the blade and clamped his iron fingers around hers. "Keep your eyes on the door, and don't let go of my hand."

Tetsuo fell into a rhythmic chant and felt the room around him fade.

* * * * *

Tor's first arrow skewered the lead soldier's foot and stuck, quivering, in his boot. At this range, with Tor's muscle behind it, the arrow punched straight through the soldier's armor. The stricken man howled and fell, almost tripping the soldier to his left.

Caleria barked more furious orders, and Tor guessed that she had not yet recovered from the mana drain Tetsuo had performed. Her protective barrier was still tactically useless.

Before, during, and after each of his shots, Tor ran in the strange serpentine pattern he had mastered to frustrate his enemies' aim. He had another arrow ready on the bowstring and carefully kept clear of the soldiers' slashing blades as they tried to surround him and corner him against the stone wall.

Tor reached with his mind back to Tetsuo's manor on Madara, where Tor had lived since he was a small boy. Tetsuo's sprawling compound was nestled between the southern tip of the Gitte-Yatay Mountains and the great salt flats that covered the western portion of the empire.

Tor's personal record was six arrows in the air at once, but that had been on an open field with much more room between him and his enemies. Here, Tor charged four of the Argenti arrowheads with mana from the mountains and sent them in a single extended volley over the heads of his foes.

The five remaining soldiers ducked easily under the attack, but Tor exploded all four arrowheads directly over them and unleashed multiple streams of fire. The streams overlapped and crisscrossed each other, their flames lingering in the air. The matrix descended on the soldiers like a great fiery net.

Tor gritted his teeth and fought to keep the magical construct together. Instability threatened to disrupt the hot streams of energy he had created. One of the soldiers rolled out from under the net, and Tor quickly shot him in the leg.

The edges of the net settled onto the floor, creating a rounded cage of flame with four of the soldiers inside. One struck at the flames with his sword.

Tor and Caleria both cried, "Wait!"

As soon as the edge of the blade touched the flames, the entire construct exploded into a wide sheet of fire. It scorched the floor, the ceiling, and the walls on either side of the room.

In the wake of the blast, thick curls of black smoke rose from two soldiers lying motionless on the floor. The remaining two screamed as they tried to shuck the red-hot armor covering their bodies.

Tor fired his last arrow at Caleria, who was taking aim at him with her own bow. Tor's shot spoiled hers, but it did not hit its target. He slung his bow over his shoulder and charged the flailing soldiers before their ruler could load another bolt.

Tor was out of arrows, but the two soldiers were now un-armored. He drew on years of hand-to-hand combat training under the imperial champion, planted his left foot, and with a wide round kick sent the first soldier's teeth scattering across the floor. Tor spun and sank an elbow into the man's jaw and watched him drop.

The final soldier had made it out of the top half of his blistering armor and carefully approached Tor. Tor circled to keep the man between himself and Caleria while he waited for the soldier to strike.

He didn't wait long. The last soldier roared and swung his sword mightily overhead. Tor easily sidestepped the clumsy blow and leaped onto the soldier's back, wrapping his arms tightly around the man's sword arm and neck. Tor tightened his grip, jerked from his waist, and was rewarded by the clean crack of the man's collarbone. Tor dropped his opponent and sprang back, narrowly avoiding another arrow from Caleria's longbow.

Tor planted his feet in front of the doorway once more. All around him, the stunned soldiers and serpents were beginning to stir. Caleria trained the tip of her arrow on Tor's chest.

"Yield, Second," she said, "and I may yet spare you. You are defeated. Admit it."

Tor quickly scanned the room. Caleria was right. She had the long-range advantage, and she didn't even need to kill him. She simply needed to keep him away from her until enough of her troops awoke and pinned him to the floor through sheer weight of numbers.

The archer met Caleria's eyes over her shining steel arrowhead. He inhaled, forcing the air deeply in and then completely out of his lungs in one slow, metered breath. He winked at Caleria and started to step forward.

The lady did not give him a full pace. Tor's foot had barely left the ground when she released.

He crouched slightly to put his eyes on the same plane as the incoming arrow. He started the next metered breath, maintaining the relaxed rhythm he had established. Then with one hand, he caught the arrow two inches from his face.

Tor straightened, his right fist clenched just behind the arrowhead. He kept his eyes fixed on Caleria, twirled the arrow in his hand like a baton, and spiked it point-first into a seam between the stones in the floor.

"I can do this all day." He grinned. "Got anymore?"

Caleria roared a furious battle cry and charged, wildly firing arrow after arrow as she came. Even as the killing bolts streaked past him, Tor was impressed. She fired five arrows in three paces before the first shot even got close to him.

As she fired the fifth, however, Tor whipped the bow off his own shoulder, snatched up the arrow still quivering in the floor, and shot Caleria through the ribs.

CHAPTER 25

Alone, Lord Dark walked his own winding path. He allowed his mind to wander as he maintained a steady flow of mana to the serpent generator. The sheer volume of artifact snakes was enough to fill Caleria's castle. He expected to hear from Xira any moment now, and he expected he'd see his greatest rival one last time.

"Assassin." In Tetsuo's voice the word was more accusation than greeting. Through his mind's eye, Dark could see the path he was on and the nondescript countryside that surrounded it, but he did not see the champion.

"Champion." Dark's tone was winning and warm. "I hear you, but I can't see you. I'm sure I would have noticed if you'd been killed. Where are you hiding?"

Tetsuo did not appear, and Dark went on.

"Don't let me distract you. I'm sure you have your hands full. Has Caleria executed the archer and the armorer yet? Or has the lovely Ayesha actually betrayed you? In which case, I suspect you've already killed her yourself." In the silence between his own sentences, Dark felt the first grim stirring of doubt.

Tetsuo was clearly preparing some sort of last-ditch effort aimed at Dark himself. The assassin would not have challenged Tetsuo physically without careful preparation, but magically he knew himself to be at least the champion's

equal. He preferred to strike rather than counterstrike, however, and he walked very lightly through the landscape of his
mind.

"Lord Dark." Tetsuo's voice sounded farther away.

Dark looked up the road and finally saw the champion.
Tetsuo came over the rise of the next hill.

"Your device has malfunctioned," Tetsuo called as he approached. "It is poised to kill not only Caleria but everyone
inside her castle."

"Has it really? What a shame." Dark stood rock still as
Tetsuo came closer. "I'll be sure to have it recalibrated as
soon as I get it back."

"Quite an impressive machine." Tetsuo stopped roughly
ten yards away. In this vision, he wore both swords, and the
separate doubts in Dark's stomach began to knot themselves
together. "And quite an impressive effort. Aren't you in
danger of overtaxing yourself, manipulating mana on such a
grand scale?"

Dark realized what Tetsuo was up to, and the knot in his
stomach slipped apart. "Don't concern yourself," he said.
"Using the device is not nearly as much effort as fighting
what it creates."

Tetsuo stared hard at Dark. The assassin's eyes did not
waver, but a small smile curled on his lips.

"You don't know where it is, do you?"

Dark showed Tetsuo his teeth. "No, but by all means,
keep trying to get me to think about it. The longer you pick
my brain, the more serpents you'll have to play with." Dark
casually raised his head and scanned the sky above. "It's
nice and quiet here, isn't it? It's probably much noisier where
you are."

"I disagree," Tetsuo said. He too looked up, but he concentrated his gaze on the area just above Dark's head.

"There's a loud, constant hum in the air." With his finger, he traced a meandering line through the sky. "It seems to be coming from . . ." His finger lowered until it pointed straight at Dark's face. "It seems to be coming from you, Lord."

"Stop playing games." Dark did not like the turn the conversation had taken. "Your colleagues need your help. Have you found a cure for the healer yet? I'm told there is none. . . ."

Tetsuo paused for the briefest moment then continued tracing his finger through the sky to Dark's left. "I can see the hum starting in northern Madara . . ." he pointed again at Dark, "continuing on through you . . ." the finger continued to Dark's right, then wavered and came to a halt. "And then it stops. I wonder if I could follow it down to its final destination. . . ."

Tetsuo suddenly faced Dark, and the champion's eyes flashed blue fire. Surprised, Dark stepped back, but the flames were not an attack. They merely rose from Tetsuo's face and circled above his head.

The blue plasma drifted up and congealed, thickening and swirling over Tetsuo until it had become a small replica of a three-towered castle. Tetsuo guided the flaming image over to Dark's right, and it expanded as it floated, eventually becoming life-sized and sinking into the hills near the road.

Dark stared in confusion at the phantasmal castle, and when he turned back, he was face to face with Tetsuo.

The champion's green eyes were cold and hard. His voice had an edge, as if he had already lost his temper and merely sought a convenient target on which to vent it.

The champion leaned even closer. "Where is the serpent generator?"

Dark was unsettled by the champion's proximity but held his ground. As soon as the shock of Tetsuo's sudden approach faded, Dark snorted and let out a loud peal of laughter.

"I don't know, Champion." Dark howled the words into Tetsuo's face. "Were you not paying attention earlier? But then, I don't have to know where it is in order to use it." Dark composed himself, and his voice became low and menacing. "Is this how you die, Tetsuo? Beaten, desperate, and childishly clutching at the illusion of hope? What a disappointment you are."

Tetsuo's eyes flashed again, and he turned to Dark's right. He nodded and spoke to the sky. "Do you have it?"

In the distance behind Tetsuo, back on the road near the top of the hill, a woman stood. She cupped her hands to her mouth and yelled, "Ready."

Tetsuo held Dark's eyes for one last appraising stare, then he and the woman vanished.

Dark turned, and saw a visible line of force stretching from himself to the nebulous horizon.

Dark jerked his head to the phantom castle, which was slowly fading away. With a mounting sense of horror, Dark followed another spectral line of force that now visibly connected him to a point on the castle's western wall, near the very top of the structure.

Tetsuo had used the stream of mana flowing from Madara through Dark to pinpoint the serpent generator. No doubt he and his mechanical savant were already on their way to dismantle it.

As the full implications of Tetsuo's trick sank in and the ghostly castle disappeared, Lord Dark brutally ripped himself out of the meditation plane and opened his eyes inside his private study.

He sat there, glaring and motionless in fury, and waited for Xira to report.

* * * * *

Tetsuo's eyes snapped open, and he sprang to his feet. "Top of the western wall. Can you reach it from here?"

Ayesha stood ready by the door. "Too far away, but if we can get to the third floor, I'm sure that'll be close enough."

She touched the handle, but the door slammed tight in the jamb and bulged inward. The snakes had found them and were forcing their way in.

Tetsuo scanned the inside of the room and walked to the exterior wall. "Can you climb a wall?"

Ayesha flexed her thin but powerful fingers, each covered in thick calluses. "I can climb, yes."

The wooden door continued to bulge and creak. Tetsuo waved Ayesha behind him and stretched his hands toward the exterior wall. With a double blast of flames, he blew a room-sized hole in the wall. He knocked a few loose stones out and let them fall to the courtyard below, then he beckoned her over.

They climbed hand-and-foot along the huge stone blocks of the castle walls until they reached the parapet. Tetsuo helped Ayesha pull herself up and bowled three of Caleria's soldiers off the wall with a crashing wave of liquid blue energy. He and Ayesha sprinted to the west face of the castle, where the wall was attached to the great hall and its complex of corridors. They rounded the corner and continued on at a quick jog. As they went, Ayesha stared down at the west wall beneath their feet, her eyes darting back and forth.

Twenty yards from the northwest corner, Ayesha stopped. She fell to one knee, her palm flat on the parapet, then she slapped the stone.

"Here," she said. "About fifteen feet straight down."

Tetsuo jerked his face to the left then the right as armored soldiers charged them from both ends of the parapet. "Close enough?"

"Normally, yes. But that's fifteen feet of solid stone. I don't know if I can reach through all that mass."

Tetsuo stepped up to Ayesha and took both her hands. "Then we'll have to get you closer." He spared one last look at the closing soldiers and said, "This will be disorienting. Keep your eyes open and break the first thing you see that looks unusual."

Tetsuo whispered an incantation and blew lightly on Ayesha's forehead.

"What are you—" she started, but her voice faded to a whisper then to nothing as Ayesha and Tetsuo both transformed from flesh and blood to a thick, blue gas.

Their bodies retained their cohesion and their shape even as the soldiers hacked and stabbed at them with their pikes. The billowing form of Tetsuo nodded to Ayesha and quickly sank into the floor below their feet. Ayesha felt herself being pulled down after him, and she tried to take a deep breath before she too sank into the stones.

Her eyes were open, but she could see nothing but grayish white. If she concentrated, she could see specks and strata inside the rock rising all around her, but she felt as if she were swimming in brackish waters.

The view suddenly changed, and they were inside the castle, in a corridor by a doorway. The entire area was nearly full, floor to ceiling, with the metallic serpents. They seemed to be pouring from an invisible point where the wall met the ceiling near the door. Ayesha waved her insubstantial hand in front of Tetsuo's face and pointed at the spot. He nodded and held up three fingers. He ticked them down—three, two, one—and waved his hands around each other.

Ayesha felt her body become solid, and she fell. Tetsuo

was a split second ahead of her on the way down, and he shouted. Another burst of black light emerged from him and engulfed the squirming mass of snakes directly below. Tetsuo landed on his feet, but Ayesha fell onto her back and side, with hundreds of rusted, corroded snake machines beneath her.

Without bothering to stand, Ayesha extended her hand toward the invisible source of the serpents. She couldn't see it, but she could feel it. Someone was beaming global amounts of mana into a receiver located right here. She felt the flow of energy, felt it being converted into physical form by the advanced artifice inside the machine, felt the machine's function . . .

It was a delicately balanced amalgamation of metal, magic, and human ingenuity. Ayesha recalled her Hyperion mentor, the one that called her a prodigy and turned her out because she knew more than he. She recalled his workshop in northern Madara where she had spent almost three years as his apprentice, mining the foothills for ore and fetching water from the nearby river. She summoned some mana of her own, shaped it with her mind, and slammed it into the delicate works of the serpent generator, like a hammer into a house of cards.

The machine choked and sputtered. It rattled free, and as it fell, Ayesha caught her first and last glimpse of the serpent generator. The device trailed smoke as it dropped. It struck the pile of snakes and burst into a thousand metal fragments.

Ayesha smiled triumphantly.

Nearby, Tetsuo grunted in pain. Ayesha turned toward the champion. He was doing his best to keep the huge mob of snakes at bay, but his spells were growing weaker, and he was starting to stumble. One of the larger members of the serpent horde had struck him on the forearm and hung with its fangs buried in his flesh. Angrily, Tetsuo crushed it against the stone wall.

"Well done," the champion growled, as his hands continued to shine. "But we haven't won yet."

* * * * *

Caleria doubled over and crumpled painfully to the stones. Tor was beside her in an instant, kicking her bow aside and pulling a handful of arrows from her quiver.

He nocked one and half-bent the bowstring, the arrowhead a few short yards from Caleria's face.

"Can you help Kei?" he said.

Pain distorted Caleria's features. Tor's arrow had gone clean through her torso, the point jutting out from her back just above her kidney. Her eyes darted past Tor's shoulder to the slowly recovering soldiers on the floor behind him. "What are you talking about?"

"The healer. Can you help him? Or Magnus? What's in that secret glen we saw?"

Caleria shook her head. "I can't help you."

"Can't, or won't?" Tor gestured with the arrow. "It's an important distinction."

"There is no distinction. I don't know how to help you, and I won't allow anyone else to. Go ahead and kill me, imperial, but do so knowing that none of you will get off this island alive."

Tetsuo lowered the bow. "We're not here to kill you, Lady. We never were."

Caleria weathered a searing jolt of pain but kept her eyes on Tor. "You'd better change your mind, boy. Because as sure as the sun rises, I will kill you all the first chance I get."

Tor sighed. "As you say, my lady." He stepped over Caleria and put the arrow in the quiver and the bow across his shoulder. "That looks pretty bad." He pointed to the arrow in her side and hooked both hands under her arms. "But it's not fatal."

Caleria actually growled as Tor hauled her onto the throne's bottom step. He took an arrow from the quiver and pressed the point into the flesh at the top of Caleria's spine.

"Why don't you order your troops to fight snakes while we wait, Lady? Or better still, have them find my master. Anything to keep them away from me.

"You see, you and I are going to sit tight, and I'm going to keep you from bleeding to death until something happens. I figure either the snakes will get us both, or your soldiers will get me, or Tetsuo will return and take me out of here. One of these things is bound to happen sometime in the next few minutes. We might as well wait together. You may be in a rush to die, but I'm not."

Caleria turned her head to speak, but this brought on a fresh wave of pain, and she stopped with a sharp intake of breath. Tor kept the arrow pressed into her neck, but he also pulled her back so she could sit as comfortably as possible.

"Sit still, Lady."

All across the great hall, soldiers and snakes were waking up, orienting themselves, and striking out at one another. Tor could hear more soldiers mustering in the courtyard outside and the sounds of metal on metal farther down the hall as Caleria's army tore into the mass of snakes.

"So," Tor said cheerfully, "is there a way to get from here to Madara without taking a boat?"

CHAPTER 26

Lord Dark had brought back his majordomo and a few other key servants, but he had kept the bulk of his staff out of the castle while he prepared his next move. Long-term success came from pressing on toward his goals no matter what gains or setbacks each day brought. Orca had been driven back to her fiery home. The serpent generator was destroyed. Tetsuo and the Edemi rulers were all still alive. He had failed.

Dark banked the fires of his fury and prepared for the reckoning he knew would soon come. There would be dire repercussions throughout the highest levels of the empire for this fiasco, and he was determined to see that they fell heavily on those who deserved it most. Umezawa and his underlings would weep tears of blood before he was through.

My lord. Xira's voice was hesitant, and Dark took some small pleasure from her fear. Xira was not at fault, however, and so she was safe for the time being. Though he was a vengeful man, Lord Dark did not allow himself to be an irrational one.

I am here.

Umezawa and the others have not left Argenti. They are lingering in the forest in the hopes they can save the healer.

They probably will. Dark glowered in his study. *This game is over, Xira. Return at once.*

With respect, my lord, I can still—

Nine hells! Dark fumed. *I am too busy to have this discussion with you again. If they catch you on Argenti, they will kill you. If you are not here in my keep within two days, I will kill you. And if you die, let me assure you that I will find your final resting place. I will decapitate your corpse and reanimate the pieces for my amusement. My catapults will use your headless body for target practice, and your pretty head shall be the ammunition. Do as you like, Lady Xira, but do not trifle with me. Ever. Do you understand?*

There was a long pause, then Xira's voice came tiny and truculent. *I understand, my lord.*

For several long minutes, Dark silently sat and considered his options. Then a knock sounded on his study door, and the majordomo entered nervously.

"An imperial courier has arrived, my lord." The majordomo held out a yellow scroll case, sealed with the imperial standard.

Dark took the scroll from the sweating man and turned it over in his hands. He looked up.

"Will that be all, my lord?"

"Get out." Dark placed the scroll on the desk in front of him, idly rolling it back and forth between his finger. "Wait," he called, and the majordomo stopped halfway through the door. "Bring me Devilboon."

* * * * *

Once again, Tor followed Hatoki the standard bearer through the dense forests of Argenti. The rest of the imperial procession kept pace behind him. There was one great difference, though: Caleria walked beside Tetsuo, a full complement of armored troops behind her.

Once Tetsuo and Ayesha had cut off the flow of new arrivals, Caleria's army had contained and exterminated the last of the mechanical serpents. Tor held Caleria at arrow-point until all of the imperials were located and escorted to the great hall. Tor gratefully turned his hostage over to Tetsuo and basked in the champion's brief but extremely satisfied expression.

Unbound and in good spirits, the four bearers were brought down from Caleria's prison tower, but Kei was tied to a stretcher borne by two hefty guards. The druids explained that he kept experiencing waves of irrational hysteria and was dangerous to himself and others. The healer's skin was slick and waxy, and his compound eyes continued to divide and expand across his face. He snarled and hissed like a mad beast when Ayesha approached him, and the armorer sadly backed away. Caleria maintained that she did not know any way to return Kei to normal.

Otherwise, Argenti's ruler was sullen but accommodating in defeat. She returned all of their weapons and agreed to remain a hostage until the imperials had left Argenti shores. Like Gosta, she had been forced to accept to a temporary truce until the champion returned to Madara.

Tetsuo had one final demand before he would depart the island: an escorted investigation of the secret forest glen. Caleria tried to beg off and negotiate an alternative, but Tetsuo was firm. Kei himself had felt knowledge there, and the champion was honor-bound to explore every possible avenue in securing the healer's cure.

In the end, Caleria had deferred to the still-absent Magnus's authority. The site was sacred ground to the local druids, and not even she could enter without their permission. She remained evasive and uncomfortable about the glen, and Tor wondered for the hundredth time what could be so valuable.

Led by Caleria, Tetsuo and his party marched to the sacred spot. In under a day, they had reached the area, and were greeted by a familiar face.

"Hold, imperials." A hundred feet ahead, Lord Magnus stepped from behind a huge spruce tree. He looked none the worse for his encounter with Orca, his stance firm and his robes immaculate. He carried a new live wood staff decorated with brass rings.

Tor casually slipped his bow from his shoulder down to his hand and prepared to grab an arrow from his quiver.

"Magnus," Caleria called. "You are well?"

"I am fully restored, my lady. The forest has been healed as well. I apologize for my long absence and trust I did not worry you overmuch."

Caleria waved his apology aside. "The champions have turned aside all attacks made by the empire. We are under a flag of truce, and I am escorting them to their vessel."

Tor narrowed his eyes at Caleria but said nothing. He didn't like her truncated version of the story, but he did like being lumped together with Tetsuo and the others as "champions."

Tetsuo stepped forward. "Hail, Lord Magnus. I am glad to see you alive and unhurt. We have business to discuss with you."

Magnus glanced at Caleria and tightened both hands around his staff. "You seek the library," he said flatly.

"We seek a cure for our comrade." Tetsuo waved the soldiers bearing Kei forward, and they laid the tightly bound youth on the grass beside the champion. "We must determine if your forest contains the answer or can guide us to it."

Magnus slowly shook his head. "Only third-laurel druids can even approach the site," he said. "It is dangerous for nonbelievers."

"But you can enter." Ayesha spoke from behind her barrow.

"I can. I wear the fourth laurel and serve as protector of this entire forest."

Ayesha stepped around her barrow and approached Magnus. "Then you can help him or tell us if help exists. Please," she said with quiet sincerity. "I fear he will not survive the trip back to Madara."

Magnus looked truly forlorn as his gaze passed from one imperial to the other and finally to Caleria. The huntress nodded to the forest lord, and he nodded back.

"Stand away from the boy," Magnus said. "I will examine him."

With his staff extended, the red-faced druid approached the stretcher. The brass rings on Magnus's staff glowed and spun, and a greenish-white glow crept from the live wood to the bound healer's hands.

The glow quickly surrounded Kei and flowed onto Magnus until both men were completely enveloped. The energy sheath bubbled and churned. Magnus's deep, melodious voice droned out, and the needles on nearby trees turned toward him like iron filings to a magnet. Magnus's song hitched, as if he had choked in midnote, but then he continued on, louder than before.

It lasted many long minutes, and Tor noticed more than a few of the armored soldiers lower their guard as they waited. Tor kept his bow ready and his eyes on Kei.

At last the glow retreated from Kei and flowed back to the brass rings. The metal seemed to absorb the energy from Magnus as well, and the forest lord wore a troubled expression as he stared at Kei.

"Very few outsiders have ever witnessed the power of the Sylvan Library first hand," he said. "It provides more than mere information. It grants comprehension."

Tetsuo bowed. "What do you now comprehend, Lord Magnus?"

"He has become something new. It is almost fully formed."

Ayesha burst out. "We knew all that, Lord Magnus. What we need to know is how to stop the process and reverse it. Whatever has taken up residence in his body has to come out."

Magnus shook his head. "That is beyond even the library's power. It is not a parasite, something you can excise. It is akin to an organic enchantment, one that binds itself to his very essence. Think of it as a seed, laying down roots and taking in nutrition from the soil. As it grows, the seed incorporates its surroundings into its body and becomes something different, a combination of many things."

"That 'soil' is my student, Magnus. How is it not a parasite? What is the difference between consuming him and incorporating him? The end result is the same."

"Perhaps, but a parasite will always be distinct and separable from the host. Your student has been changed . . . *evolved* into the creature you see here. There is no longer any distinction between them."

"Rot," Ayesha said. "Kei is still in there."

Magnus bowed his head. "Not for long, I fear."

"I refuse to accept that. Look again." Ayesha turned angrily to Tetsuo. "There has to be more. Something we can use."

Tetsuo glanced at Magnus, who shook his head.

"Ayesha. You are certain some portion of Kei still remains?"

"I am. I taught him deep meditation, and we have spent many long hours together on the path." She nodded savagely. "I can feel him. He's still in there, somewhere."

"Insects don't meditate," Magnus said. "Bugs don't dream. Your student's mind has been remade and his body restructured. There is no way to undo these things."

"With respect, Lord Magnus," Tetsuo said, "if, as you say, there is no distinction, then we must create one. Ayesha says Kei is still there." He pointed to the struggling form on the stretcher. "So we must go in and get him."

Tetsuo called out to Caleria. "Clear this area, my lady. Pull your troops back at least fifty feet." He glanced at Hatoki at the head of the parade. "You, too. Everyone but Kei, Ayesha, and I must withdraw." He then addressed the healers and the soldiers who had been assigned to Kei. "You may stand down. Thank you for your assistance."

Tetsuo knelt, drew the jade talisman from around his neck, and placed it in Kei's hand. The healer thrashed and screeched on the stretcher, but his hand closed so tightly around the phoenix token that its edges cut into his skin.

"I am Tetsuo Umezawa." The champion spoke softly as he rose to his feet. "To the thing at my feet I say, face me. I challenge you for the life of Kei Takahashi."

* * * * *

Xira hugged the trunk of a tall evergreen as she watched the soldiers and bearers back away from the stretcher. From her camouflaged position high in the tree, she overheard Magnus's diagnosis and laughed. She didn't need a red-faced druid to tell her the new eumidian was nearly ready. She could feel it watching through Kei's eyes, thinking with Kei's brain, and reacting with his body. All it lacked was a little more time and some guidance from her.

Once all the soldiers were clear, Umezawa beckoned to his harridan armorer, and they both sat cross-legged beside

Kei. They closed their eyes, and Xira could just hear their low, chanting voices. Were they praying?

Xira silently snapped her jaws. They were wasting their time. If the champion thought there was no danger to him in the forest, Xira would happily prove him wrong.

She widened her eyes and waited for the opportunity to strike.

* * * * *

Ayesha drifted for a moment and felt the dream path firmly beneath her feet. Tetsuo's hand wrapped around hers, and they both started down the dusty paving stones.

"Champion," she said, "I am eager to help, but what are we doing here?"

Tetsuo's eyes were fixed on the road ahead. "We are going to separate Kei from the creature."

"But Magnus said it couldn't be done."

"Magnus is powerful but too awed by nature. He sees the battle for Kei's life as one of survival and extinction, two creatures competing for the same territory. In those terms, he is correct: Kei has already lost."

"What can we do, then?"

Tetsuo drew his sword. "We can give Kei an unfair advantage. Call your student to us. Use your angriest tone."

Ayesha smiled. Anger was easy for her to summon, at this point. She took a deep breath and whistled so loudly her own ears rang. Her voice pealed out like a great cathedral bell.

"Kei," she thundered, "to me! The longer I wait, the longer I have to think of your punishment!"

The road ahead was silent. Tetsuo glanced to Ayesha by his side and said, "Again."

Louder still, Ayesha whistled and shouted for Kei. Here on the meditation plane, her frustration magnified her volume past the limits of human ears. The entire world echoed with her cries.

In the dust ahead, something materialized. A humanoid shape with misshapen arms and legs and a painted white face. Kei screeched at them and charged.

"Insects don't meditate," Magnus had said. *"Bugs don't dream."* How, then, was the Kei-thing here?

Ayesha felt a rush of hope. She had been right about Kei's continued existence. All along, they had been looking for a schism between Kei and the parasite, but perhaps Magnus was correct: There wasn't a schism, and the forest lord couldn't create one.

She and Tetsuo could.

The champion sheathed his sword but raised his arm up as if he still held the blade. Tetsuo brought his arm down to his right hip and pointed a nonexistent weapon at the ground behind him. He hummed, something crackled, and a gleaming sword appeared in Tetsuo's hand. The blade and the handle were both made of vivid blue-black light, and the air shimmered around its edge.

The Kei-thing stopped its charge, staring warily at the sword.

"Don't let Kei go," Tetsuo said softly to Ayesha. "Call to him as a mentor, a parent, a friend, but don't let him leave."

Ayesha nodded.

"Thing," Tetsuo called. "You recognize the power of this blade, don't you? Even the lowest form of life recognizes a dire, naked threat. This blade can kill you, thing. It is a soul-sword, the distillation of my essence and a lifetime of discipline. Leave this place, or I will halve you where you stand."

The creature hissed angrily but did not retreat. It eyed Ayesha, and the armorer smiled.

"Kei," she said gently. "Come here." She spread her arms invitingly. "You're not safe there."

Screeching, the creature took a step forward then a step back. It hooked its sharp-fingered hand into a claw and raised its arm as if to strike at the armorer.

Tetsuo sprang forward and swung the glowing blade through the Kei-thing's wrist. Its howl of agony stabbed into Ayesha's brain, and its severed hand fell to the dusty road. Tetsuo raised the sword again.

"Kei," Ayesha said. "Come here." She crossed her arms into her sleeves. "Now."

Tetsuo slashed at the creature again. It turned and ran, but its pace was slow and leaden. It could not pull its left leg free of the path, as if it were mired in quicksand.

Ayesha heard a double scream as Kei's voice and the thing's overlapped. Then, the twisted mockery of her student tore free. It left an emaciated, translucent figure on the path in its wake, a figure with one foot stuck in the ground and a face smeared with white.

The creature was gone. Tetsuo was gone. Ayesha scanned the road ahead and behind then ran to Kei and gathered his weeping form into her arms.

* * * * *

Xira watched the champion and the armorer twitch and tremble through their trance. Then, Tetsuo's eyes snapped open, and he sprang to his feet. "Cut him loose, Tor."

The archer spared one second to stare at his master then cut the ropes.

Xira snapped her jaws hungrily, admiring his grace and

power. Someday, she mused, she must bestow upon Tor the same gift she had given Kei.

It took the creature on the stretcher a moment to realize it was free. Then it scrambled up off the stretcher and eyed Tetsuo menacingly.

Xira didn't know exactly what Tetsuo was planning, but she knew he wouldn't succeed. If he struck her offspring, he would also strike the healer. If he didn't strike, Xira would merely swoop in and spirit the new eumidian away. She could hide it for months in the forest, feeding it and protecting it until it was ready to fly on its own. When she was sure it was entirely loyal to her, she would finally return to Lord Dark's keep and turn it loose on him.

Xira remembered her master's ugly little threat and bristled at the indignity. Target practice, indeed.

The Kei-thing realized it still held Tetsuo's phoenix talisman and hurled it into the woods. The creature's movements were short, staccato bursts of blinding speed followed by bouts of sniffing and scanning. It dropped to its knees and pressed sharp fingers into the dirt, and then lifted them to its lips.

The thing's elbows had sprouted tiny hornlike spikes that now tore through the sleeves of its robe. Its joints all flexed slightly in the wrong direction as it moved. It turned multiple eyes to the champion, tasted the air around it, and snapped its jaws hungrily.

Xira fairly beamed with pride.

The creature issued a grating cry and rushed the champion, arms and legs swinging wildly. Tetsuo stood firm as it approached, his sword extended out and down to his right. The champion's eyes were clear and steady, fixed on his opponent.

At the last possible second, Tetsuo dropped his blade and swung his arm up and forward. The metal sword hit the ground while another formed in Tetsuo's blurred hand. The mystic weapon was composed of ghostly blue-black light, and it tore through Kei's chest without resistance until it emerged from his opposite side.

The Kei-thing screamed and froze where it stood, paralyzed by agony in midstep.

The sound it made punched through Xira's head like a metal spike, and the branch dissolved under her powerful fingers. She felt the blade in her chest as if she herself had been its target, and a rush of fever surged up her spine.

Tetsuo reversed the direction of his swing and slashed his energy blade back through the creature's torso. This time the blade caught on something halfway through, and Tetsuo shouted as he pulled it free.

The Kei-thing's scream died in its throat, and it collapsed onto its back. Xira's scream echoed across the forest from tree to tree, and she struggled to stay upright on her perch high above the forest floor.

Tetsuo still held the energy blade high in the air. Something clung to the bruise-colored weapon, something amorphous and oily that glowed with a greenish light. Tetsuo lowered his sword and examined the dripping blob. Then he yanked the blade out and spun in place, slashing the greenish thing in half before it had time to fall. The clinging sphere burst into ragged, ephemeral bits.

Xira felt something explode in her head. She choked, her lungs collapsed, and her fingers tingled. The supporting branches slipped out from under her hands and feet, and the needle-covered forest floor rushed up to meet her.

"Healers, to your work," the champion called. In a completely different tone: "Xira's here, Tor. She's all yours."

Barely conscious and bleeding, Xira leaped into the air. Lord Dark's flight enhancement held her body up, but her own wings had to beat to build any real speed.

She was twenty feet up and climbing when Tor's arrow pierced the large wing on her left side. Xira screeched and dropped several yards, but Dark's spell kept her aloft. She rose above the smaller trees and climbed even higher, trying to put as much distance as she could between herself and her enemies.

Her main wing on the left was useless, but she had enough power in the other three to keep moving. She beat them as fast as she could. Her pride, her offspring, and her assignment were all forgotten. Only one thought repeated in her pain-wracked mind:

Escape.

* * * * *

"I could see you," Kei sobbed. "I could hear you. But I couldn't *reach* you."

Through sheer will, Ayesha held Kei's ghostly form. "You're safe now, my student. I'm proud of you, you know. A fourth-level druid said you wouldn't make it back, and yet here you are." She paused. "Stop crying," she added. "The worst is over."

Kei settled down, breathing in gasps. "Someone's calling me," he said dreamily. "There's somewhere I need to be."

Ayesha glanced down at her hip. Her meditative form wore a tool belt instead of her short sword. The blade was safely sheathed on her physical hip, however.

"You and me both." She rose, carefully guiding Kei's ghostly form up with her. "Come on," she said. "I'll take you back, and then catch the beast that did this. We have unfinished business in the forest."

* * * * *

The wound in Xira's wing continued to hamper her as Caleria's troops harried her from below. Between the pursuing troops and the thick canopy overhead, Xira had not gained the altitude she needed to keep herself safe.

Xira circled back to where she had started, and as she had hoped, most of the soldiers were searching elsewhere. Tetsuo, Magnus, and a handful of healers stood around the fallen figure of Kei. He was propped up for the druids to examine, but his large eyes remained closed.

Suddenly, Xira felt thin, powerful fingers take her by the scalp and haul her face roughly back.

"There you are," Ayesha growled. She floated freely, surrounded by a powdery cloud of blue dust.

The eumidian twisted and tried to struggle free. Growling savagely, Ayesha stabbed her short sword in Xira's neck.

The eumidian retained enough of her reflexes to turn her shoulder into the blade, and thus Ayesha's strike was not lethal. The sword skidded across her collarbone and lodged in her shoulder. Green blood spattered Ayesha's face, and Xira howled in pain and fury. With the last of her fading strength, Xira pushed free of the armorer and flew straight up.

Dangerously weak, Xira burst through the forest canopy and disappeared among the clouds.

*　*　*　*　*

"You got her," Tor said angrily.

Ayesha landed beside him, the nimbus of blue dust settling on the ground and vanishing. Her sword dripped eumidian blood. "And you got her, too, I'm told."

"Then how did she make it out of here?"

"She's been enchanted," Ayesha said. The armorer stared

at the point in the sky where Xira had vanished. "Pretty basic flying spell, too." She smiled at Tor. "I'm good with those."

The archer grimaced. "I remember."

"If I had wings, too, I could have—" Ayesha started. "Kei!" She sheathed her sword and dashed over to where her student lay. Tor followed her as she pushed her way through the ring of druids and soldiers that had formed around the fallen healer.

Tetsuo cradled the youth's head in his lap. He looked up at Ayesha and carefully slid out from under Kei, transferring his head to Ayesha's gentle hands.

"The thing Kei had become is dead," Tetsuo said. "Kei himself has reclaimed what's his."

Ayesha stroked the hair away from Kei's face, and the healer groaned. His eye lids fluttered, and the throng of onlookers all fell silent. Kei's eye sockets were still twice as wide as they had been, and he retained his compound pupils.

"Is he going to stay like that?" Tor asked.

"Of course not," Ayesha snapped. She added softly, "I think. Lord Magnus?"

The forest lord shrugged. "I cannot say. You will have to wait and see." Magnus turned to Tetsuo and bowed. "Congratulations, Champion. If I may, I would like to understand exactly how you cured your friend."

"So he can add that information to the library we're not allowed to see," Ayesha said sharply.

Tetsuo retrieved his sword from the ground and sheathed it. He crossed his arms into his sleeves and spoke to Magnus. "It takes a great deal to pull someone from his chosen path. Kei always stayed true to his. I merely lightened his burden."

Magnus seemed less than satisfied with the answer, but he did not press Tetsuo for more.

"If you will accompany us the rest of the way," Tetsuo turned to Caleria, standing just outside the ring around Kei, "you can see us off. We are at last ready to depart."

Caleria marshaled her troops into ranks, and the druids began to melt away into the trees.

Tor knelt down next to Ayesha and whispered, "I just wish we had caught her. She deserves worse than two little wounds."

"I agree," Ayesha said, a nasty gleam in her eyes. She took Tor's hand in hers and gave it a conspiratorial squeeze. "We'll talk more once we're on the water."

Ayesha then spoke to Tetsuo but did not hold his gaze. "Thank you. I knew you wouldn't let us down." She lifted Kei's long body and placed him back on the stretcher.

Tetsuo watched her for a moment then nodded at Tor. "If you and Hatoki are ready, Second?"

Tor jumped to his feet and quickly made his way to the front of the procession. A few minutes later, they were trekking through the forest, bound for the southern coast, the sampan, and eventually, home.

CHAPTER 27

Lord Dark sat at his desk, the imperial scroll rolled out before him. He kept his emotions in check, careful to feel nothing that might express itself on his face. He was utterly still and silent, aloof from the world around him.

A timid knock sounded, and the majordomo spoke. "Boris Devilboon to see you, my lord. As you requested."

"Enter," Dark said.

The majordomo opened the door and stood beside it. Devilboon came into the room, his face all excitement and his eyes scanning the high ceilings and black marble walls.

"My lord," he said breathlessly, "it is truly an honor to be—"

"Leave us."

The majordomo bowed and vanished into the hallway, closing the heavy wooden door behind him.

Dark stared at the little man until Devilboon swallowed nervously. "You wanted to see me, my lord?"

"Yes, my friend. It is time to reward you for your role in the Edemi affair."

Devilboon tilted his head quizzically. "Really, my lord? I don't recall contributing—"

"Oh, you contributed. Ours is a complicated and subtle business. Often my operatives don't realize how much their actions affect our service to the emperor."

Devilboon bowed. "I am overwhelmed, my lord."

Lord Dark rose and came around the huge oaken desk. "The emperor contacted me a short time ago." He took the scroll from the desk top and offered it to Devilboon. "A three-word communiqué. Would you like to see it?"

"I would be honored, my lord." Devilboon took the scroll, stared at the stark characters written there then looked up in hopeful confusion.

" 'Come at once,' " he read. "Is this for me as well, my lord?"

"No." Lord Dark gently took the scroll from Devilboon's hand. "But on to your reward. When I bestow gifts upon my agents, I like to give them things that make them more powerful. More useful to our cause. Like Xira's camouflage or your own prophetic utterances."

Devilboon's face wrinkled in puzzlement, but he waited for Dark to continue.

"I suppose I should have been more rigorous in decoding your latest proclamation." Dark spoke in a calm, resigned tone. He sat lightly on the edge of the desk. " 'Fangless in a serpent's bed' can mean a great number of things. Though I expect that Umezawa is never truly fangless . . . and perhaps there weren't enough snakes to qualify as a 'bed.' But I digress." He rose to his feet and offered his hand to Devilboon.

"I need powerful agents, Boris. And more, I need reliable ones. Take my hand now, that you may serve me even more effectively."

Devilboon hesitated but a moment then smiled nervously. He reached out his hand, which vanished inside Lord Dark's powerful grip.

Dark snarled as he clapped his other hand around Devilboon's and sent a withering surge of black mana into the smaller man's body. Devilboon screamed in high-pitched agony, and his feet rose off the floor. Lord Dark held on, pumping more black mana into his underling. Smoke rose from Devilboon's flesh, and his eyeballs burst.

Dark pulled his left hand back and slammed the ball of his thumb into Devilboon's larynx. The little mage's scream choked off, and he let out a sickening gurgle. Through it all, Lord Dark maintained his grip and continued to flood Devilboon's body with energy.

Finally, a loud crack sounded, and Devilboon was hurled backward into the hard stone wall. He dropped to his knees, his empty sockets pleading to his pitiless master then fell face-first to the floor. He wheezed out one long, protracted breath, and Boris Devilboon died.

Phantasmal streams of black smoke circled above his fallen body like eels in a tank.

Dark readied another wave of mana, held his right hand out with the fingers splayed, and said, "Rise."

Black sparks flickered around Devilboon's corpse. Like a tiny swarm of insects, the sparks fastened onto the dead mage's robes and lifted him to his feet. His hood had fallen over his head and face, and as soon as he was completely vertical, the sparks gently peeled the fabric back so Lord Dark could see.

The skin on Devilboon's neck and hands was mottled and splotchy, a chaotic mixture of shades ranging from dark ashen gray to a rich aubergine. The flesh on Boris's face was gone, replaced by a layer of thick, crazed black glass that was smooth on the surface but riddled with tiny hairline cracks below. His oily hair was now stiff and brittle, and strands of it crumbled and fell as he floated before Lord Dark. His eyes were open, but the sockets were empty holes, windows to a dark and terrible place where light had never been. He retained his ratlike features and his ridiculous mustache, but Lord Dark was willing to accept some deficiencies in his reconsecrated servant. At least he had made sure to crush the little irritant's throat. That should keep him from yammering and fawning every time Dark spoke to him.

The sparks holding Devilboon up began to fade, and they gently lowered him onto the floor. His legs wavered but held, and soon he drew himself up to his full height and stood patiently, waiting for a command from his master.

"You are dead, Boris." Dark rolled up the imperial scroll and held it out to the monster before him. "What do you see? Proclaim."

Dead Boris took the scroll in one hand and held it cupped it between his palms. His voice was a painful mixture of a gurgle, a whisper, and a cough:

This failure you may safe ignore
Hold to the path ye chose before
For in the gath'ring clouds of war
The champion will be no more.

Dark smiled. "Well done," he said. "Your efficiency has already increased threefold. Time will tell about your accuracy." He took the scroll from his underling's upturned hands.

Dead Boris said nothing, moved not at all, and continued to stare.

*   *   *   *   *

The sampan was not where they had hidden it, but under Magnus's direction the forest beasts quickly brought it back to the spot where it had landed. Hatoki and the other bearers loaded the boat and prepared for launch, while Ayesha directed Kei and his stretcher to the stern.

"This is all for naught," Caleria said. She was standing away from the sampan, Lord Magnus and two plumed soldiers behind her. "Within days, your emperor will send you back to kill us all. Hear this, Champion. There will be no more imperial duels on Argenti. Once you depart, I will issue orders for you and your entire entourage to be killed on sight. Any unrecognized vessel discovered off our coast will be sunk without warning, and any survivors will be fed to the forest."

Tetsuo remained impassive. "So be it, Lady. Although my return here is perhaps the best you can hope for at this point."

Caleria bristled. "Is that a threat?"

Tetsuo shook his head. "The emperor does not make threats."

"Just go," Caleria fumed, "and tell everyone on Madara that the next boatload of imperials will not find Argenti so hospitable."

Caleria turned and stormed off, her armored lieutenants keeping perfect formation behind her. Magnus stood for a moment longer, bowed to Tetsuo and Tor, then walked off into the woods.

Tetsuo headed up the gangplank.

Tor followed him. "Do you think the emperor will send us back to fight them again?"

Tetsuo turned for one last look at the forest. "I think things will become very unpleasant for Madara and the Edemis alike before this matter is finally settled."

Ayesha escorted the last of the armored soldiers down the gangplank and returned to root through her barrow. On the deck beside her, she placed a stick of chalk, a coin made of white gold, and the vial of blue powder she had used on Tor and the sail-kite.

She paused and looked up at Tetsuo. "Ready to cast off when you are." The piece of chalk cracked and flaked as Ayesha dragged it across the wooden deck planks.

"What are you doing, armorer?" Tetsuo asked.

"I think I have a handle on the enchantment Xira was using to augment her wings," Ayesha said. She flashed her sharp, white teeth. "I'm a breaker, remember? It's my sincere hope that there aren't any predators in the water between here and the Talon Gates. I'd hate to miss the opportunity of seeing her drowned corpse. Say, how well do wasps swim, anyway?"

Tetsuo pretended not to hear as he walked back to the rudder of the ship.

Tor allowed himself a small grin, which Ayesha returned before going back to work with the chalk and the blue powder. Then the archer went below to check on Kei and lash himself to something sturdy for the voyage home.

*　*　*　*　*

Xira Arien had cleared the shores of Kusho and was on her way across the wide expanse of ocean between her and Madara. Her main left wing was still holed and useless, but she had stopped the bleeding around her neck and shoulder. She was not traveling at top speed but would be back in Dark's castle long before the deadline he'd given her.

She skimmed along the waves, mere feet above the choppy seas and whitecaps. She was cold and tired, and her wounds ached, but she kept her spirits up by imagining what Lord Dark would do to the champion and his servants.

Perhaps, she thought, with a snap of her jaws, he will even turn some of them over to me.

Xira heard a sizzling sound and suddenly dropped several feet. A large wave broke across her face, and she sputtered, struggling to regain altitude. Only her right wings buzzed, but she was able to climb in a clumsy diagonal up and away from the waves.

The sizzle sounded again, louder than before. Xira had time to wonder what was happening to her before the sizzle became a soft pop, and the blue glow around her winked out.

Xira howled in outrage, flailing and spinning down through twenty feet of space. She slapped into the sea face-first, stunned by both the impact and the frigid water. Dazed, Xira floated for a few seconds as the stinging salt water burned into the slash across her neck and shoulder. She struggled a few strokes, but the wound prevented her from using her right arm to swim.

A wave broke over her head, shoving her below the surface and dragging her up. She sputtered and gagged, spitting seawater from the back of her throat and inhaling more painfully into her lungs.

Xira weathered a few more large waves. Once she had learned how to keep from being ducked, she stretched her left arm out in front of her and started kicking. As often as the searing sensation in her shoulder and wing allowed, she reached forward with her right arm and attempted a few clumsy, infrequent strokes.

Xira rode another large swell and took advantage of her position to scan the seas ahead. There was no sign of land, either before or behind her. She was bleeding into the sea, on a tight deadline, miles away from land.

Xira swore that she would see each and every member of

the champion's entourage bled dry for this humiliation. Even if she saw it through decapitated zombie eyes, she would see them pay.

Another wave broke over her, and it started to rain.

E P I L O G U E

At the foot of the altar, the burly man knelt in the supplicant's position. He had spoken the words and offered the sacrifice hours ago, but still the emperor kept him waiting. He bore it all in silence, the very picture of a dedicated and abject servant.

Finally, the candles flared and the room cooled. The emperor's face slowly appeared over the altar, all piercing eyes and feral hunger. His mouth was tightly closed, and he stared at Dark, the criticism in his expression far more eloquent than any words could have been.

"Your imperial—"

"Is Caleria dead?" The emperor's voice was no longer a soft hiss. Instead, it was the sound made by the wind just before it tears the roof off a house. "Is Magnus? Or Gosta? What happened to your schemes, little assassin?"

"Majesty," Dark did not raise his head or attempt to stand. "I warned you about the champion's interference. But for his actions and those of his underlings, all your enemies in the Edemis would be dead."

The emperor mouth flew open, and he roared.

The flesh on Dark's face pressed tightly against his skull as the emperor's fury raged past him like a hurricane wind. Dark convulsed and felt every coherent thought being ripped from his mind.

"Mind your tone," the emperor said.

Dark steadied himself and forced his agonized muscles to hold the bowed posture of the supplicant. When he could think clearly enough to form words, Dark said, "Forgive me, Your Eminence."

"I do not. Offer me another option, Ramses, for I have not yet decided what I am going to do to you." The emperor's voice dropped, becoming softer and more sinister. "You won't like what I'm coming up with on my own."

"Eminence." Dark kept his clenched fists tight against the floor and his head bowed. "I accept whatever punishment you decree, but Umezawa is not blameless in this matter. In resisting me, he resisted you. I ask that whatever befalls me, also befalls him."

"Tetsuo will be punished," the emperor said. "Though he acted within the boundaries of his office, he acted against my best interests. There will be a reckoning."

Dark smiled.

"And you," the emperor continued, "have behaved childishly. Remember this, my assassin: Tetsuo has frustrated *your* methods, kept you from *your* goals. He has only delayed my success in the Edemis, not canceled it.

"Caleria claims she is ready for war. She sends beasts to my shores and stockpiles spells and musters troops to resist me. But white mana fights a very specific kind of war, one that is ordered and civilized. She is not ready for our kind of warfare."

The emperor turned his face to a darkened corner of the room. At his unspoken signal, two men stepped from the shadows, each in the uniform of a kentsu officer.

General Elsdragon and Marshal Hage both stepped in between Lord Dark and the altar, turned, and knelt before the emperor.

"When can you be ready?"

Elsdragon lifted his face. "Within two weeks, my lord. Hage will begin storming the beaches of Kusho while I prepare a larger force to follow."

"Excellent. I will summon you all again before the kentsu sets sail."

Dark peered at the officers from under his heavy brow. When their heads bowed, he could see the back of Elsdragon's neck, but Hage's was obscured by his long Ærathi tresses.

Dark lowered his eyes and smiled. "All hail the glory and wisdom of the emperor," he said.

GO BEHIND ENEMY LINES WITH DRIZZT DO'URDEN IN THIS ALL NEW TRILOGY FROM BEST-SELLING AUTHOR R.A. SALVATORE.

THE HUNTER'S BLADES TRILOGY

The New York Times *best-seller now in paperback!*

THE LONE DROW

Book II

Alone and tired, cold and hungry, Drizzt Do'Urden has never been more dangerous. But neither have the rampaging orcs that have finally done the impossible—what for the dwarves of the North is the most horrifying nightmare ever—they've banded together.

June 2004

New in hardcover!

THE TWO SWORDS

Book III

Drizzt has become the Hunter, but King Obould won't let himself become the Hunted and that means one of them will have to die. The Hunter's Blades trilogy draws to an explosive conclusion.

October 2004

THE THOUSAND ORCS

Book I

Available Now!

Forgotten Realms and its logo and Drizzt Do'Urden are trademarks of Wizards of the Coast, Inc. in the U.S.A. and other countries. ©2004 Wizards.

CHECK OUT THESE NEW TITLES FROM THE AUTHORS OF R.A. SALVATORE'S WAR OF THE SPIDER QUEEN SERIES!

VENOM'S TASTE
House of Serpents, Book I
Lisa Smedman

The New York Times Best-selling author of *Extinction*.
Serpents. Poison. Psionics. And the occasional evil death cult. Business as usual in the Vilhon Reach. Lisa Smedman breathes life into the treacherous yuan-ti race.

THE RAGE
The Year of Rogue Dragons, Book I
Richard Lee Byers

Every once in a while the dragons go mad. Without warning they darken the skies of Faerûn and kill and kill and kill. Richard Lee Byers, the new master of dragons, takes wing.

FORSAKEN HOUSE
The Last Mythal, Book I
Richard Baker

The New York Times Best-selling author of *Condemnation*.
The Retreat is at an end, and the elves of Faerûn find themselves at a turning point. In one direction lies peace and stagnation, in the other: war and destiny. *New York Times* best-selling author Richard Baker shows the elves their future.

August 2004

THE RUBY GUARDIAN
Scions of Arrabar, Book II
Thomas M. Reid

Life and death both come at a price in the mercenary city-states of the Vilhon Reach. Vambran thought he knew the cost of both, but he still has a lot to learn. Thomas M. Reid makes humans the most dangerous monsters in Faerûn.

November 2004

THE SAPPHIRE CRESCENT
Scions of Arrabar, Book I
Available Now

Forgotten Realms and its logo are trademarks of Wizards of the Coast, Inc. in the U.S.A. and other countries. ©2004 Wizards.

R.A. Salvatore's
War of the Spider Queen

THE EPIC SAGA OF THE DARK ELVES CONTINUES.

New in hardcover!

EXTINCTION
Book IV
Lisa Smedman

For even a small group of drow, trust is the rarest commodity of all. When the expedition prepares for a return to the Abyss, what little trust there is crumbles under a rival goddess's hand.

January 2004

ANNIHILATION
Book V
Philip Athans

Old alliances have been broken, and new bonds have been formed. While some finally embark for the Abyss itself, others stay behind to serve a new mistress—a goddess with plans of her own.

July 2004

RESURRECTION
Book VI

The Spider Queen has been asleep for a long time, leaving the Underdark to suffer war and ruin. But if she finally returns, will things get better... or worse?

April 2005

The New York Times best-seller now in paperback!

CONDEMNATION
Book III
Richard Baker

The search for answers to Lolth's silence uncovers only more complex questions, allowing doubt and frustration to test the boundaries of already tenuous relationships. Sensing the holes in the armor of Menzoberranzan, a new, dangerous threat steps in to test the resolve of the Jewel of the Underdark, and finds it lacking.

May 2004

Now in paperback!
DISSOLUTION, BOOK I
INSURRECTION, BOOK II

Forgotten Realms and its logo are trademarks of Wizards of the Coast, Inc. in the U.S.A. and other countries. ©2004 Wizards.

FATHER AND DAUGHTER COME FACE-TO-FACE IN THE STREETS OF WATERDEEP.

New in hardcover!
ELMINSTER'S DAUGHTER
The Elminster Series

Ed Greenwood

Like a silken shadow, the thief Narnra Shalace flits through
the dank streets and dark corners of Waterdeep. Little does
she know that she's about to come face-to-face with the
most dangerous man in all Faerûn: her father. And amidst a
vast conspiracy to overthrow all order in the Realms, she'll
have to learn to trust again—and to love.

May 2004

ELMINSTER: THE MAKING OF A MAGE

ELMINSTER IN MYTH DRANNOR

THE TEMPTATION OF ELMINSTER

ELMINSTER IN HELL

Available Now!

Forgotten Realms and its logo are trademarks of Wizards of the Coast, Inc.
in the U.S.A. and other countries. ©2004 Wizards.

FORGOTTEN REALMS®

THERE ARE A HUNDRED GODS LOOKING OVER FAERÛN, EACH WITH A THOUSAND SERVANTS OR MORE. SERVANTS WE CALL . . . THE PRIESTS

LADY OF POISON
Bruce R. Cordell

Evil has the Great Dale in its venomous grip. Monsters crawl from the shadows, disease and poison ravage the townsfolk, and dark cults gather in the night. Not all religions, after all, work for good.

July 2004

MISTRESS OF NIGHT
Dave Gross

Fighting a goddess of secrets can be a dangerous game. Werewolves stalk the moonlit night, goddesses clash in the heavens, and a lone priestess will sacrifice everything to stop them.

September 2004

QUEEN OF THE DEPTHS
Voronica Whitney-Robinson

Far below the waves, evil swims. The ocean goddess is a fickle mistress who toys with man and ship alike. How can she be trusted when the seas run red with blood?

May 2005

MAIDEN OF PAIN
Kameron M. Franklin

The book that **Forgotten Realms®** novel fans have been waiting for—the result of an exhaustive international talent search. The newest star in the skies of Faerûn tells a story of torture, sacrifice, and betrayal.

July 2005

Forgotten Realms and its logo are trademarks of Wizards of the Coast, Inc. in the U.S.A. and other countries. ©2004 Wizards.

Adventures in the Realms!

THE YELLOW SILK
The Rogues
Don Bassingthwaite

More than just the weather is cold and bitter in the wind-
swept realm of Altumbel. When a stranger travels from
the distant east to reclaim his family's greatest treasure,
he finds just how cold and bitter a people can be.

February 2004

DAWN OF NIGHT
The Erevis Cale Trilogy, Book II
Paul S. Kemp

He's left Sembia far behind. He's made new friends.
He's made new enemies. And now Erevis Cale himself
is changing into something, and he's not sure exactly
what it is.

June 2004

REALMS OF DRAGONS
The Year of Rogue Dragons
Edited by Philip Athans

All new stories by R.A. Salvatore, Richard Lee Byers,
Ed Greenwood, Elaine Cunningham, and a host of
Forgotten Realms® stars breathe new life into the
great wyrms of Faerûn.

December 2004

Forgotten Realms and its logo are trademarks of Wizards of the Coast, Inc.
in the U.S.A. and other countries. ©2004 Wizards.